For all of us who dreamed of a roommate who was tall, dark, and handsome but only ever got ones who were loud, late on rent, and left their socks in the couch cushions instead. Life isn't fair, but at least books exist to make us dream.

THE ROOMMATE EXPERIMENT

CAMILLA ISLEY

Boldwood

First published in Great Britain in 2025 by Boldwood Books Ltd.

Copyright © Camilla Isley, 2025

Cover Design by Alexandra Allden

Cover Images: Shutterstock and iStock

The moral right of Camilla Isley to be identified as the author of this work has been asserted in accordance with the Copyright, Designs and Patents Act 1988.

Every effort has been made to obtain the necessary permissions with reference to copyright material, both illustrative and quoted. We apologise for any omissions in this respect and will be pleased to make the appropriate acknowledgements in any future edition.

A CIP catalogue record for this book is available from the British Library.

Paperback ISBN 978-1-83633-383-8

Large Print ISBN 978-1-83633-382-1

Hardback ISBN 978-1-83633-381-4

Ebook ISBN 978-1-83633-384-5

Kindle ISBN 978-1-83633-385-2

Audio CD ISBN 978-1-83633-376-0

MP3 CD ISBN 978-1-83633-377-7

Digital audio download ISBN 978-1-83633-378-4

This book is printed on certified sustainable paper. Boldwood Books is dedicated to putting sustainability at the heart of our business. For more information please visit https://www.boldwoodbooks.com/about-us/sustainability/

Boldwood Books Ltd, 23 Bowerdean Street, London, SW6 3TN

www.boldwoodbooks.com

1

HUNTER

There are exactly eleven steps between my door and Dylan's new room; I've counted them obsessively since morning as I waited for him to arrive with his boxes.

Ironically, each step represents a year I've known him, a year of stolen glances, hidden smiles, and unspoken feelings. Eleven years since the summer after freshman year when I went to visit my best friend Nina at her parents' house and met her impossibly tall, impossibly handsome brother for the first time.

He was sunbathing by the pool. A hint of a smirk on his lips, eyes closed under dark sunglasses, one arm lazily draped behind his head as he soaked in the warmth.

I nearly tripped over when Nina introduced us, my tongue suddenly tied in knots as I gazed up (and up, and up) into those mesmerizing blue-green eyes. Dylan smiled, and the world tilted on its axis.

From that moment on, he's had my heart in a headlock. My entire stay at Nina's became a secret study of him. I'd watch him toss Nina into the water, his abs rippling as he laughed, and imagined what it would feel like to be in his arms. I even resented it was never me being thrown into the pool.

After that first year, summer visits turned into regular hangouts when my college roommates and I all moved to New York after graduation, where Dylan already lived. Recently, since Nina and Dylan's best friend, Tristan, started dating, we've been seeing a lot more of each other. And now, we're living together.

The physical distance between us has been narrowing and shrinking, but I suspect Dylan still sees me only as his baby sister's friend. I'm not even sure I can call it being friend-zoned. I'm a step lower. Friend zone *adjacent*. An accessory friend, the friend of a friend you're used to having around but don't really consider *your* friend.

While for me, he's been the man I've compared every date, every boyfriend to. I've memorized every detail of him: the way his eyes crinkle when he laughs, the little scar on his chin from a childhood skateboarding accident, the freckle behind his left ear that I once noticed when he bent down to tie his shoe. I know his coffee order by heart—large Americano, extra espresso shot with a splash of oat milk. And I can pick out his laugh in a crowded bar from a mile away.

All these details are pieces of him I've tucked away, each one a small, treasured artifact stored in a corner of my heart, carefully collected in all the time I've known him.

Eleven years. Eleven steps.

It's ridiculous how much significance I'm assigning to this narrow stretch of hallway. But I can't stop. Every step between us represents a chance that I've never been brave enough to take. But now, with us living under the same roof, maybe things will be different.

I lean against my doorframe, listening to the muffled thuds and rustles coming from Nina's old bedroom. Dylan is unpacking his stuff. As of two hours ago, we're officially roommates.

A prickly spike jolts my nervous system as I realize this is the first time we've been alone. Unjustified butterflies surge in my belly at the sound of him humming under his breath. I need to get a grip. I can't be on pins and needles whenever I'm home, waiting for his next movement. Even if every little thing about him is a tiny hook in my heart.

"Hunter? You out there?" Dylan's voice floats down the hall, and my stomach does a somersault.

"Yeah, I'm here," I call back, wincing at the slight high-low wobble I don't control.

I cross the hall, counting each step under my breath again. *One, two, three...* By the time I reach eleven, I've plastered what I hope is a casual smile on my face.

Dylan is standing in the middle of the bedroom, surrounded by boxes and looking unfairly ravishing in a faded T-shirt and jeans. His blond hair is tousled, and there's a smudge of dust on his cheek that I immediately itch to wipe away.

"Hey, roomie." He grins, making my knees go weak.

I lean against the doorframe, trying to look nonchalant. "Hey yourself. Need help unpacking?" I should've offered to help him get settled right away.

Dylan runs a hand through his hair, messing it up even more. "Nah, I've got it under control."

"Oh." A flicker of disappointment tightens in my chest. Of course, he doesn't need my help. Or want to hang out. He probably just wants the Wi-Fi password.

Before I blurt out it's PrettyFlyForAWiFi, he adds, "But I was wondering if you have a spare set of keys, or if I should go get one made?"

"Um, didn't Nina give you hers?"

"No. She was all over Tristan, gushing about moving in together." Dylan rolls his eyes in an unconscious move; he might've openly accepted his best friend and younger sister are dating, but I suspect he still isn't entirely comfortable with their constant PDAs. "Must've slipped her mind."

"I have Rowena's old keys. You can use those." Rowena was my other roommate, who also moved out today to shack up with a dude, but for entirely different reasons from Nina.

Dylan's face lights up, and the warmth of his smile travels all the way across the room. "Really? That'd be perfect, Hunt. You're a lifesaver."

My heart dances a little jig at the praise. I feel like one of those small, over-excitable dogs running in a circle and chasing my tail while yapping eagerly. "I'll grab them for you."

"Thank you."

I wave off his thanks. "No problem."

"No, really. You saved me a trip." Dylan drops a heavy box and looks out the window at the bright sunlight filtering in. "I wasn't looking forward to going to a hardware store in this heat."

I'm making his life easier. That's good. What else could I do to make him feel at home? "Hey, do you want me to lower the temperature on the air conditioning?"

I try not to stare as Dylan lifts his arms to stretch, his T-shirt riding up to reveal a tantalizing strip of skin above his waistband.

"That'd be great." He wipes a bead of sweat from his forehead with the back of his hand. "Maybe turn it a couple of degrees lower?"

I nod, trying not to fixate on the way his T-shirt clings to his chest, slightly damp from exertion. "Sure thing."

I turn and skip down the hallway. In my room, I grab the keys from where I tossed them earlier in one of the desk drawers. I almost expect to find them dusty with cobwebs. My best friends moved out only a few hours ago, but it already seems an eternity.

Rowena's keychain jingles in my hand as I shuffle-dance into the living room, stopping at the thermostat. I turn the wheel all the way down to sixty-eight degrees and shiver when the vent kicks in, the cool air raising goosebumps on my bare arms. Despite the cold, I smile to myself, imagining cozying up with a blanket on the couch later, Dylan sitting beside me as we watch a movie.

Wishful thinking, I know. Dylan sees me as a friend, nothing more—perhaps something less. But I can't stop daydreaming about the countless romantic possibilities of cohabitation. Movie nights that turn into cuddling on the couch, cooking dinner and sharing intimate meals, our hands brushing as we do the dishes together, passion taking over, Dylan grabbing me by the waist and bending me over the counter before he—

I close my eyes against the vision. I need to stay grounded in reality. At the rate I'm building castles in the air, I wouldn't be surprised if woodland creatures showed up and started cleaning the house while they sang.

I head back to Dylan's room.

"Here you go." I toss him the keys.

He catches them effortlessly, his reflexes as quick as ever. Dylan looks at the keychain, a mini ax encased in clear plastic, the same as a fire-emergency tool, and at the writing on the back:

Break Glass in Case of Bad Decisions

He flashes me that heart-stopping grin again, and I have to remind myself to breathe. "Interesting key ring."

I wince despite myself. "Yeah, Rowena should've kept it. I don't know what's gotten into her to agree to marry a complete stranger for money while pregnant with her ex's baby." Dylan raises both eyebrows and before he can tell me I'm being judgmental, I lift my hands. "I know it's her decision, but I worry. She's my best friend."

Dylan's expression softens. "Nina's the same. But, hey, we know who this guy is. If Adrian West tries anything funny, Tristan and I will make sure he regrets it." His jaw sets into a determined line.

Damn, he's so hot when he threatens to protect the people he cares about. It's one thing I admire the most about him—his fierce loyalty to those he loves. And while he doesn't exactly love me or Rowena, his sister does, and for the transitive property, he feels protective of us, too.

"Well, I hope she won't regret moving in with the guy."

Dylan lifts another box, biceps bulging. "It might sound selfish, but I'm glad the roommate re-shuffling worked out despite everything. I couldn't have handled living with strangers."

I'm one step below a true friend but one above a total stranger. Yay, me. "Hey, with what you're paying for both rooms, you could've gotten a place of your own."

Dylan groans dramatically. "Eh, I've never lived alone. I'm not sure I would've liked it."

Not a stranger and preferable to total loneliness. At the speed things are progressing, he'll propose by the end of the week. "Don't worry, I'll keep you from turning into a crazy cat lady."

Dylan chuckles, which makes me giggle. We dissolve into laughter, and it feels like it has always been us—playful, effortless, pulsing with... *togetherness*.

When our chests stop shaking, his gaze holds steady on mine, and I can't handle it. I look away first. "I'll let you finish. Call out if you need anything else."

"Sure thing. Thanks again for the keys."

I nod and start to walk away, then turn back, pretending a thought just entered my mind and that I haven't been strategizing this move for days. "Hey, I was thinking of throwing something together for dinner." My voice pitches only slightly higher than normal. "You want to share?"

Dylan's face lights up. "Yeah, would love to. Need help cooking?"

I shake my head, pointing at all the unopened boxes littering his floor and thinking of the ones still scattered in the living room. "No, no, you've already got your hands full."

"Okay, thanks." Dylan tilts his head and studies me for a few electric seconds, giving me the unsettling impression he can see right through me. But then he nods and opens a new box. "I'll try to get finished fast, then."

With one last wistful glance at his biceps, I exit the bedroom and head for the kitchen, zigzagging through the boxes strewn in my path.

I open the fridge and throw myself into making lasagna. I stocked all the ingredients to make his favorite dish yesterday, after obsessively scouring cooking blogs for the best lasagna recipe that'll win me his heart. Dylan will love my food and then he'll love *me*.

As I layer the sheets of pasta with the sauce, another daydream takes over. I imagine him having his mind blown by how good the lasagna is. I picture heated glances across the dinner table that will once again inevitably lead to our first passionate kiss. But then my practical side intrudes into the fantasy as I try to envision the logistics of how we'd kiss across a table. Would he wipe the surface of everything, same as it happens with desks in movies? Set me on the table, push between my legs, and kiss the living daylights out of me? Or would he scoot closer and go for a more understated side hug where the food and dishes are spared a trip to the floor?

Which bears the question if making out with someone after eating lasagna would be more sexy or gross. I should've gone easier with the garlic in the sauce. Whatever. Dylan could eat raw onions, and I'd still want to kiss him.

I'm pushing the pan into the oven when the man himself emerges from the hall, looking sweatier than ever—and good thing I turned the thermostat down because the room immediately feels ten degrees hotter.

"All unpacked?" I squeak.

"Nah, but I've decided I'm done for the day." He sniffs the air. "Hey, smells delicious. What are you making?"

"Lasagna."

His eyes widen. "That's my favorite."

"Oh, really?" I laugh a little too hard. "I had *no* idea."

"Do you mind if I take a shower before dinner, or is it ready?"

"Go ahead, I just put the pan in the oven. It'll be done when you come out."

He goes, and I fan myself. Perhaps making a dish that requires firing up the oven in mid-June wasn't the best idea. But the things we do for love.

I lay the table, focusing on the familiar routine instead of the fact that Dylan is down the hall, in my shower—*naked*.

Our shower now, I suppose.

Another wild vision takes over, and I let myself get lost in the mindless dreaming of Dylan and me showering together. No risks of woodland creatures showing up this time because it's not the kind of wholesome fantasy that'd take place in a fairytale—unless it was the after-dark version.

A while later, the oven timer dings, jolting me out of my

reverie. The lasagna's cheesy aroma fills the kitchen as I pull it out. The crust looks just right—golden brown and bubbling.

I'm setting the pan on the table when Dylan walks in, and a lump of air catches in my throat. He's wearing basketball shorts and nothing else. I'm blinded by an expanse of flat muscles and pale skin so perfect it belongs between the pages of *Twilight*.

At least he doesn't glitter.

But his chest is a work of art—broad and perfectly sculpted, with droplets of water still clinging to his body, tracing glistening paths down the planes of his abdomen. His six-pack abs are so clearly defined they could've been carved from marble. And his hair, damp from the shower, curls slightly at the ends, so casually sexy, it's almost insulting.

"Oh, there it is." Dylan grabs a T-shirt from one of his boxes still lying around and pulls it on, granting my brain permission to resume a few basic functions. "Smells even better than before." He inhales deeply. "You're going to spoil me."

I laugh, ignoring the way my heart flutters at his words. "It's only dinner."

Dylan's eyes meet mine, and I could swear there's something —a flash of... interest? Curiosity? But then he blinks, and it's gone.

We sit down to eat, and I have to admit, the lasagna is one of my best. Dylan moans appreciatively around his first bite, the sound landing a punch somewhere in my lower belly. I take a large gulp of water to distract myself.

"How does it feel to be officially moved in?"

Dylan grins. "Pretty great, actually. Thanks again for letting me crash here. I know it was kind of last minute."

"I should be the one thanking you. Without you, I would've had to move out and I love this place. I hate change."

"Change is good sometimes." He winks, taking another bite of lasagna.

I almost choke on my bite. Change is good. Change is *great*. I am converted. Let's shake up things right away. Delicious as the lasagna is, I'm ready for it to be thrown to the floor.

My head is spinning so fast with fantasies I've turned into Sleeping Beauty twirling in the woods, surrounded by singing birds and squirrels, ready to dance my dreams away with my prince.

"Oh, by the way," Dylan interrupts my daydreaming. "I wanted to ask you something."

My heart leaps into my throat. This is it. He's going to say he's always had feelings for me too, that even if it's only been a few hours, moving in together made him realize—

"I was wondering if it'd be okay for my girlfriend to visit sometimes?"

I nearly drop my fork, catching it at the last second with a clumsy scrape against my plate—my heart hammering as if I've just rescued something far more precious than a piece of silverware. Not that it matters as everything else shatters around me.

The singing in my head comes to a screeching halt. All the birds explode under the pressure of a shrill, too-high note like in *Shrek*. And I'm left shell-shocked, staring at my new roommate.

Girlfriend? When did he...? How did I not know...?

"Hunter? You okay?" Dylan's looking at me with concern, and I realize I haven't spoken for several long seconds.

"Yeah, sorry," I croak out. "Just... surprised. I didn't know you were seeing someone." Then my voice turns unnaturally bright as I add, "A girlfriend—wow, Dylan, that's amazing." Amazingly devastating. "First Nina and now you. New relationships are the best! Like walking around with glitter in your veins." Or push pins, in my case. I need to shut up.

Dylan's face relaxes into a smile. "It's pretty new. Her name's Olivia. She's great; I think you're really going to like her."

I think I'm really going to hate her. But I nod mechanically. "Oh, I'm sure I will!" My fake grin is wide enough to break my cheeks. The lasagna, which tasted sublime moments ago, turns to ashes in my mouth. But I force down another bite, determined to pretend everything is fine, super. A-okay!

"So, is it okay if she comes over sometimes?" Dylan prompts, still waiting for an answer.

"Of course," I hear myself say as if from a great distance, my voice bubbling with forced enthusiasm like I'm a morning talk show host. "This is your home, too. She's welcome any time— seriously, no need to ask."

Dylan beams at me, completely oblivious to the way my world is crumbling around me. "Thanks, Hunt. You're the best."

I force another smile, but inside, I'm splintering. The fairytale I've been spooling in my head all day shatters, replaced by a grim reality where my Prince Charming has shown up at the castle gates with a different princess in tow.

As Dylan launches into the improbably romantic story about how he met Olivia, I nod along, making appropriate cheerful noises at the right parts. But my mind is elsewhere, counting those eleven steps again. Only now, they don't represent the years of knowing Dylan. They symbolize the insurmountable distance between us, a chasm I foolishly thought I could bridge, but that has never been wider.

Eleven steps away. An entire world apart.

2

DYLAN

I've fucked up, but have no idea how. Hunter hasn't stopped smiling since we sat down to dinner. But halfway through the meal, something about it has started to feel off, like that forced grin has been ironed onto her face. Her energy is different—too bright, too bubbly, like she's overcompensating for something. I do a mental inventory of our conversation, but I can't pinpoint what I said or did to upset her, or when exactly the shift happened. I just know it did. Things were going well—friendly banter, easy quips. And now this synthetic politeness has wrapped around us like a creeping fog.

I look at her, and she gives me a thirty-two-tooth smile in return. But it doesn't reach her eyes, their usual warmth replaced with a glossy, distant sadness.

I sound insane, but I'm sure something is up. I'm not making things up. Like when I got up to refill the water pitcher and I caught her off guard. She thought I had my back turned and had dropped her head in her hands, her shoulders sagged in a way that confirmed my instincts. And now, even though she's smiling at me and offering cheerful quips, she's barely touching her lasagna. When she does take a bite, it's small, mechanical, like she's forcing herself to swallow it against a gag. Which doesn't make sense; the lasagna is delicious.

Since I've scarfed down all my pasta and Hunter doesn't seem interested in finishing hers, I offer to do the dishes. Anything to ease the strange disconnect. "I'll clean up." I give her my most charming smile. "Only fair, since you cooked this amazing meal."

Hunter glances up, meeting my eyes briefly. "Sure, thanks." She nods, but her tone lacks real warmth. As she stands up, her long, dark hair falls down her back, swaying slightly as she moves to the counter. She tears off a sheet of aluminum foil with a crisp, metallic sound that slices through the quiet, jagged and precise. Her movements are rigid as she carefully wraps the metal sheet over the casserole of lasagna leftovers. Hunter drops it in the fridge and closes the door too enthusiastically, making it slam. "Should be good also tomorrow."

"Lasagna always tastes better the next day." I give her an open smile.

"Lasagna magic, right?" Hunter flashes a quick, robotic smile, her jaw tight as her eyes flick to the doorway, betraying her eagerness to escape. Fuck, the awkwardness is painful.

Stretching my back, I stifle a yawn, exhausted from hauling a thousand boxes. I gather our plates and deposit them in the sink. Hunter jumps out of my way almost comically.

I eye the pots and pans and suddenly feel too tired to tackle the washing tonight.

Tomorrow. I'll deal with them in the morning when I'm not dead on my feet.

I'm about to head to the living room and collapse on the couch when I catch Hunter's gaze lingering on the sink, her dark eyes fixed on the unwashed dishes. She presses her lips into a thin line, and I can sense the disapproval radiating off her. Well, at least it's a genuine reaction.

I sigh, a familiar frustration bubbling up inside me. "Please don't tell me you're one of those," I half-joke.

Hunter raises an eyebrow. "Those what?"

"You know, a neat freak. Like Tristan." I shrug to keep the mood light.

"I'm not a neat freak, Dylan." Her eyes flash with annoyance. "You offered to do the dishes. I didn't ask."

"Yes, but does it have to be right now?"

She grabs a dish sponge. "I can do the washing."

Perfect. I've made things worse. "Please don't. I'll take care of them *now*." I backpedal, attempting to smooth over the faux pas.

"Thank you." She nods, dropping the scrubber. And from her tone, she might as well have told me to go fuck myself. "Goodnight."

"Night."

Her stiff posture as she turns and walks away drips with irritation. And the decisive click of her bedroom door closing sounds meaner than if she'd slammed it.

"Oh, hell."

I roll up my metaphorical sleeves and get to work, scrubbing the plates and pots with a bit more force than necessary before transferring them into the dishwasher. As I dry my hands on a kitchen towel, a sudden thought hits me—*this is the first night in fifteen years that Tristan and I aren't roommates*. No more late-night video game sessions, no watching college basketball reminiscing about our days at Duke, or marathons of ridiculous reality shows we'd never admit to liking in public.

Craving a bit of fresh air, I step out onto the balcony. *Not exactly fresh*. Without the air conditioning, the heat is stifling. But I stay.

The city stretches out before me, a glittering sea of lights and distant sounds. Car horns and the murmur of nightlife drift up from the streets below, a reminder that New York truly never sleeps. I lean against the railing, letting the warm night breeze ruffle my hair and the energy of Manhattan wash over me. The vast stretch of lights makes my problems seem small in comparison. Still, I can't shake the nagging worry that I've started on the wrong foot with Hunter.

I'll have to make it up to her, show her I'm not some inconsiderate slob, explain that I was just tired tonight.

My phone buzzes in my pocket, interrupting the self-flagellation. I fish it out and smile as Tristan's name appears on the screen.

"Miss me already?" I tease, keeping my tone light.

There's a beat of silence before Tristan replies, his voice uncharacteristically serious. "Yeah, Thirty-Three. I do." We still call each other with our old team numbers from when we were playing basketball at Duke. A reminder of how far our friendship stretches back.

The admission feels strangely comforting. A shared acknowledgment of how much our lives have changed in such a short time. That it's okay to be happy for him and Nina, but also to miss my best friend.

I click my tongue, wanting to lighten the mood. "Well, I warned you that your girlfriend is a super-annoying roommate," I joke, hoping to coax a laugh out of him.

But Tristan scoffs. "Nah, Nina's great. No complaints there." His voice takes on that slightly goofy, love-struck tone he always gets when talking about my sister.

"I take it you're not calling to report she kicked you out?"

"Nope, she's showering," Tristan replies, and I can practically hear the smirk in his voice.

I groan, holding up a hand even though he can't see me. "Please don't tell me it's a post-sex shower."

Tristan chuckles, a deep, rumbling sound that's so familiar it makes my chest ache. "Then I won't tell you."

Rolling my eyes, I change the subject. "Remember our first place together? That tiny dorm room where the beds were too short?"

"How could I forget?" There's a note of amusement in his voice, and I can picture him lounging on the couch in his apartment, one arm draped over the back as he stretches out comfortably. "Those beds are still the reason I'll never sleep in the fetal position again."

I laugh, the tension from earlier easing a bit as I reminisce with my best friend. "Those were the days, Eleven. Remember that time we tried to sneak that keg into our room?"

"And we dropped it down the stairs?" Tristan chuckles. "I was sure the RA would catch us."

"Good times, man. Now, you're shacking up with my sister, and I'm..." I trail off, not sure how to finish that sentence.

"How're things with Hunter?" Tristan must sense my hesitation.

I sigh, pinching the bridge of my nose. "I've already fucked up. Left some dirty dishes in the sink like a slob, and I've committed some other obscure offense I haven't figured out yet."

Tristan laughs, but there's a sympathetic edge to it. "Poor bastard. Can't even smooth things over with mind-blowing sex."

And just like that, for the first time in my life, I get a mental flash of Hunter in a sexual context. Long, toned legs wrapped around my waist, dark hair fanned out across the pillow, those obsidian eyes burning into mine as I—Woah. Where did that come from?

I banish the inappropriate image. "Yeah, well, I'll resort to the traditional forms of groveling."

I hear my sister's voice yelling his name in the background.

"I should head inside. Early day tomorrow and all that."

"Same here." Tristan stifles a yawn. "Night, Thirty-Three."

"Night, Eleven. And thanks for calling."

"I thought you might need to hear my voice, honey." Tristan uses a mock-romantic tone.

"Asshole."

"Love you, man."

"Same."

I hang up, slipping my phone back into my pocket. The skyline glitters in the distance, but I don't really see it. My mind is stuck on that fleeting, vivid image of Hunter, limbs tangled with mine. I need to get that out of my head, and fast. The last thing I want is for things between us to grow even more complicated.

With a sigh, I make my way back inside, the cool air of the apartment a welcome relief from the cloying humidity. As I pass Hunter's door, I pause, wondering if I should knock and apologize. But then I reconsider. I'll make it up to her by becoming a better, cleaner roommate. In my room, I flop down on the bed and stare up at the ceiling fan whirring above, its shadows casting playful shapes across the walls as my mind refuses to shut off. My thoughts ping-pong between guilt over arguing with Hunter and that damn mental image of her pinned underneath me that has imprinted in my brain.

I mean, sure, she's attractive. I'd have to be blind not to notice. But that's always been a passive observation, a fact filed away without much thought. But tonight, it feels different. That image of her tangled in the sheets with me came out of nowhere, blindsiding me like a sucker punch. Maybe it's because we've never spent this much time alone together before. Sharing a space like this changes things—it strips away the buffer of other people, leaving just the two of us. I tell myself it's nothing, just a stray thought brought on by the new dynamic.

She's my roommate now. And even if seeing more of her messes with the wiring in my brain, I can't go there. We're in too close quarters. Living together means there's no escape if things get messy. And, more importantly, I'm seeing someone. Things with Olivia are pretty new; we've only gone on a couple of dates. But I still have no business fantasizing about another woman. Already, Olivia wasn't super thrilled when I told her I was moving in with a woman—a single, smart, gorgeous woman...

I groan, covering my face with my hands. This is not how I pictured my first night in the new apartment going. I need to fix this, and fast. Tomorrow, I'll wake up early, make breakfast as a peace offering, and apologize for whatever incomprehensible offense I committed. It's a solid plan.

Just as I doze off, my phone lights up with a message.

OLIVIA

How's the new place? New roommate nice?

I stare at the screen, guilt churning in my stomach as Hunter's face flashes in my mind. How do I even begin to answer that?

3

HUNTER

I'm sprawled on my bed, the buttery glow of the nightstand lamp softening the edges of my room. Shadows stretch lazily across the pale-blue walls, turning the dark wood of my bookcase into an inky silhouette. The earthy scent of paper and wax drifts from the candle I've lit, heavy and clingy, more oppressive than soothing. My gaze catches on the bookshelves, their carefully organized rows of novels, textbooks, and engineering manuals stacked with obsessive precision, each one perfectly aligned by subject and size.

Across the room, my laptop glows faintly on the tidy desk, surrounded by carefully labeled files and a mug of perfectly aligned pens. The screen is stuck on a spreadsheet of color-coded data—an unfinished report for the engineering consulting firm I work for. The closet door is slightly ajar, revealing clothes hung in perfect rainbow coordination, all facing the same direction on identical hangers.

Okay, maybe I'm a bit of a neat freak. But if anyone asked, I'd deny it.

I shift uncomfortably, fingers brushing the cool sheets covered in tiny constellations and math formulas. I trace the white shapes over the pastel-lilac cotton, wishing an equation could solve the mess in my head. But the cute, starry patterns bring no solace as regret claws at my insides.

Groaning, I bury my face into the pillow, cringing at the memory of how I acted like a total bitch to Dylan. I took out my frustration about his new girlfriend on him, griping about dirty dishes. Yeah, it annoys me when someone leaves them in the sink to get that gross, slimy residue that's impossible to scrub off afterward and that attracts every fruit fly in New York. But let's be real. I snapped at him because I was mad my roommates-to-lovers dream had gotten crushed.

My stomach churns anxiously. Did I completely ruin our semi-friendship? Is Dylan already regretting taking up his sister's lease?

Footsteps echo in the hall and my heart stops. Two shadows take shape under my door. Dylan's feet? Why is he standing outside my room? Is he as upset about our fight as I am?

I hold my breath, pulse pounding, waiting for him to knock, to speak, to reassure me he's dumped his girlfriend and all my fantasies can still come true—probably not this last one.

But then the silhouettes move on and I hear Dylan go into his bedroom.

Sagging back onto the mattress, I stare at the ceiling, bewildered and wondering.

A sharp ding pierces the stillness. Rolling over, I grab my phone from the nightstand. It's a text from Nina.

NINA

Hey, how are you doing?

I hesitate, then type back.

HUNTER

I'm fine, why?

Even as I hit send, I have a sinking premonition of what her next question is going to be.

Nina's response comes quickly, confirming my suspicions.

NINA

Tristan told me that Dylan said he upset you earlier

I let out an even louder groan than before. My body curls inward as if to physically reject the mortification. Great, so Dylan is already complaining about me. My bitchiness has made its way through the friendship grapevine.

Honestly, I deserve it. Of course Dylan's telling people what a disaster I am. I don't even blame him for saying something. If I were Dylan, I'd be texting all my friends too, warning them about my neurotic roommate with a chip on her shoulder. Why wouldn't he? I've gone from friendly to unhinged in less than an hour.

Instead of coming across as the cool, easy-going roommate he might've secretly imagined spending late nights laughing with, I've cemented myself as the uptight control freak who gets irrationally upset over a couple of dirty dishes. I've officially tanked any chance of being seen as fun, chill, or—heaven forbid—someone worth dating. The kind of person he'd look forward to coming home to.

He probably thought I was at least normal when we moved in together. Now he knows the truth: I'm a dickhead who vented her frustration on him for no good reason. He has no idea why I really flipped out on him. Dylan must be so confused. *Way to go, Hunter.* Even if I were remotely on his radar before tonight—which I wasn't—this just solidified my place as not-girlfriend material. No, scratch that—not even want-to-casually-hang-out-with material.

That's probably why he was lurking outside my door. To tell me this has all been a mistake, that he's moving out, and going to live happily ever after with *Olivia.*

My fingers fly across the screen, tapping rapidly as I go all out to play it cool.

HUNTER

I was tired and snapped at him about the dishes

You know how I can be about that stuff

I'm sorry if I upset him. It's no big deal. I'll smooth things over tomorrow

Nina's reply pops up.

NINA

Yeah, typical. When my brother says he'll do something, he means... eventually

But are you sure there's nothing else? Tristan thought there was more, based on what Dylan told him

Holy fucking hell, what did Dylan say to Tristan? Did he guess the reason I was upset? No, that's impossible; I practically asked to become BFF with his girlfriend and have regular sleepovers. He can't know it's about Olivia.

I prop myself on one elbow as I re-read the message, chewing my lip. Should I confess to Nina about my massive crush on her brother? My gaze flickers to the framed photo on my nightstand

—me, Nina, and Rowena in matching pink Elle Woods costumes, drenched but grinning ear to ear on the Halloween night we first became friends.

Could I really admit my fixation on her brother after all this time? My thumb hovers over the keyboard, my heart squeezing. What would I even call it? An infatuation? Obsession? It feels so intense, so all-consuming, but can you truly be in love with someone who barely knows you're alive? And what's the point now that he's officially off the market? After staying silent for eleven freaking years, do I tell Nina the second her brother is no longer available?

I almost confide in her. But I chicken out at the last second, typing a deflective response.

HUNTER

No, no, it was definitely the dishes thing, promise

I close my eyes, letting out a shaky exhale—crisis averted, suspicions brushed off. But an uneasy dissatisfaction lingers. I bite my lip, torn between the fear of exposing my true feelings and the urge to pry, to find out more about the woman who's stealing my dreams.

Before I can stop myself, my thumbs are flying across the keyboard again.

HUNTER

Hey, random question...

Did you know Dylan had a girlfriend?

The moment I hit send, my stomach drops. What am I doing? I want to reach through the screen and snatch the words back, but it's too late. Nina has already read the text. *Crap.* I bite my lip harder as I roll over the bed, waiting for her response, wondering if I've said too much. If my best friend can read past my bullshit.

The three dots signaling Nina is typing pop up immediately, but her actual reply takes forever to come through. I shift restlessly, running an agitated hand through my hair and tugging it over my shoulder as I stare unblinking at the screen. Shit, did my question about Dylan's girlfriend give away what's really on my mind?

The suspense is killing me. I hop off the bed, pacing around the room to work off the nervous energy. I blow out the candle on my desk, crack open the window to let the smoke drift outside, and snap my laptop shut. Once the air clears and the summer heat starts to creep in, I shut the window again and settle on the bed, hugging my knees to my chest just as a new message from Nina pops on the screen.

> **NINA**
> Yeah, he mentioned going on a first date last week. Didn't know it had progressed to something official. Why?

A prickle stings my eyes and I rapidly blink it back. Call it a hunch, but I get the distinct sense that this carefully neutral response isn't what Nina initially wrote. As if she's figured out my pathetic crush on Dylan, but we're both studiously skirting around the topic.

I sigh heavily, the phone resting limply on my thigh until it vibrates with another incoming text from Nina.

> **NINA**
> How do you know about the girlfriend thing?

Chewing on my thumbnail, I debate how much to reveal.

> **HUNTER**
>
> Dylan asked if he could bring her over sometimes

I type back, attempting a casual tone.
Nina's reply has an oddly cryptic vibe.

> **NINA**
>
> If you're not comfortable with a stranger in your space, you can say no...

I scoff. Right, because I really need to come across as even more of a psycho bitch to Dylan.

> **HUNTER**
>
> No, I'm fine with it. Not a big deal. Just wanted to know if you'd met her and if she's cool

I also want to know if she's beautiful, have all her social handles so I can low-key cyber-stalk her, and would asking for her social security number be overkill?

> **NINA**
>
> Sorry, haven't met her yet

I roll my eyes at the non-committal reply and I toss the phone aside on my pillow. I'm done with this conversation.

After a few minutes, a different notification dings from our group chat—code name Gossip Girls. It's Rowena, reassuring us everything is fine in her tower—a swanky Manhattan penthouse —and that Adrian is cool. I don't even know how to reply to that. The message at least reassures me I'm not the only one messed up in our group of friends. I send a hug emoji back. After that, we wrap things up with brief goodnights.

Slumping down, I flick off the bedside lamp, flooding the

room with inky blackness. I can only make out the shadowy outlines of my bookshelves in the faint glow filtering through the blinds from the street.

I squeeze my lids shut, but my mind won't quit whirring. Frustration simmers in my veins as I toss and turn futilely, haunted by the disastrous start of my cohabitation with Dylan. *Ugh.* I need to find an anti-cringe setting for my brain *stat.* Is there an app for that?

4

HUNTER

I blink awake at 5 a.m. without an alarm, the sky outside just turning pink. At once, I'm alert, straining my ears for any sound in the apartment. But the house is silent. Dylan must be asleep.

A knot uncoils in my stomach. I don't have to face him. Not yet. I can slip away before he wakes up and avoid a morning repeat of yesterday's debacle—the sting still burns like a thousand red ants biting all over my skin. Even a shower is out of the question. The noise might wake him; his room is right next to the bathroom. I'll wash up at the gym instead.

After slipping into something comfortable, I gather a change of office-appropriate clothes, trying not to wrinkle the outfit too much when I stuff it into my gym bag. As I pull my bedroom door open, the hinges protest with a slight squeak. I silently curse and vow to oil them as I step through the threshold. I need stealth, but the entire apartment fights against me. The floorboards creak under my feet as the hallway stretches impossibly long. And the pipes groan somewhere in the walls, adding a muffled grumble to the stillness.

I glare at the flat surface; *can't you wait five minutes before starting a wind section concert?*

Finally reaching the front door, I slip out, inhaling deeply as the humid morning air envelops me.

At the gym, I swipe my membership card and push through the glass doors. I almost make a beeline straight for the showers, but since I'm here, I might as well squeeze in a workout.

I go check the course schedule, not in the mood to mindlessly exercise on the machines. That kind of training never appeals to me. I get bored too easily, lose interest fast, and bail before getting any benefit. I prefer guided instructions and the structure of a group. Keeps me accountable, and there's no slipping out halfway through.

The gym is nearly deserted this early, the sterile scent of disinfectant and rubber mats still unspoiled by the inevitable tinge of sweat. I pass by the rows of treadmills, their blank screens mirroring the dim overhead lights, and read the bulletin board. Mindfulness yoga is the sole pre-dawn offering.

I could use some mindfulness.

I drop my things in a locker and head to the yoga studio. The room is awash in soft, warm light, the walls a calming neutral shade. A hint of incense lingers, even if nothing appears to be actively burning. I grab a mat from the rack by the door and unroll it near the back, hoping to remain inconspicuous. While not a total novice, I'm far from a yoga master.

A loud gong kick-starts the class. With a deep exhale, I sit up straighter, determined to embrace this small slice of peace before the day truly begins, pushing aside all thoughts of a certain tall, blond distraction living under my roof.

As the instructor guides us into the first pose, her voice soothing, I try to concentrate on my breathing, on emptying my mind, but my thoughts refuse to cooperate. As I move through the positions, my brain continues to churn, making me wince each time I replay last night's events.

I redouble my efforts to focus on the instructions, but my mind stubbornly drifts back to Dylan. Every stretch becomes a reminder of our uncomfortable dinner, each deep exhale a sigh I couldn't release in his presence. The yoga teacher keeps shooting me pointed looks, my constant wincing and teeth-grinding likely a dead giveaway that inner peace is eluding me.

As the class winds down, I'm no more relaxed than when I started. I sigh, rolling up my mat and returning it to the rack before heading out of the studio. The hot shower is a welcome relief, washing away the sweat and some of the stiffness in my muscles, but doing little to quell the persistent thoughts of Dylan.

I dress quickly, shoulder my bag, and stride out of the gym, making my way to the closest subway station. As I descend the steps, the familiar rumble of the trains and the bustle of morning commuters envelop me. I find solace in the journey's anonymity, my thoughts finally quieting as I lose myself in the city's rhythm.

By the time I exit the subway, I need another shower. Thankfully, a blast of air conditioning engulfs me as I step into my office building. The sleek, glass-walled lobby is already bustling. Business suits brush past each other, briefcases in hand, as they head toward the elevators. It's another Monday morning at Winton Engineering Solutions, and the office promises the usual battlefield of egos and power plays. But today, I'd rather be at work than face the minefield of conflicting emotions waiting for me at home. I want to see Dylan; I crave our next encounter. But I also want to avoid him like the Plague.

The elevator ride to the twenty-fourth floor is as quick as it is silent. The doors glide open onto a series of interconnected hallways lined with glass-walled offices, each door bearing the name of a different engineer, and larger meeting rooms that make up the heart of the firm. From up here, the Hudson River glitters in the distance, the sun catching the ripples of water in a dance of light and shadow. The Manhattan skyline stretches out beyond it, a steel and glass jungle that is both a comfort and a cage.

I head toward my office, one of the smallest for a team leader, but that I've made the most of, decorating it with a few personal touches: a framed picture of my mom and dad from my college graduation, a cactus plant I've kept alive for two years, and a collection of engineering manuals stacked neatly in the corner of my desk. I've also hung my master's degree on one of the drywalls, in case someone still doubted I'm really an engineer. There's the proof, folks, printed on watermarked paper.

I drop my bag on the chair, fire up my computer, and take a minute to gather my thoughts before the daily grind pulls me under. Since I'm early, I take my time sorting through unopened emails that accumulated over the weekend.

When I come up for air, the clock on my computer reads 8.55 a.m. The team leaders' morning meeting is in five minutes. I grab my notepad and pen, checking my reflection in the glass wall. I've pulled my hair back into a neat ponytail to hide the lack of access to a flat iron this morning. And I'm wearing only basic makeup—mostly concealer, to cover the signs of a sleepless night. I smooth down the wrinkles in my cream blouse and straighten my pencil skirt. Ready as I'll ever be.

The conference room is already half-full when I get there. A large, crystal table dominates the space, surrounded by high-backed, leather chairs. The vast windows frame a breathtaking, full-scale view of the city cut in half by the partially drawn blinds —a shield against the summer glare.

"Morning, everyone," I say as I take my seat toward the end of the table, my usual spot.

A chorus of mumbled greetings responds. Most of my colleagues are buried in their phones or tablets, also catching up on emails or reading through reports. Soon, the last of the stragglers file in. I flip open my notepad, ready to jot down the latest updates. Daniel, the company's COO, takes the seat at the head of the table. His gray hair and perpetual scowl give him a gruff appearance, but I like him. He's fair.

Mark, the team leaders' coordinator for the infrastructure division, sits next to him, his blond hair perfectly gelled, and a smug smile on his face as he thumbs through his phone. I make a point not to look at him.

Daniel clears his throat, tapping a pen against his laptop to get our attention. "Alright, let's get started. We've got a lot to cover."

I straighten in my seat, pen poised over my notepad.

"First order of business," Daniel continues, "the Upton Bridge project. How are we looking on timelines?"

Mark jumps in, his voice smooth and confident. "We're on track to meet the end-of-month deadline. The team worked through the weekend to ensure the foundations were set. We're coordinating with the subcontractors to complete the steel deliveries next week."

"Good." Daniel nods, making a note. "We can't afford any delays on that one. The client is already breathing down our necks. What about the harbor-front redevelopment?"

I glance at my notes, ready to speak up, but Mark beats me to it. "We've run into a few snags with the city permits, but I've got

Jim on it. He's been in touch with the zoning commission daily. We should have it sorted by next week."

My fingers tighten around the pen. Jim's been on it? Last I checked, Jim, while being the team leader assigned to the project, was on vacation last week. I was the one who spent hours on the phone with the zoning commission, navigating the maze of paperwork and red tape. But I bite my tongue. No point in sounding petty or whiny.

Daniel turns to me, finally acknowledging my presence. "Hunter, you've been overseeing the new green-energy initiative. Any updates?"

I force a calm smile. "Yes, we've made significant progress. I've been in talks with SolarTech, and they're on board with our proposal to integrate solar panels into the new office building designs. We're also exploring options for geothermal heating."

Daniel nods, but his eyes have already moved on. "Good. We'll need that report ASAP. Now, on to the next item..."

As the meeting drones on, I tune out the undercurrents of office politics. Mark keeps hogging the spotlight, and my contributions are acknowledged only when it's unavoidable.

We Rolodex through the various projects: the renovation of the old city hall, the expansion of the subway line, and the new residential complex in Queens. I keep jotting down notes but find it harder than usual to pay attention to the developments that don't involve me directly. My mind keeps drifting back to Dylan and the mess I made last night.

"And last," Daniel's voice pulls me back, "we've got a new project coming in. A big one. The North Shore initiative. A new office complex with avant-garde design. The client is Carmichael Corp. They want to get a LEED certification." *Green energy, this is my field of expertise*, I think with a jolt of excitement. "It's going to be a massive undertaking, lots of moving parts, tight deadlines.

We'll need someone to take the lead, someone who can handle long hours and the pressure."

A new project, a massive one with a time crunch and endless challenges. It's a shot at recognition, a chance to show I can handle more than minor infrastructures—something that could finally get me noticed. My brain races with possibilities: impressing the higher-ups, adding a significant project to my portfolio, and stepping out of the shadows. But it's more than that. The thought of demanding work and long hours ironically sounds like a lifeline, a reason to leave the apartment early and come back late, an excuse not to be home. To avoid the reality of Dylan and his new girlfriend.

I raise my hand, my voice cutting through the room. "I'll do it."

Heads turn in my direction.

Mark snickers. "You, Hunter?"

"Yes, me." I meet his eyes for the first time since he entered the room, my voice steady. "I'd love to take on the North Shore project."

The room goes so quiet you'd think I'd just announced pineapple belongs on everything—yes, even spaghetti. My gaze switches to Daniel, who's looking around the table as if hoping for any other takers. Calculations run behind his eyes. His gaze flickers to Mark, who shrugs noncommittally. No one else appears eager to volunteer.

"Are you sure?" Daniel hesitates. "This project will be extremely complex. Someone with more seniority would be better suited." He looks around the room hopefully.

When nobody else steps forward, Daniel glances at Mark again. "You could work on it with Mark's supervision."

Before Mark can say anything, I nip that option in the bud. "If

Mark wants the project, I'd happily leave it to him. If it has to be my project, I'd rather proceed alone."

Working with Mark as my "supervisor" would only mean doing all the work and getting zero credit. And I don't know, the whole Dylan situation has dosed me with a sizable helping of "fuck it" attitude. Last week, I wouldn't have volunteered, or I would've accepted Mark's oversight. But yesterday, I witnessed firsthand what not going after the things I want does. It leaves the door open for someone else to swoop in and snatch them from right under my nose. Fuck that. Fuck Mark. And fuck Olivia.

Daniel hesitates a beat longer, weighing his options. He could appoint one of the guys to the project, but then he'd have two unhappy team leaders. "Alright," he concedes. "Let's see how the preliminary design phases go. You'll coordinate directly with Carmichael Corp. If you make the client happy, The North Shore project will be yours officially. Otherwise, Mark will take over." He nods at me and I nod back. "I'm going to need weekly updates."

"Understood." I try to hide the grin that's threatening to break through. "I won't let you down."

Never have I been more eager to spend time at the office and bury myself in work.

5

DYLAN

Monday mornings at an investment bank are nothing short of chaotic. A rush of movement and chatter engulfs me as I enter the open-plan office. Phones ringing off the hook, voices raised in conversation, and the clatter of keyboards—all of it blends into a symphony of controlled entropy. The faint smell of fresh coffee wafts through the air, mingling with the scent of expensive cologne and the unmistakable tang of stress and high stakes. I tug at the knot of my tie, straightening it, its dark, solid blue, matching the tailored suit I put on without thinking this morning. Presentation in my field is everything, and in a world where first impressions can make or break a deal, looking the part is half the battle.

My office is a minimalist's dream: a polished desk, a few framed certificates on the wall, and a stack of papers that multiply every time I look away. Floor-to-ceiling windows offer a sweeping view of Manhattan. The skyline is breathtaking, even more so with the city still waking up, its skyscrapers glinting in the rising sun. Pausing outside my office, I glance at my reflection in the glass. Hair in place, suit perfect, eyes a little tired—nothing a coffee can't fix.

And this morning, I'm going to need more than one cup. Mondays are always brutal, but today has an extra kick. There are several mergers on the table, and everyone's scrambling to get their hands on the best deals.

Kelly, my assistant, is already at her desk next to my door, her fingers flying over the keyboard with the kind of focus I can only manage after my second cup of coffee. She looks up as I stop by her station, offering a bright smile. "Morning, boss. Ready to dive in?"

"Morning, Kelly." I flash her a grin. "As ready as I'll ever be. How was your weekend?"

"Too short." She sighs. "Yours?"

I picture the stack of boxes I still have to unpack and the situation with Hunter that I wasn't able to fix earlier this morning since she was nowhere to be found. "Too messy." My smile tightens.

"Oh?" Kelly raises an eyebrow at me.

"Moving houses, remember? My best friend kicked me out to shack up with my sister?"

Kelly nods sympathetically, as if she can sense my mood, but mercifully doesn't prod for more.

"What's on the docket for today?"

She hands me a print-out of the day's schedule, neatly organized, in a large, clear font, double spaced, and printed on cream paper instead of white—the basics of my survival. She'll have also sent me an electronic copy I can use text to speech on.

I have dyslexia, something I don't like to parade around, and these little adjustments help me function at the highest level without anyone noticing.

"You've got a meeting with the mergers team at nine." Kelly

gives me the highlights of my day. "Followed by a client call at ten. A lunch meeting with potential buyers for the Horizon deal. And later tonight, you have a call with the Tokyo office at seven."

I nod, scanning the schedule. "Got it. Thanks, Kelly. Any updates on the Lione acquisition?"

"Still waiting on confirmation from their legal team," she says. "I'll let you know as soon as I hear anything."

"Perfect. Thanks. I don't know what I'd do without you."

Kelly waves me off. "You'd be lost and late to everything, that's what."

She's not wrong. I chuckle, heading into my office and closing the door behind me. I settle into my chair, the leather creaking under me, and soak in the silence. The calm before the storm. I flip open my laptop, and emails flood the screen instantly, piling on top of the stack of reports on my desk that I need to get through.

I pull up the meeting agenda Kelly prepared, skimming the major points to cover. But I lack my usual focus; my thoughts keep yanking me back to this morning. The apartment was eerily quiet when I woke up, Hunter noticeably absent. I'd planned to make her breakfast, bribe her with something sweet—pancakes, waffles, the works. A peace offering of sorts. But as I crossed the hall, her door was closed, her room dark, and her shoes were no longer in their spot in the entryway.

A made-up mental image of Hunter sneaking out in the early hours, tiptoeing past my door, flickers in my mind. I didn't hear her leave. I'm not sure what her morning routine is. But is she always gone before 6 a.m.? Or was she avoiding me? I can't shake the nagging sensation that it is the latter option.

I rub a hand over my face. No time to dwell on it now.

A knock on my door pulls me from my thoughts. Kelly pokes her head in. "Five minutes till your meeting."

I nod, closing my laptop. "Right. Thanks."

My assistant leaves, and I stand, smoothing down my suit. Time to put on the game face. Whatever's going on with Hunter, it'll have to wait.

The nine o'clock mergers meeting is what I expect: intense and fast-paced. We go over the latest reports, each merger dissected down to the smallest detail. Numbers fly across the table, financial projections and risk assessments, each figure representing millions of dollars and the future of entire companies. I keep my focus sharp, pushing thoughts of my new roommate into a corner of my mind. Here, I'm all about business.

After the meeting, I sort my calls, go to lunch with clients, and by the time I'm back in my office, it's already mid-afternoon. But I still have hours of work ahead.

My phone buzzes on the desk. A message from Olivia.

OLIVIA

Hey, handsome. Want to hang out tonight? I could come over and check out your new place ;)

I frown at the message, setting the phone down. I want to hang out with Olivia, but the thought of her coming over to the apartment makes me uneasy. Hunter said it's okay to have Olivia over whenever. But I don't really know how she rolls—if she prefers not to have people over during the week, and it's okay only at weekends, until what time. Last night was our first living together, and I've messed up already. I didn't get a chance to apologize this morning, and bringing a third person into the mix before we've cleared the waters might not be smart. I press the microphone button and dictate my reply.

DYLAN

I'd love to see you, but the place is still a wreck. Haven't finished unpacking. How about I come to yours instead?

OLIVIA

Aww, okay. But you owe me a tour soon. I want to see where my boyfriend lives

Boyfriend. The word tastes strange as I roll it over my tongue, unfamiliar. We've been dating only for ten days, but she's moving at light speed. True, I've called Olivia my girlfriend, too, but only because it's shorter than "the woman I've been seeing." I wonder if she's on the same page or if she assumes this is already a serious relationship after two dates.

DYLAN

Soon, I promise

I send the text and dive back into work. I skim through the numbers, the lines of text blurring as I focus on the bottom line. Profit margins, market share, risk factors—it's all a balancing act, a delicate dance of data and projections.

Another buzz, another text from Olivia.

OLIVIA

What time tonight?

DYLAN

I'm stuck here for a while. I'll text you when I leave the office

I toss the phone onto the desk, screen down, and crack my neck, the familiar popping sound a brief relief from the pressure mounting in my head as the busy afternoon stretches out before me.

By the time I resurface, the sun is already setting, casting long shadows across the city. I'm exhausted, my mind buzzing with fatigue. I'm half-tempted to cancel on Olivia and go home. But I'm not positive the situation there would be any more relaxing. Plus, I'm not a dick. I'm not gonna ask for a rain check at the last minute.

I pack up my things, slipping my laptop into my backpack. The office is quieter now, the evening calm settling in. I nod to Kelly as I pass her desk, offering a tired smile. "Heading out."

She stretches her arms above her head, grinning. "Finally."

"See you tomorrow."

"Night, boss."

I order a car on the ride down in the elevator, shooting a quick text to Olivia next.

DYLAN

On my way. Should I stop to get takeout?

Her reply arrives as I step out of the building, the air still simmering with the day's heat, the city alive around me—the noise of traffic, the whisper of a breeze slipping through the tall skyscrapers, the buzz of thousands of lives all moving at once.

OLIVIA

No need, I cooked. Can't wait to see you

Good thing I didn't cancel after she made me dinner.

My car arrives. I slide into the back seat and lean my head against the headrest, closing my eyes. A vague sense of something left undone sweeps over me. But then the car starts moving, and I tell myself it's nothing, only a long day getting to me.

6

DYLAN

Tonight at Olivia's was... *weird*. We had dinner—turns out she's an amazing cook, then we talked. I broached the subject of how fast our relationship was progressing, and she was cool about it. At first, she hesitated, asking if it was because she'd called me her boyfriend. I said, yeah, in a way. Olivia had the cutest reaction. She covered her face with her hands, but still smiled, and said she regretted sending the text right away. I told her it wasn't a problem, but that I wasn't sure how serious she thought we were. She agreed to keep it casual for now.

Then, after dinner, we started making out on her couch. But when things got heated, she shut me down, explaining she prefers to take it slow at the beginning and get to know the other person better before sex, which, of course, I respected. And the weirdest fucking thing? I was relieved she didn't want to have sex with me. Which has never happened to me, and I'm not sure how to fucking explain it.

Back at my place, I unlock the front door and kick off my shoes, stumbling into the dark apartment well past midnight. I grope the wall, searching for the light switch that eludes me in this new space. I'm completely disoriented, my mental map of my old apartment clashing with the unfamiliar layout of my sister's —mine now, I guess.

Moving cautiously down the hall, I bump into something solid. A loud crash pierces the silence as glass shatters against the hardwood floor, the sound as sharp as a gunshot in the stillness. I take another step and cry out as a shard slices into my foot, sending a jolt of searing pain up my leg.

"Shit," I hiss under my breath, hobbling forward, bumping into more stuff. Suddenly, something hard slams into my groin, and agony explodes behind my eyes, whitening my vision. I double over, gasping for air.

The impact sends me reeling backward and I land flat on my ass, thankfully avoiding the minefield of broken glass. A loud groan escapes me as I curl into myself, hands instinctively cupping my throbbing privates.

"Dylan?" a familiar voice asks tentatively in the darkness.

I can only muster another pitiful moan in response. Light floods the room and I squint to see Hunter standing over me, wild-eyed and panting. She's wearing tiny shorts and a tank top that leaves little to the imagination, her raven hair a tousled, wild mess. And she's gripping a baseball bat, while a bead of sweat trickles down her flushed face. I take in these details in a dazed blink.

"Oh my gosh," Hunter squeaks, voice high-pitched with shock and remorse as I hunch over in pain. The bat clatters to the floor. She presses her hands to her mouth, eyes wide. "What the hell were you doing creeping around in the dark like some cat burglar?"

"I was just... trying to find... the damn light switch," I grit out, each word a struggle to breathe through the nauseating waves of pain radiating from my groin. "Guess I haven't figured out... the layout of this place yet."

Hunter's brow furrows. "Why didn't you use the flashlight on your phone?"

"I was getting to that... before you went all Babe Ruth on my family jewels." I grimace.

Her face crumples with guilt. "I'm so sorry." She hurries over and carefully helps me to my feet, looping an arm around my waist to support me. As she presses close, I notice how amazing she smells—bright citrus and lush berries. Like an Italian summer, she's sunlight and turquoise seas. For a second, I almost forget the throbbing ache in my privates. *Almost.*

We hobble awkwardly to the couch, Hunter bearing most of my weight. As she eases me down, her gaze darts to the hardwood floor behind us. "You're bleeding." She gasps, taking in the glistening trail of crimson droplets. "Wait here," she orders before rushing off to the kitchen, leaving me drowning in the sweet scent of her shampoo and a growing sense of embarrassment.

Hunter returns a minute later carrying a bag of frozen peas.

I eye it dubiously. "Uh, not sure how peas will fix a bleeding foot, Hunt."

"The peas are for your..." She gestures vaguely in the direction of my crotch, cheeks flushing an adorable shade of pink. "You know."

"Ah. Right." I accept the makeshift ice pack with a grateful wince, gingerly pressing it against my bruised man bits. The cold seeps through the fabric of my suit, blessedly numbing the worst of the throbbing. I let out an involuntary moan of relief.

Hunter's eyes nearly bug out of her head at the sound. Cheeks blazing, she spins on her heel and flees to the bathroom, returning with a first aid kit. Kneeling down in front of me, she chews her plump bottom lip uncertainly.

"I need to check that cut." She reaches for my leg, fingertips grazing my ankle. "Is it okay if I strip your sock...?"

My mind short-circuits at the sight of her on her knees before me, at the soft caress of her touch. For a wild, inappropriate second, I mishear her request. Blood rushes to my face... and other extremities. I'm grateful for the frozen peas on my "sock" preserving the last shreds of my dignity.

I nod mutely, not trusting my voice. Hunter flashes me a reassuring smile and rolls up the leg of my suit pants. Delicate fingers hook into the top of my sock, peeling it down inch by tantalizing inch. The slide of fabric over my calf is electrifying, each brush of her fingertips against my ankle sparking currents that zing up my shin, through my thigh, straight to my... other *injured part*.

As she assesses the damage, dark hair falling in a silky curtain around her face, the thrum of pain fades away, replaced by a different kind of tension. One I shouldn't be feeling for my roommate.

She trails a featherlight touch over the arch of my foot and I twitch, both from the tickle and the unexpectedly sensual sensation. "The glass is stuck in," she informs me, glancing up with those impossibly dark eyes. "It's best to get it out. I can do it, or we can go to the emergency room and have a professional look at it?"

I force myself to ignore the way my pulse quickens at her proximity. "Is it in deep?" I mentally kick myself for another double entendre. *Real slick, Thompson.* But she can't be thinking what I'm thinking.

Hunter's cheeks bloom again. "No, it's not in too deep," she replies, and I could swear there's a slight catch to her voice. Is it my imagination, or is the air between us suddenly charged?

"Then hopefully, I won't need the emergency room." I

attempt a grin, even though my heart is pounding so hard I might still require an ECG.

Hunter tears open a gauze packet and uncaps a bottle of disinfectant, soaking the white square. She locks eyes with me, her expression serious. "This could hurt."

I shift on the couch, ignoring how the innocuous words sound intimate. "It can't be worse than the bat," I joke feebly.

Hunter's face falls, her eyes shimmering with remorse. "I thought you were a home invader." Her voice is small, laced with genuine regret, and a pang of guilt twists in my chest for upsetting her.

"Hey, no, it's my fault," I assure her. "I'm sorry I scared you."

She gives me a tight-lipped smile before turning her attention back to my foot. "Do you want me to count before I remove it?"

I nod, bracing myself.

"Okay. One, two—"

On "two," she swiftly pulls out the glass and presses the gauze to the wound. I yelp in surprise, more from the unexpected timing than the pain.

Hunter smirks up at me, a naughty glint in her eyes. "Thought you might need the distraction."

I stare at her, dumbfounded. Has Hunter always been this beautiful? In the dim light of the living room, her olive skin glows, and her dark hair tumbles over her shoulders. I'm suddenly aware of how little she's wearing: a thin tank top and shorts that expose her sculpted, lean thighs. One of which she's using as a prop for my injured foot as her fingers deftly wrap the gauze around it, each barely there touch sending currents pulsing through my body.

"There." She secures the bandage. "The bleeding should stop now that the wound is wrapped." Hunter gently lowers my foot to the floor and stands up, her movements graceful and fluid.

In an unguarded lapse, I let my eyes roam over her figure, lingering a second too long on her chest. I do my best not to notice how she's not wearing a bra underneath her top and decide my interest is purely scientific. I'm getting to know my roommate's habits and preferences, that's all. When I meet her gaze again, the fiercest blush of the night colors her cheeks, and she self-consciously crosses her arms.

Mentally kicking myself for being a total creep, I avert my eyes. "Thanks for the medical attention."

She offers me a small smile and backtracks. "I'd better scoop up all that glass before anyone else gets injured."

I don't have the strength to get up yet, so I don't offer to help. I listen as she sweeps the floor and throws the shards into the recycling. Then presumably mops my blood from the floor before she's back in front of me, pointing her thumb toward her bedroom. "Well, if you don't need anything else, I should head to bed. I have to wake up early tomorrow for work."

Her words remind me of how she disappeared this morning, plunging us back into an awkward tension. I can't let her go without addressing the topic. "I know it's late, but can we talk for a second?" My voice comes out almost desperate. The question sounds more like a plea.

The seconds stretch, taut and wavering, as I silently pray she won't brush me off. I need to clear the air, to understand what's wrong. I brace myself for rejection.

But then, miraculously, Hunter nods. "Okay. Let's talk."

7

HUNTER

Night one, I go psycho bitch on Dylan about dirty dishes. Night two, I whack him in the privates with a baseball bat. My instinct would be to flee to my room, hide inside, and never come back out again.

But when he asks me to talk, looking like he does now—golden hair disheveled, white shirt with a few undone buttons, tie hanging loose around his neck—he's so mouth-watering irresistible, I can't say no. He might be the one who got hit, and me the basher, but I'm the one left unsteady, as if the rug had been pulled out from under me.

Now that the medical emergency is over, I realize I'm wearing next to nothing. Heat creeps up my neck and face. "Do you mind if I go put on something a little more... covering before we talk?"

Dylan's gaze flickers down my body before darting away. He clears his throat. "Uh, yeah. Sure."

I scurry to my bedroom, heart racing. This cohabitation is going to give me premature gray hair. I grab a strapless bra and fasten it over my PJ tank top for damage control—no time for finesse—and cover the fashion crime with an oversized T-shirt. As I return to the living room, I make a silent vow to not let my emotions get in the way of me acting like a normal, half-decent human being and be cool with Dylan.

He's still on the couch, frozen peas balanced precariously on his lap. He looks up as I approach, a crooked smile playing on his lips. "Better?"

I nod, perching on the edge of the seat cushion as far from him as possible. "I should be the one to ask you that."

"Peas are working magic." He scrunches up his face in that cute half-frown that knocks me off my feet every single time. "But aren't they going to go bad?"

"Even if they don't, I'm not cooking crotch peas."

"Hey, crotch-to-table could be a new trend."

"The food critics would go bananas."

Dylan chuckles, then winces. "Oof, laughing still hurts a bit." He shifts the peas, his expression turning more serious.

I tense up, bracing myself for the awkward conversation I've been dreading since dish-gate.

"About last night." He runs a hand through his hair, mussing it. "I'm sorry if I made you uncomfortable. I didn't mean to... you know, make a mess of your space or anything. And I know I outdid myself tonight going for full-scale property damage, but hey, at least I'm setting the bar so low, any future disaster will seem mild in comparison."

My inner groan is so loud I fear he might still hear it. "No, Dylan. I should apologize. I overreacted about the dishes, and then tonight... I basically attacked you. I'm really sorry."

The crooked grin is back, causing all kinds of inappropriate reactions in my internal organs. "Hey, no harm done. Well, maybe a little harm." He gestures to the frozen peas. "But I'll survive."

I let out a shaky laugh. "I promise I'm not usually this neurotic. Or violent."

"Could've fooled me," he teases, eyes twinkling. "You seem pretty dangerous to me. Should I wear a cup around the apartment?"

I fiddle with the ribbed neckline of my T-shirt, my fingers twisting the fabric as I look everywhere, the floor, the couch—not the *peas*—but at him. "We should invest in glow-in-the-dark light switches."

"Uh-huh, so we *can* have nice things."

"Sure." I smile because how can I not. "We'll get them with little glowing basketballs for you."

"Great, then I'll stop running into trouble." He keeps his eyes on me, unblinking.

This time, I can't look away; I drift in the deep blues and greens of his irises as we fall into a silence that if it isn't exactly comfortable, at least is no longer tense.

Dylan flicks at the condensation forming on the bag of peas, like icing his crotch is just another Monday night activity. "What did I even break? Can I replace it?"

"It was just a vase. Rowena used to fill it with flowers."

"Did you like the flowers?"

"I mean, sure, they were nice. But then they all just died in a few days."

"Sure I can't buy another one for you?"

I shake my head. "No need."

Dylan stands, still holding the bag of peas and keeping the weight off his left leg on his heel, the bandaged part of the foot raised. "Same time tomorrow?"

I snort, crossing my arms. "If you survive the night."

"I'll see you in the morning, Brolin." Dylan tilts his head.

"Unless you're always up and out of the house at the crack of dawn?"

I can read between the lines of what he's not asking—if I was avoiding him this morning? But I'm not ready to admit that I was. Because then he'd ask me why, and I would have to explain to him things I can't say. Things no one knows. Things that are buried so deep inside me, sometimes even I can pretend they're not there.

I stand from the couch as well. "I'm on a new, massive project. So, yeah, I might have longer hours for a while."

Our gazes meet again and hold. If he smells my bullshit, he doesn't call me out on it.

For a wild instant, I wish that he would. That this boat I've been drifting on for eleven years finally got rocked.

Instead, Dylan gives a slight nod, accepting my answer. "Goodnight, Brolin."

"Night, Thompson."

I watch Dylan limp down the hallway and wait until his bedroom door clicks shut to release a long, shaky exhale.

I pad back to my room, sagging on the bed with too much adrenaline flooding my system to fall asleep right away. What time is it even?

The digital clock on my nightstand reads 1.30 a.m.

A horrible thought hits me in response: why was Dylan returning home so late? Long day at work, or was he coming back from seeing his girlfriend? Did I whack him in his post-coitus willy?

My inner villain lets out an evil laugh. *I hope I've broken it and that they can't have sex for at least a month.* But unfortunately, it's my tragic inner princess who gets the last word as unwanted mental images of Dylan making love with a faceless (but impossibly gorgeous) woman float before my eyes.

Flopping onto my bed, I grab a pillow and press it over my face, muffling a frustrated groan.

And the worst part?

Now I'll have to set the alarm to 5 a.m. every day and pretend to be a fucking morning person indefinitely.

8

HUNTER

After a relatively quiet week, disaster strikes on Saturday night. Before the weekend arrives, I'm out the door each morning at dawn. Safely avoiding Dylan.

But as I return home each evening, exhausted from work and days that keep getting longer, I brace myself, expecting the worst. That this will be the night I find Olivia and Dylan smooching on the couch—or, even more painfully, locked in his bedroom.

Some evenings, Dylan isn't home at all. Part of me wonders if he's with Olivia, and my insides yank at the thought. Other nights, he's chilling in the living room, playing video games or watching sports. His long legs casually sprawled before him, his hair in that effortless, just-woke-up style that has my fingers itching to run through it. Whenever I find him like that, I try not to stare at how his sleeveless hoodies show off his sculpted, ex-basketball-player arms or how he looks like he's just rolled out of bed. Unfairly irresistible, and so forbidden.

The only solution is to physically tear my gaze away, focusing on whatever task I've invented for myself in the kitchen. Or altogether disappearing into my room.

Each night that passes without Olivia making an appearance is a small victory, though I'm not sure what battle I'm fighting. I exist in a constant state of fear, waiting for when Dylan will bring his girlfriend over and shatter the illusion I'm safe in my home.

But after a week of nothing, I start to relax, getting complacent, lowering my guard—and that's, of course, when I'm caught in the storm.

The weekend has started weirdly already. I have zero plans. Nina is all loved up in the honeymoon phase of having moved in with her boyfriend, and she doesn't call. Rowena is off somewhere in the Hamptons, playing pretend. As for me, I'm strangely untethered, adrift in my apartment. And most of all, alone. My two best friends have been a constant presence in my life since college. The three of us used to do everything as a group. Even with boyfriends in the picture, we'd hang out during the day—all together, or me and Nina, or me and Rowena. Now the distance —physical, that's quickly transforming into emotional—feels unsettling.

With no plans, and after a grueling week of early wake-up calls and late nights, I sleep in on Saturday. But when the sun pours through the windows, too bright and warm for my groggy mood, I can't ignore it's morning any longer and get up. I pad into the kitchen, my hair a wild tangle around my face, only to stop short when I find Dylan at the stove, making pancakes.

His presence is as jarring as it is comforting, the smell of warm batter and maple syrup clouding my brain. He wasn't home last night, and I had assumed he'd be sleeping over at Olivia's. Otherwise, I would've showered, slipped on a subtly sexy outfit, and added a touch of makeup.

His broad shoulders are turned to me as he flips a pancake with unthinking grace. The sight sends a pang through my chest, a longing for something I can't have. Maybe I can still run back into the bathroom and make myself presentable.

I must groan my frustration aloud because he turns, his face breaking out in a bright smile as he spots me.

"Morning, sunshine," Dylan greets me in a teasing voice, his eyes sparkling with amusement as he effortlessly flips another pancake. "Not as much of a morning person as you claimed, huh?"

I scrunch my face, increasingly self-conscious of my wild hair and rumpled pajamas. But he's seen me now. I can't run back down the hall and go "powder my nose." To sound nonchalant, I mumble, "I'm not a morning person unless I *have* to be for work."

Dylan cuts one of the perfect spongy disks into quarters and offers me a sample, holding it out as if he wanted me to eat straight from the utensil. The golden fluffiness is too tempting to resist, and despite my hesitation, I lean in, plucking the fluffy morsel off the spatula with my fingers. The first bite melts in my mouth, buttery and light, distracting me from my disarrayed thoughts. "Oh wow." I moan mid-bite, momentarily forgetting my appearance. "These are amazing."

Dylan's grin widens, his eyes crinkling at the corners. "Secret family recipe." He winks. "Stick around, and I'll teach it to you someday."

I nearly choke on my pancake. *Stick around? Say the word, and I'll stick to you harder than maple syrup.*

Calm down. He's just being nice. I shouldn't read too much into it.

"Secret family recipe, uh? Nina never shared it with us." I frown. "She never made pancakes. Her most cooking was ordering off the takeout menus."

Dylan, looking a little self-conscious, admits with a shrug,

"Baking is kind of my thing." His eyes flicker down to the pan as if he's just shared a scandalous secret.

I give him a questioning look at this unexpected revelation. "You mean cookies and cakes?"

He flips the last pancake. "Yeah, it's not the most 'macho' hobby, but I enjoy cooking, baking in particular. The precision that goes into it."

He says it so casually like it's another thing on his list of endearing qualities, and I inwardly curse the love fairies. Because, of course, he loves to effing bake.

He sets a stack of pancakes on the small kitchen table, and they look straight out of a cookbook stock photo. Couldn't he have at least botched one? Be a little less perfect?

As if to confirm his lack of human flaws, Dylan also pours me a mug of freshly brewed coffee.

I wrap my hands around the warm ceramic and keep my tone light as I ask, "Any plans for the day?" When what I really mean is, *Do you plan to see your girlfriend? When? How? For how long? Doing what? Is she coming over? Because in that case, I need to beg for asylum somewhere.*

No, I retract, I don't want to know doing what. I hope his ding-dong is still bruised and out of commission.

Dylan shakes his head, replacing the coffee pot on the hot plate. "Nah, I want to finish unpacking. Tackle the pile of boxes left in my room. I haven't even touched the office. I ordered a new desk, by the way; it should arrive next week in case you have to sign for a big package."

He still hasn't sat down after pouring me the coffee, and the second he says *big package*, I peek at his crotch. *And he catches me.*

I'm boiling from the inside out.

I avert my gaze quickly, wishing I could pretend it never

happened. But he saw me—I have to acknowledge it somehow. "And have your *manly parts* recovered since the other night?"

Fuckety. Fuck. Tell me I didn't just say that. Can the sea witch please come and steal my voice?

Dylan smiles awkwardly as he sits down. "No long-term injuries to report. Those peas did not sacrifice in vain."

I stare firmly at my plate, focusing on cutting my pancakes into neat squares. "Glad to hear."

He drops his elbows onto the table, crossing his arms. The movement makes his T-shirt stretch across his biceps, fueling my inner turmoil.

"What about you?" He thankfully reverts to our previous topic. "Any plans for today?"

I wish I could tell him I'm doing something extremely cool like joining a sustainable urban gardening class in Brooklyn.

But the question is salt in the wound of my non-existent social life now that my roommates have moved out. I shrug, vaguely gesturing with my fork. "Not really. I'm going to catch up on some reading, do a bit of cleaning. Finish some work stuff."

It's a lame answer, I know, but it's the best I can come up with when my brain is short-circuiting from proximity to a man who redefines the expression "out of my league."

Still, as we continue to chat and eat, the knot of tension in my chest loosens. Sharing breakfast with him feels natural, effortless almost, when I'm not blabbering nonsense.

For a heartbeat, I can pretend everything's fine. It's a dangerous illusion, I know. But for now, I let myself sink into it, savoring the warmth of his laughter and the sparkle in his blue-green eyes, as if this were just another typical weekend morning. As if my heart weren't fluttering at every smile, glance, or accidental touch. And that's my mistake.

9

HUNTER

After a day wasted doing chores and little else, I decide to at least treat myself to dinner. I'm about to leave the house to go to my favorite Mexican place around the block—sadly, they don't deliver—when I bump into Dylan, looking pleasantly disheveled as he carries a stack of cardboard boxes down the hall. His T-shirt stretches across his sculpted chest as he balances the load in his arms.

"Hey, Hunt," he greets me with an easy grin. "Where's the recycling? These empty cartons are taking over my room."

I take the boxes from him, offering a small smile in return. "I can bring them downstairs. I'm headed out, anyway. We'll do a full tour another day."

"Oh, thanks, you're the best." His eyes crinkle at the corners when he smiles, and I have to look away before I say something stupid like, *How's your ding-dong?* Once a day is enough.

"No problem. I'm going to grab tacos from my favorite Mexican place. You want in?"

A grin spreads across Dylan's face, his eyes shining. "That would be amazing. I'll get a..."

I mentally recite his order to the last detail. *Pollo asado with corn tortillas. One quesadilla. Nachos with guacamole and pico de gallo, no cheese.*

Dylan echoes my thoughts and I nod along, hoping he doesn't notice I'm not writing any of it down. Or that if he does, he'll chuck it down to me having an exceptional memory. With a quick wave, I escape out the door, wondering if our second dinner together will go better than the lasagna letdown. How could it be worse? Haha... wait for it.

A short walk later, I step into the taco place, greeted by thick, warm air heavy with the comforting scent of spices and sizzling meat.

I relate my order to the guy at the counter, then throw in an extra burrito and nachos for good measure. Because carbs are the only certainty in my life right now.

When I come back to my place, I shuffle the takeout bags weighing down my arms to free a hand, about to put the key in the lock, when I hear a feminine giggle coming from the other side of the door. My stomach drops. That could only be *her*. Cruella D'Olive. Dylan's girlfriend.

There's no other possibility. Nina doesn't laugh that way. Rowena is in the Hamptons. And my building is not one where neighbors visit at random.

Panic rises in my throat. I don't know what to do. Should I flee? But I'm wearing a crappy T-shirt and baggy shorts, and I only took my phone to the Mexican place. Plus, Dylan knows I'm supposed to come back. He'd worry if I disappear—or worse, ask questions.

Pursing my lips, I brace myself and enter the house. My eyes snag on the other woman occupying my space at once.

Olivia.

Dylan's girlfriend is a beautiful blonde with warm amber

eyes, wholesome, all-American, so perfect she could appear in a toothpaste commercial. Seriously, she probably wakes up in the morning and birds braid her hair.

She is also my exact opposite. The awareness cuts through me as a sharp prick burns behind my eyes. She's everything I'm not: polished, put-together, blonde—did I say blonde? Then there's me, in my ratty clothes, holding bags of greasy takeout, my hair a dark mess, and my heart in pieces.

Before I can even process my anguish, Olivia greets me with a dazzling pearly-white smile that could outshine the sun. "You must be Hunter. I hope you don't mind I paid Dylan a surprise visit." Her voice is so sweet, it gives me a toothache.

I blink, still clutching my mountain of takeout bags like a security blanket, wondering if I should've added a bottle of tequila to my order—carbs might not be strong enough for this. "Uh, hi." I force a smile that probably comes off as a grimace.

When I don't add more, Olivia explains she was too curious to see the apartment, her enthusiasm bordering on manic. "And it's so nice to finally meet you." Finally? How long has she been waiting? Didn't they just start dating?

Olivia interrupts my mental drift, going in for a hug, and not even my takeout bags can save me from the much-unwanted embrace.

I'm appalled at the personal-space invasion. Over Olivia's shoulder, I shoot a look at Dylan that screams, *What the fuck?*

He makes an apologetic face that says, *I didn't plan this.*

Stepping back from the sticky hug, I do my best to remove myself from the situation. "I'll leave you two some space and eat in my room."

But Olivia, still beaming with that impossibly bright, polite smile, tells me not to be ridiculous. "We can all have dinner together."

Desperate to avoid this nightmare, I scramble for an excuse. "There isn't enough food for three."

Olivia, ever prepared, chimes, "Oh, don't worry. I brought one of my specialties, so there's plenty."

I stammer, "It probably won't pair well with tacos."

Unfazed, Olivia counters, "I made tamales. Isn't that a serendipitous coincidence?"

Even more appalled by how accomplished she is—and yes, I'm aware we don't live in Jane Austen's England but accomplished is the right word for her—I ask, "You mean from scratch?"

When Olivia confirms with an enthusiastic nod, I wish I could drop into a hole and disappear. Who even makes tamales by hand? Is she planning an appearance on *MasterChef*?

As I set down the takeout bags on the kitchen counter, Olivia glances at the table. "Hmm, there isn't a lot of space here. How about we get comfy on the couch?"

Dylan nods enthusiastically, his eyes lighting up. "I've been dying to watch the pilot of that new *Star Wars* spin-off."

In a galaxy far away, my heart explodes—it breaks into pieces so small no one will ever be able to find them and put it back together. I wanted to see that show, too. Why does he have to love everything I love?

Let at least Olivia hate *Star Wars*.

"The one where the Jedi are still a thing?" she asks instead. "I'd love to."

Dylan looks over at me, eyebrows raised in a silent question. "You good with that?"

Despite wanting nothing more than to retreat to the solitary confines of my room, I nod. "Yeah, sure. I was curious about that show, too." The words taste like self-betrayal.

That's how we end up on the couch, our feast spread out on

the coffee table. Dylan grabs the remote, sets up his premium streaming subscription, and presses play. As the opening credits roll, a sense of dread settles in my stomach. How long is each episode? How will I survive till the end? Please tell me at least it's one of those shows where they still release one episode per week and not dump the entire season at once.

I discreetly check on my phone. One episode, forty-two excruciatingly awkward minutes. Let the countdown start.

I spend the entire dinner as the world's most uncomfortable third wheel. Dylan and Olivia are cuddled up on one side of the couch, acting all lovey-dovey and short of hand-feeding each other. They're two peas in a pod, and I'm the lonely turnip wondering how I got thrown into this stir-fry.

Then I take my first bite of Olivia's tamales and the spicy blend bursts across my taste buds. The savory, perfectly seasoned filling, the tender masa—it's the most delicious thing I've ever tasted. And I'm fighting the urge not to throw it up.

I want to crawl out of my skin and forget I exist. How can one person be so perfect inside and out? Does Olivia volunteer at animal shelters and knit sweaters for orphans in her free time, too?

To add insult to injury, Dylan's girlfriend keeps dropping clever jokes about the show, making him laugh. Each chuckle carves at my insides, eviscerating me slowly and methodically, leaving nothing untouched.

At least if I were Taylor Swift, I could take this low point in my love life and write soul-wrenching lyrics about it, channeling my heartbreak into a song and then moving on.

It's her, her, *she's the problem*, it's her.

But unfortunately, my songwriting isn't up to par. I finish my food—I've never enjoyed Mexican less—and wait for the episode to be over before I excuse myself. I wish the happy couple goodnight and retreat to my room. I'm about to close the door when I hear them talking in hushed tones. Curiosity gets the better of me, and I tiptoe back out into the hallway to eavesdrop.

"Do you think Hunter doesn't like me?" Olivia's voice carries through the apartment. Her sweet tone is textbook passive-aggressive.

"No. Why would you say that?" Dylan reassures her, but his tone betrays a sliver of hesitation.

"I have this feeling..." Olivia persists. I picture her perfect brows furrowed in worry. Fake or real remains to be determined.

Dylan sighs, and I can tell he's choosing his next words carefully. "Maybe Hunter prefers not to find strangers at home unannounced?"

"We haven't seen each other all day." Olivia sounds defensive now. "And you said you were too tired to go out. I thought it'd be a pleasant surprise."

"Yeah, but I don't live alone. Next time, let me check with my roommate if she's okay with you coming over."

"Why wouldn't she be?"

Dylan doesn't reply. At least not verbally. He could be shrugging, but I don't dare peek around the wall.

There's a pause, and then Olivia suggests, "We should spend more time at my place. I live alone, so we wouldn't be bothering anyone."

My heart rams itself against my ribcage. Great, now I'm the bothersome roommate who needs to be managed.

"You live on the opposite side of Manhattan," Dylan points out. "I've been coming over a lot, but I can't do it every night."

"I know, and I appreciate the effort you're putting into our relationship," Olivia replies, her voice dripping with sweetness.

Next, I hear the unmistakable sound of kissing, my cue to

leave before the crack of my heart shattering alerts them to my presence.

I tiptoe back down the hallway. Earplugs, that's what I need. Before Dylan and Olivia move things to the bedroom. I embark on a frantic hunt for sound blockers, certain that the airline from my Miami conference a few months back gave me a courtesy kit. I always keep that shit. It must be here somewhere.

I turn my entire bedroom upside down, taking out my rage and frustration on innocent clothes and defenseless furniture. I toss pillows across the room, yank open drawers, and rummage through my suitcases like a possessed woman.

Finally, I find the kit buried at the bottom of my carry-on. I jam the earplugs into my ears, cheering at the blissful insulation. My last act before collapsing into bed is ordering a family-size supply of replacement earplugs online.

As I lie still, tears streaming down my face and soaking into my pillow, I wonder how I'll survive this living arrangement. I should move to Alaska—just me and the bears. Perhaps Brooklyn could be enough. I could claim I got a sudden hipster calling.

I close my eyes, picturing myself renting a quaint brownstone and not shaving my armpits. Can body hair cure unrequited love? *Afraid not.* And I can't afford a house on my own, anyway.

For now, I'll have to coexist with the happy couple, even if it means investing in a lifetime supply of earplugs and turning my heart into stone.

10

DYLAN

That sound again. It's Monday morning, and I'm lying in bed, cocooned in my freshly changed sheets, the fabric cool against my skin. I stretch and sink deeper into the pillow, determined to tune out the weird noises. Still half-draped in the fog of sleep, I pull the covers closer as if they could shield me from the world. When the disturbance persists, tugging at my awareness, I roll over and blink at the clock on my nightstand: 5.50 a.m.

By now, Hunter is usually gone, already at the gym or on her way to work. Whatever that obnoxious sound is, it's not coming from inside the apartment.

I groan and flop onto my back, staring up at the ceiling. Ten glorious minutes before the alarm goes off, and I intend to enjoy them to the last second. I close my eyes again, drifting back to that sweet spot between wakefulness and dreams. Monday morning can wait a little longer.

Then I hear it distinctly. A low grunt, followed by a muffled curse. I frown, pushing myself up on one elbow. Another grunt, louder this time, then a strange rustling sound. Curiosity piqued, I sit up, rubbing the sleep from my eyes. The room is still dim, the sun not fully risen, leaving everything bathed in a cool, bluish tint.

My gaze drifts over the last few unpacked boxes scattered across the floor of my new bedroom. Nina's old room. I'm still adjusting to the idea that this place is mine. It'll be a while before I stop thinking of this as a temporary crash pad. But perhaps now's not the time to get philosophical.

Reluctantly, I swing my legs over the side of the bed and shuffle out of my room, my bare feet padding on the hardwood floor.

"Hunter?" I call out but receive no response.

I walk to her door, hesitating a second before knocking. "Hey, everything alright in there?" My voice comes out still gravelly from sleep.

After a brief pause, she responds with a frustrated, "I'm fine," that doesn't sound *fine at all.*

I raise an eyebrow, suddenly more awake. "You sure? It sounds like you're wrestling a wild animal in there."

More rustling, another grunt, and a soft thud. I knock again, this time a little louder. Okay, maybe it's not a beast she's fighting, but whatever it is, it sounds like it's winning.

"Hunter? Can I help?" I offer, concerned now.

There's a pause, then an exasperated sigh. "Alright, just... don't laugh."

Not reassuring, but definitely intriguing. I wonder what could be happening behind that door. Is she assembling IKEA furniture at 6 a.m.? Practicing some bizarre new yoga pose?

"Promise. No laughing," I pledge, unsure if I can keep my word. It'll depend on what I'll find on the other side.

After a reluctant, "Come in" from Hunter, I cautiously open her door and step inside her bedroom. And freeze.

I blink, processing the scene before me. Hunter is thrashing in the center of the room, tangled in a too-tight shirt that's stuck over her head. The top covers her face and most of her upper torso, *thank goodness*. Her arms are raised above her, trapped in the sleeves as if in a sort of straightjacket. During the struggle, her bra has lost the fight to stay clasped and is now dangling beneath the blouse. There is a little under-boob showing.

Hunter looks like she's been wrestling this outfit for a while, and the shirt is definitely winning. My eyes trail down to her flat stomach where a sparkly belly button stud pierces her skin. Has she always had that? I shuffle to my mental catalog of all the summer visits she's paid to my parents' place, but I can't remember... The fact that I can't recollect bothers me more than it should, and I don't know why.

Hunter lets out another muffled cry.

The scene is comic, but somehow, I can't find a single laugh within me. Instead, there's this burning warmth settling in, something that twists low and leaves me rooted on the spot. I swallow past whatever it is I'm feeling at the sight of that belly ring and the peek of under-boob.

I tear my eyes away and scan the rest of the room—immaculately tidy, ready to pass a military inspection. The bed is pristine, not a single crease or pillow out of place, and every surface is spotless. Even the books on her shelves are stacked with precision. The only thing out of order is an overflowing laundry basket near her bed.

I take a step closer to Hunter to figure out the best way to help her out of this predicament without making things more awkward.

"Uh... need a hand?"

"No, Dylan, I'm practicing a new interpretive dance routine," Hunter retorts, her voice muffled by the fabric. "Yes, please, help me."

I approach her with the same caution I would use for a wild animal that might bolt at any sudden movement and reach for the hem of the shirt, trying to untangle her without accidentally copping a feel.

"Okay, just... hold still," I instruct, grasping the fabric and tugging. "We need to coordinate. Exhale on three and I'm going to pull."

She nods, the shirt bobbing with the movement. I count down, "One, two, three," and tug.

The blouse doesn't budge. Hunter lets out a frustrated groan that would be adorable if she wasn't so clearly annoyed.

"I'm going to try again," I reassure her.

"Put more elbow grease into it."

"I won't take the bait and make a joke about lubricant."

"Dylan, please, I can't breathe." Even underneath the frustration, she sounds amused.

"Okay, one, two, three..."

We manage to pull the shirt down on the third try.

The fabric slides down her torso, snapping into place. Her bra stays twisted underneath. Hunter, her face flushed, tugs her top down further, avoiding eye contact.

"There. You're free. Fashion emergency averted." I keep my gaze high, away from her chest and the tantalizing lacy pink fabric of her bra.

Hunter looks part mortified, part defiant as she meets my eyes, 100 percent deliciously tousled. "Not a word."

I make a zipper-over-mouth gesture as Hunter's gaze drops from my face and she gasps, making me realize that I came straight from bed and am not wearing anything except for my boxer briefs.

I cough, and her eyes dart up from my bare chest.

"You're in your underwear," she mumbles, then catches herself. "I mean, thank you."

"I'll go get dressed."

She nods.

But as I backtrack blindly, my foot catches onto something. I stumble, arms flailing to steady myself as my feet get more tangled into whatever tripped me. Something hard hits my calf, and I kick it away on instinct, sending clothes flying everywhere as I fall flat on my butt.

I land a little stunned, surrounded by scattered garments—jeans, shirts, and, to my horror, a collection of bras and lacy underwear—and Hunter's laundry basket capsized on the floor.

I contemplate the possibility that I'm being punished for something I did in a past life because, amidst all the chaos, a lacy thingy has landed on my head. My eyes widen under the lace. The soft fabric—pink and racy—is draped over my nose. And I don't need to inspect it to know it's one of Hunter's thongs hanging off my face like a deflated superhero mask.

For a long, painful moment, neither of us moves. My face burns red as I gingerly pluck the underwear off, holding it up. "Uh... this yours?"

Hunter stands there, equally shell-shocked. She stares at the thong in my hand as if it might explode at any second. Her cheeks are as pink as the lace, and she's pressing her lips together. My roommate looks like she'd gladly crawl under the nearest piece of furniture instead of answering me. Finally, she moves. "Thanks." She takes the unfortunate underwear from me and stuffs it back into the basket, avoiding my gaze as she collects the rest of her laundry, her long, dark hair falling forward to shield her face.

I stand, waiting for her to be done. Neither of us knows what to say. But I can't stand the silence. "I, uh... didn't mean to touch, t

—to trip on... you know." I rub the back of my neck. *Real smooth, Dylan.*

We share a look—embarrassed, horrified—and that has us both silently agreeing to never mention this again. "Well, uh..." I scramble for something to say to defuse the awkwardness. "I'll... go pretend this never happened."

Hunter nods, her face still flushed. "Yeah... solid plan."

Making sure there's no more laundry to stumble upon, I turn and slip out of the room. As I shut the door behind me, I lean against the wall and exhale, staring at the ceiling in disbelief. I try to focus on literally anything other than Hunter's lingerie and the accidental peek-a-boob. Taxes. Yeah, taxes. Those are neutral. "Taxes. Think about taxes," I mutter, as I head back to my room, hoping I've hit my embarrassment quota for today.

11

HUNTER

I stand frozen in my room after Dylan leaves, my cheeks still burning with mortification. I double-check the door is closed, leaning against it as if a wooden barrier could block out the humiliation that just unfolded. But the image of Dylan bare-chested lying on the floor, tangled in my laundry, with my thong draped over his face, is burned behind my retinas.

I can't believe that happened. I press the heels of my palms over my eyes, wishing for a time machine that'll bring me back to earlier this morning when I picked an old shirt from the closet and thought, *Hey, it'll stretch, it's what viscose does, right?*

Wrong.

I tug at the blouse in question, which is still squeezing me worse than a boa constrictor, and head to the desk. Scissors in hand, I slice the fabric open from the navel up with immense satisfaction. I put on a different, size-appropriate shirt that hasn't shrunk from too many dryer cycles, and fix my hair, looking in the dresser mirror over my desk. With three women who used to share a single bathroom, we all had stacked emergency beautification supplies in our bedrooms.

The person staring back at me is unhinged. My hair is a mess, skin botched with shame, and the eye circles worthy of a raccoon. I haven't slept all weekend, plagued by nightmares of Dylan and Olivia together—knowing what she looks like, how they touch each other, and the sounds they make when they kiss magnified the weight crushing me and invited insomnia.

With a deep sigh, I spray perfume on my neck and try to shake off the exhaustion. But the dark circles under my eyes are stubborn. Not even a double layer of concealer can do much.

I scold myself for letting the Olivia situation get to me. But Dylan is my kryptonite, and living together has only added fuel to the fire. Unfortunately, I'm as equipped to handle the flames as a marshmallow at a bonfire.

Desperate to escape, I grab my bag and creak my bedroom door open, listening to trace Dylan's whereabouts in the apartment. Mercifully, the shower is running, and I can avoid another mortifying interaction. I'm outta there faster than Neo dodging bullets in *The Matrix*.

As I speed-walk down the hall toward the elevator, I wonder what Dylan must be thinking. I'm glad I don't have a visual of the situation he found me in, trapped in a shirt like a total moron. I groan, pressing the down button repeatedly as if that will make it come faster.

"Just forget it happened," I mutter to myself as I step into the elevator. "It can't get any worse." But even as I say it, I know that's tempting fate. With Dylan and me under the same roof, it's only a matter of time before I find new and creative ways to humiliate myself.

A ding chimes overhead, and the doors slide open. I straighten my shoulders and step out, ready to face the day. Or at least, as ready as I can be with the memory of a half-naked Dylan tangled in my underwear replaying on a loop in my mind. I hope work will provide the distraction I desperately need to chase away all the Dylan angst. Getting lost in engineering schematics and project timelines sounds a lot better than dwelling on my disastrous personal life.

After a grueling subway ride, I push through the revolving doors of my office building, the cool blast of air conditioning a welcome respite from the heat outside and the simmering embarrassment still clinging to my skin.

An even greater sense of relief settles over me as I reach my office, which has become my only private, safe space. I drop my bag by my desk and slump into my chair, the supple leather cradling my tired body. As I log into my computer, the day's schedule fills the screen, and I'm thrilled not to have a single free minute.

"I'd say good morning, but you look like you've been run over by a truck."

I startle at the voice and glance over the monitor to find Clara leaning against my office doorway. She's part of the small group of women at the firm and one of the few colleagues I consider a friend—easy to talk to, always ready with a quip or a sympathetic ear, and never afraid to tell it like it is.

I force a smile. "Yeah, I didn't sleep much this weekend."

Clara crosses her arms, studying me. "Is it because of North Shore? You've got some serious balls taking on such a huge project. Everyone in the office is talking about it."

I shake my head, even if she's given me an out. It'd be easy to blame my current state on work. What I'd give for my problems to be something a budget revision could fix. "No, it's not the project. That's... manageable. It's more of a personal matter."

Clara's eyes light up with interest, and she steps into my office, perching on the edge of my desk. "Want to talk about it over lunch? Sometimes, it helps to unload, especially on someone who doesn't know your entire life story."

I hesitate, biting my lower lip. Part of me wants to keep everything bottled up, to push it down and pretend everything's fine. But there's another part—the part that's tired of carrying this weight around, of feeling my lungs are deprived of air, constantly drowning—the me desperate to let go, who wants to lay it all bare instead of holding back.

And talking to a person outside my usual circle of friends who doesn't know Dylan or is related to him could help me gain some perspective.

"Yeah, lunch sounds great." I blink, a surprising calmness settling in as if my thoughts cleared of static at the prospect of unloading the emotional baggage.

Clara grins, hopping off my desk. "Cool. Meet you in the lobby at one?"

I nod, mustering a smile more genuine this time. "I'll be there."

As Clara walks out, throwing a wave over her shoulder, I turn back to my computer screen, adding the lunch to the schedule.

* * *

Clara and I snag a table at a cozy café with mismatched furniture and the best paninis in town. I order my usual—a turkey and avocado sandwich—but when it arrives, I barely have the appetite to take a bite, the restlessness of the weekend still tangling my stomach.

Clara jumps right in. "Alright, lay it on me. Why do you look like you've got a week's worth of Monday blues crammed into a single day?"

I let out a humorless laugh, fiddling with a paper napkin. "Would you think me pathetic if I told you I'm actually relieved it's Monday? That I'd rather be at work than dealing with what's at home?"

Clara leans forward. "Ooh, color me intrigued. Tell me everything."

I wonder where to even begin. "I live with this guy, Dylan." Just his name sits heavy on my tongue. "We've known each other for years—he's my best friend's brother—but we've only been living together for a week. And, uh... it's been complicated."

Clara nods, sipping her water. "Complicated how? Roommates stuff, or something more?"

My throat seizes up as if refusing to release the confession I've never voiced to anyone. But it's time. I can't go on like this. "I have feelings for him... serious feelings. But he's seeing someone else. He started dating a new woman, Olivia, a short time before moving in. And she's... perfect: beautiful, sweet, polite, a superb cook. *Blonde*."

"Gah, very Ally McBeal. She's your Georgia."

"Except Dylan and I never dated." I force myself to take a bite and swallow. "Anyway, Saturday night, she surprised him at the apartment, and I was trapped into having dinner with them. I've been losing sleep over it."

Clara exhales, leaning back in her chair. "That's rough."

"Tell me about it." My eye twitches simply discussing it. "I didn't sleep this weekend because I kept imagining them together. And this morning, I got stuck in a stupid, old shirt, and he had to help me. Then he tripped over my laundry basket, and..." I trail off. "It was so embarrassing." Clara's eyes widen. I wave my hand, brushing it off. "One of my thongs was on his face... It was a disaster."

Clara snorts, trying not to laugh but clearly amused. "Okay, wow. We have a lot to unpack. Is your problem that he has a girl-friend, or that she's coming over to your place? You don't want to live with him anymore? What is it?"

"That's the issue." Frustration seeps into my voice. "I don't know. I can't sit around and watch them together, but I also can't tell him how I feel now that he is with someone else."

Clara stabs a tomato from her salad and leans in. "You need to get out of the house more. Give yourself a break from all that tension. Get your mind off him. Have you thought about dating someone else?"

I blink at her, caught off guard. "Like who? If I had someone to date, I wouldn't be obsessing over my roommate."

"Yes, but are you actively looking for a date or just hoping Prince Charming falls in your lap?"

More waiting for Prince Charming to dump Cinderella and decide he prefers Esmeralda.

"Please don't tell me there's plenty of fish in the sea."

"In the sea, maybe not." Clara grins. "But dating apps are filled with eligible bachelors. Download one on your phone and explore the options. Even if you're not looking for anything seri-ous, it could be a good distraction. And who knows? You might meet someone cool."

I frown, not sold on the idea. The thought of swiping through profiles, making awkward small talk with strangers... it's daunting. Especially when my heart is still clinging to the hope that Dylan might wake up one day and realize he loves me back.

But as I nibble at my barely touched sandwich, I can't dismiss the truth in Clara's words. Sitting around the apartment, watching Dylan and Olivia play house, will chip away at my sanity. I need a diversion, something to yank me out of the endless pining and self-pity. But online dating?

I'm about to say no when Clara cuts me off with a wave of her hand.

"Come on, Hunter. You said it yourself, you need a distraction. Meeting new people could help you move on. You don't want to keep torturing yourself over Dylan."

The idea of dating seems... premature. The only serious boyfriends I've had since I met Dylan fell in my lap like Clara said. I didn't seek the connections. There was Bret, the guy who literally swept me off my feet at a wedding when my heel broke on the dance floor. He offered his shoulder as I hobbled around for the rest of the night, using him as my personal crutch. And Troy, the Samaritan who returned my wallet after I'd left it at a laundromat. He'd tucked a note inside that read, *You owe me a coffee for the return*, with his number scribbled underneath. But with both, even at the start, when things were going well in the relationships, I couldn't help measuring them up to Dylan—and they always lost. How could a random dude I meet on the internet compete?

But I can't deny the logic in Clara's suggestion. I need something—anything—to keep me from spiraling further into the Dylan-and-Olivia vortex.

"Alright," I concede. "I'll think about it."

Clara grins, looking entirely too pleased with herself. "Good. Try it. What's the worst that could happen?"

Those could be the famed last words. But for the first time since Dylan moved in, my stomach flips at the promise of something new, exciting, and freeing. Nothing left to lose.

I wipe my mouth on a napkin, leaving the second half of my sandwich untouched. "I'm stuffed."

Clara nods. "Love woes always make me lose weight if nothing else." She leans forward. "Have I convinced you to give online dating a shot?"

I sigh dramatically. "Okay, okay, you win. I'll create a profile."

Clara claps her hands together. "Yes. How about we grab drinks after work and set you up?"

The idea of putting myself out there twists my stomach with a blend of excitement, nerves, and a tiny flicker of hope that I'll get away from under Dylan's spell. I open my mouth to confirm the evening plans when my phone buzzes with an incoming text.

It's from Rowena in our group chat.

> ROWENA
>
> Hey, can you gals meet me after work today? I need to talk to you both

At once, my mind flies to worst-case scenarios. Did something happen in the Hamptons? Is she having second thoughts about moving in with a stranger? Is Adrian mistreating her in any way? I type back a response.

> HUNTER
>
> If you've changed your mind, we can kick Dylan out of the third bedroom, he hasn't set up the office yet

Her reply comes in a minute later.

> ROWENA
>
> No, nothing like that. I just need to talk

I frown at the cryptic message but send back a thumbs-up emoji. Drinks with Clara will have to wait. I glance up at her apologetically. "Rain check on tonight? A friend needs me, some kind of crisis."

Clara waves a hand. "No worries. You show up for your girls. We can have lunch again tomorrow and kick off Operation

Online Dating." She wiggles her eyebrows at me and I can't help but laugh.

"Deal."

We settle the bill and walk back to the office, my mind still wondering what Rowena could need advice on.

The rest of the work day flies by, my new project keeping me busy. But when my phone pings with an alarm reminding me of the meet-up with Rowena, I'm out the door without hesitations.

12

DYLAN

After fleeing Hunter's room, I quickly hop into the bathroom for a cold shower. Five minutes later, I step out, the fire in my veins still far from cooling. I wrap a towel around my waist, droplets dripping from my hair onto my shoulders. The bathroom mirror is fogged up. I wipe a hand across the glass, clearing a circle to catch my reflection and shave.

As I walk into the living room, I notice the silence. Hunter must have already left for work. My lungs twinge with... relief? After our last super-cringy interaction, I'm not eager for a repeat. Or maybe it's shame. Or disappointment. All three are equally possible.

When Tristan and Nina first told me they were moving in together and kicking me out, albeit lovingly, taking over Nina's room seemed the fastest, most logical solution. The New York rental scene is no joke, and while I'm doing well at my investment firm, I don't want to throw away my savings on some overpriced bachelor pad—to rent at least. I want to save until I'm ready to buy.

But as I pour myself a mug of the coffee Hunter left in the pot and glance around at the empty apartment, I wonder if I've been naïve thinking living with her would be the same as staying with Tristan. Yes, we've known each other forever. She's a friend, but being roommates is different. Is it because she's a woman? Would it be the same with any other woman on the planet?

No.

The answer rings in my ears before I even have time to fully form it. It's instinctive. Immediate. And I know it to be true.

I scratch my head. This whole platonic living arrangement might be trickier to navigate than I expected. And it doesn't help that Hunter looks the way she does: all dark eyes and flawless skin.

And I should stop having these thoughts. Especially now that I have a girlfriend.

I finish my coffee and drop the mug in the dishwasher—I've learned my lesson about the sink and leaving dirty dishes in it. I go change for work while still analyzing the situation. Hunter and I are friends. So, yeah, I saw her underwear, and it was sexy as hell. The memory of her belly piercing had me turn the water to cold in the shower. But I need to lock those thoughts away before they spiral into something I can't control.

I didn't think it'd be this hard to adjust. Nina and Tristan moving in together was inevitable, but I wasn't ready for how it'd turn my life upside down. Those two have been my rocks, Nina as my literal sister and Tristan as the brother I never had. But now that they've become a thing, I've been pushed out by both. I'm watching from the sidelines while they build their life together. Sure, I'm happy for them, but it feels like I've been demoted. I'm the backup player no one needs anymore. And I so desperately wanted to grab on to something familiar. Not to live with strangers or by my fucking self.

But maybe next time, I'll think twice before signing up to

share an apartment with a woman who looks like she stepped out of a Victoria's Secret catalog. *Rookie mistake, Thompson. Rookie mistake.*

I stride into the office, the familiar Monday chaos swirling around me. But today, I'm off my game. As I settle into my corporate fishbowl, the usual start-of-the-week energy eludes me.

The June sun slants through the glass walls, bright but not yet oppressive, glinting off the brushed steel seams of the skyscraper. Outside my door, phones ring, cutting through the tense atmosphere on the M&A floor. And analysts argue over spreadsheets and upcoming deals, their voices rising and falling like waves.

I'd usually check how the juniors are doing to detect potential red flags. But today, my mind is elsewhere, wrapped up in lace and lingerie.

I stare at my computer screen, willing myself to focus. But it's no use. Hunter's lacy pink thong haunts me—the color, the feel of the soft fabric draped across my face, and worst of all, the fantasy of what it must look like on her.

I massage my temples to snap back to reality. On the screen, a financial report waits for my attention, but the figures dissolve into meaningless shapes. Words swim in front of me, blending into each other as my brain is even less cooperative than usual.

I open a text-to-speech app to read the report for me instead of slogging through it myself, hoping it'll be easier to follow. The robotic voice drones on, reciting numbers and percentages that usually captivate me but that this morning can't hold my attention.

I've just finished listening to the report when my assistant pops her head into the office. "Everything's good for the 11 a.m. meeting? Need anything from me?"

I nod. "Could you please pink the report?"

Kelly raises an eyebrow. "Pink?"

"Print," I correct, as heat rises to my face. That lace really did a number on me.

Kelly frowns, amused. "Got it, boss. Do you want me to use pink paper instead of the usual cream?"

I scowl and flip her the bird. She laughs and flips me a mock military salute. "Cream it is."

Kelly leaves the office, and I drop my face into my hands, letting out a groan as my phone buzzes. It's a message from Olivia —right, my girlfriend. Guilt churns fresh in my gut at how much time I've wasted thinking about another woman's lingerie.

> OLIVIA
>
> Morning, babe. Hope your week is off to a great start. I miss you already. When can I see you again?

I hesitate before dictating a response. I'm not in the mood for Olivia today. The week is off to a brutal start, and I've been at work since 7 a.m. I need space to think—or rather, to stop thinking about other women's lingerie.

> DYLAN
>
> Hey, work's crazy at the moment. I'll be swamped all week.
>
> But let me make it up to you with dinner at a nice restaurant Friday night.
>
> There's this new French place I heard about that we could try

Waiting until the weekend will give me time to breathe, to

figure out what's wrong with me and how I'm going to deal with the strange, inappropriate thoughts I'm having about Hunter.

Also, Olivia's nice, but the constant pushiness—like showing up unannounced at my place on Saturday—is rubbing me the wrong way. I hit send and toss my phone on the desk, leaning back in my chair with a sigh.

I need to screw my head on straight. A glimpse of lace shouldn't derail my day or my relationship. It's lingerie, for fuck's sake. It's not like I haven't seen it before.

Olivia replies instantly.

> OLIVIA
>
> Sounds great. I love French cuisine. I'll wear something nice for you ;)

My eyes glaze over the screen again. Why does my girlfriend promising a sexy outfit leave me completely indifferent? I gulp down the lump in my throat and silence the phone, putting it face down on the desk.

I dive back into the merger reports, determined to make sense of them. My brain is still foggy from lingerie-induced madness, but I power through.

The 11 a.m. meeting is a video call, so I don't even need to leave my office. I join the video conference and take the lead on presenting a new merger. I'm walking the others through the assets of the company to be acquired, starting with their real estate holdings, when I mix out my words again, "The risk is that the rent on the warehouse could double since the lace agreement will expire next year, and the owner knows they need it."

My team stares back in confusion through the screen. The tips of my ears grow hot, and I correct myself, "Sorry, lease agreement. The lease agreement will expire."

I apologize to my colleagues for the slip-up, hoping they'll attribute it to stress or lack of sleep. Anything but the truth—that I can't stop obsessing over my roommate's underwear.

Finally, I'm done with my part of the presentation. I put my mic on mute and sit back, relieved I no longer have to speak and am required to provide only minimal input. I keep tapping my fingers on my desk as the video call continues.

It's not the first time my brain scrambles words, but today, it's happening more often. My usual misfires are on overdrive, likely triggered by my preoccupation with Hunter. I don't know why my brain switches words on me—pink for print, lace for lease—but it's always been like this. Once I was diagnosed, I've gotten good at compensating.

But "compensating" doesn't mean it's been easy. I've spent my entire life building a fortress of coping mechanisms, layer after layer, to keep anyone from noticing the cracks. Teachers, friends, even my parents for a while. No one needed to know just how many nights I stayed up late, staring at words that refused to make sense, trying to memorize entire pages because reading them wasn't an option. I've rewritten more notes and summaries than I can count, not because I'm thorough, but because it's the only way to retain anything.

In school, I was forced to reveal this weakness. Teachers thought I was lazy. Classmates called me dumb. Even my parents, as supportive as they were, didn't fully get it at first. The humiliation of being called out in class for misspelling simple words or misreading instructions is something I wouldn't wish on anyone. It stayed with me all my life, that sense of being different in a way that isn't celebrated, just noticed and pitied—or worse, mocked.

Sports were the one thing where I didn't need to read a fucking thing, so I threw myself into athletics. I was tall, so basketball was the obvious choice. I didn't get into Duke for my stellar grades. But if basketball got me through the door, once I was there, I made sure I did my best to excel also academically. No one knew me, no one thought of me any less, and I kept things that way. Hid my daily struggles.

I've made it so far. But the fear never leaves—the constant dread of someone catching on. A boss noticing I skimmed instead of read. A colleague spotting a typo I didn't realize I'd made. Every email I send is triple-checked, every report reviewed until my eyes feel like sandpaper. When dictation was integrated into phones, I almost cried with relief.

It's exhausting, always staying one step ahead of the truth. The worry is always there, keeping me sharp, keeping me afraid. And when I'm stressed, it gets worse.

By lunchtime, I'm practically useless at work. My inbox is flooded with unread emails, and reports are still waiting for my input. I order a salad but barely touch it, pushing the lettuce around with my fork.

I have everything a man could want. A great job. Amazing friends. A gorgeous, kind girlfriend. What's my problem?

Olivia is perfect—on paper. But why doesn't it feel right? Even the idea of dinner on Friday doesn't bring the excitement it should. Olivia is beautiful, smart, thoughtful, and totally into me, but something is not clicking.

And then there's Hunter. She's been in my life for years, and we never had a problem. But now she's slipped under my skin in a way I can't ignore. And I still can't figure out how long she's had that damn belly button piercing.

Thankfully, more meetings keep my head off things until it's time to go home. As I pack up for the day, my phone pings with a text from Olivia.

OLIVIA

Hey, what time are we meeting on Friday?
Should I make a reservation?

Shit, I should've taken care of the booking already and sent Olivia the details. But I haven't thought about the dinner at all. I send a quick vocal text to Kelly to book the restaurant for me and dictate my reply to Olivia.

DYLAN

I've requested a table for 9 pm

Just waiting for the confirmation

She replies instantly.

OLIVIA

Perfect. Can't wait :)

An enthusiasm I'm not sharing. My disposition leans more toward a sense of obligation, which is ridiculous mere weeks into dating someone. But hopefully, dinner on Friday will give me clarity.

13

HUNTER

When I arrive at the coffee shop, Nina is already waiting, fidgeting with her mug of tea.

"Hey," I greet her, taking a seat. "Any idea what this is about?"

Nina shakes her head, blonde hair swishing. "Not a clue. But I hope everything's okay."

I glance toward the sidewalk as if expecting Rowena to appear. "Me too. How are things with Tristan? How's the Co-ed?"

Nina gives me such a bright smile in response, I consider putting on my shades. I click my tongue. "Lots of sex, then?"

"Yep, but also lots of cuddling." She chuckles. "Who could've guessed the Prince of Darkness was a teddy bear?"

A server interrupts, taking my order.

When he goes away, Nina asks, "What about you? Is my brother still being a pig?"

The compulsion to be honest with her grips me again like it did the other night when we were texting back and forth. But Dylan has a girlfriend. It's a complicated situation, and I don't want to put her in the middle of it.

Just then, Rowena arrives, saving me from having to answer

as we both focus on her. I had expected to find her frazzled or stressed. Instead, Winnie is glowing, her hazel eyes bright behind her black-rimmed glasses. The fake engagement suits her.

After we exchange hugs and she orders her drink, Rowena catches us up on the latest developments in her pregnancy and new home. She's seven weeks along now, and things with Adrian are going smoothly. But what she wanted to discuss is whether she should tell Liam, the biological father, about the baby.

Nina is the first to respond, her green eyes wide. She insists that Rowena should not tell him, and I nod in agreement. After everything that jerk put her through, Liam doesn't deserve to be let back into Rowena's life.

"Winnie, that guy is bad news. All he ever did was make you doubt yourself and feel small. What if Liam were the same with the baby? Don't invite that toxicity back in."

Rowena bites her lip, clearly torn, her gaze shifting between us. "You're right, both of you. It's not fair to my baby to willingly expose them to a manipulator when they're too little to protect themselves."

We toast to leaving deadbeat dads where they belong—far away—and the mood brightens as we talk about Adrian. Rowena shows us the ring he bought her and mentions that we'll get to meet him at the engagement party in three weeks.

I slam my palm on the table, sending our coffee mugs rattling. "Three weeks? Oh, hell no, we can't wait that long to meet the mysterious Adrian West! It'll be way too awkward if the engagement party is the first time we're introduced."

We insist a bit, and Rowena reluctantly agrees to ask him if we can get together sooner. With the promise she'll introduce us to Adrian soon, we all hug goodbye and go our separate ways. The café is close to my apartment—it was one of our favorites when we lived together—so I walk the few blocks home, enjoying the early-evening sun that is still bright but not as hot. It's late-ish when I get back.

I let myself in, feeling like an intruder. I listen for signs of Dylan's presence, but he mustn't be home yet. The apartment is quiet, too quiet. Empty without Rowena's laughter or Nina's chatter. I head to the kitchen and rummage through the freezer, settling on a frozen dinner.

The microwave dings and I grab my food, locking myself in my room. I refuse to risk running into Dylan after what happened this morning. I eat my unremarkable chicken fried rice in bed, watching video tutorials on my phone on how to create the perfect online dating profile.

Step one: don't look like you've been eating sad microwaveable dinners alone.

I apply the newly gained expertise to draft a semi-decent, witty bio but don't post it yet. I'll wait until tomorrow when I'm with Clara for validation. Baby steps.

* * *

The next day, I meet up with my colleague for lunch as promised. Over Caesar salads, I show Clara my draft profile.

"Oh, Hunt, this is perfect." She scrolls through my pics next. "Your bio is hilarious, and these pictures? Absolute fire."

A smile breaks across my face, but my fingers fidget with the edge of my napkin. "You think so?"

"Absolutely. You're going to have matches flooding in." She hands my phone back, grinning. "And that's great because online dating is a numbers game, Hunt. It sounds awful, but you've got to go on as many dates as possible."

I wrinkle my nose. "That seems exhausting."

Clara shrugs. "But it's the best way to find someone you click with. Come on, let's make the profile live and see if we've got any keepers."

We spend the next half hour swiping through potential suitors, giggling at the more outrageous profiles. By the end of lunch, I have four dates, one each night from tonight through Friday.

Look at me, living my best rom-com dreams. I can almost hear the upbeat music in the background as the down-on-her-luck heroine turns around her sad love life. Should I get a makeover, too? Maybe not. At the rate I'm going, I'm pretty sure even Bridget Jones would tell me to slow down.

* * *

That night, back at the apartment, I rummage through my closet to find the perfect outfit for tonight. I settle on a sleek, black dress that's at the same time simple but sexy. As I apply the finishing touches to my makeup, I hear the front door open and close. Dylan must be home.

I freeze, listening for any signs of Olivia tagging along. When I don't catch her voice or laugh, I consider it safe to go.

Grabbing my clutch, I take one last peek in the mirror and give myself an encouraging nod.

The self-confidence lasts as long as it takes for me to step out of my room and almost collide with Dylan in the hallway. His eyes widen as they roam over me. "Wow, Hunt. You look... amazing. Where are you off to?"

He's wearing a suit and looks like a hotshot banker fantasy in the flesh. My brain short-circuits.

"I've got a date tonight. And tomorrow. And the next day. And the day after that. All different guys."

Oh my gosh, where is the sea witch?

Dylan's eyebrows disappear under his blond fringe, a hint of something unreadable in his expression. "Well, good for you. I hope you have a great time." He steps aside, letting me pass.

As I walk out of the apartment, I almost face-palm myself, then remember the fresh makeup and settle for an inward cringe. When will I ever stop acting like a total moron around Dylan?

14

HUNTER

The wine bar where my date has asked to meet is the kind of place I imagine corporate types frequent. Sleek, modern, with an air of sophistication that's a little too forced. I spot Ethan sitting at a table by the window. He's even more striking than his profile picture, with his perfectly styled sandy hair and impeccable suit.

As I approach, he stands up, flashing a polished smile and extending his hand. "Hunter, it's great to meet you in person."

"Likewise," I reply, matching his level of formality. We sit down, and I barely have time to peek at the menu before Ethan launches into his first question.

"What's your five-year plan?" His hazel eyes bore into mine, giving me the impression I'm in a job interview rather than on a date.

I blink, taken aback. "My five-year plan? Well, I haven't thought about it…" I trail off, unsure how to respond. Does he mean in my personal life? Or professionally?

Ethan raises an eyebrow, looking unimpressed. "But how do you expect to move forward without a roadmap?"

I resist the urge to roll my eyes. "I prefer to stay flexible?"

He frowns, clearly not satisfied with my answer. "Flexibility is important, but if it's not paired with a solid plan, you're drifting." Ethan leans forward, his expression serious. "How about short-term goals, then, how do you structure them?"

I laugh awkwardly, hoping he's joking. But the intensity in his gaze tells me otherwise. "How about we start with something a little lighter?" I suggest, desperate to steer the conversation in a different direction. "What do you like to do for fun? Any hobbies or travel plans?"

But Ethan seems uninterested in casual chatting. And after a while, he smoothly transitions back to the topic of productivity. "What's your biggest time-management challenge?" He takes a precise bite of his avocado toast, waiting for an answer.

I fidget with my untouched glass of wine. Right now, having wasted an evening on this date is quickly becoming my biggest time-management challenge. As Ethan drones on about his morning-routine app, I draft a polite "thanks, but no thanks" text to send later.

After splitting the bill, Ethan walks me out, shaking my hand once more. "You seem like you're on top of things, Hunter. It's been great meeting you."

I wonder if he's going to follow up with a performance-review email.

As I make my way home, I sigh, vowing to swear off corporate types for the foreseeable future. Even if Dylan, theoretically, is a corporate type. But with his easy-going nature and goofball attitude, it's so easy to forget. If only all investment bankers were more like him... I wouldn't like them, anyway. Because they're not Dylan.

What I should wish for is a version of him who's single and into me.

I stare up at the night sky, searching for a sign. But no stars shoot across the firmament to offer me hope, so I walk my sorry ass home.

* * *

Wednesday evening rolls around, and despite a terrible first experience, I'm getting ready for another date. Last night with Ethan was a total disaster, but I'm positive the guy I'm meeting tonight, Malik, can't be any worse. And as Clara keeps reminding me, it's a numbers game. The more dates I go on, the higher the chances of finding someone I click with.

At the front door, I nearly collide with Dylan again. He's the spitting image of the hot guys on the covers of billionaire romance novels. Dark suit, white shirt, blue tie. Hair sleeked back for once instead of tousled in that endearing way of his. *Move over, Christian Grey.*

The sight is as unsettling as ever. But at least this time, I manage to keep my mouth shut and only wave him goodbye.

A short cab ride later, I step into an understated Italian bistro. The place smells of garlic and bread with twinkling lights hanging from the ceiling that cast a warm glow over the checkered tablecloths. It's the perfect setting for a cozy evening.

Malik is at a table near the back. He's tall and lean, with smooth, dark skin and an impeccably groomed, short beard. His broad smile drew me to his profile on the app. But the body that goes with that smile isn't bad at all. His fitted charcoal T-shirt and black jeans make him look like he stepped out of an upscale magazine ad for casual summer fashion.

We settle into a booth, and the conversation flows easily. Malik talks about his job as a graphic designer, his favorite indie bands, and the best spots in the city to get coffee. I relax, thinking that maybe first dates don't have to be grueling.

But halfway through dinner, something shifts. Malik's smile falters, and he gets this distant look in his eyes. "My ex, Samantha, loved this place."

I freeze, my fork hovering in mid-air. *Uh-oh. Mentions of the ex on a first date can't be good.*

"We were together for three years. She was... amazing." Malik's staring into his plate of spaghetti as if it were a portal to the past where he could see himself and Samantha sharing a noodle with the same demure sweetness of *Lady and the Tramp*.

As Malik lists everything he misses about Samantha—how she made spaghetti with meatballs like the ones we're eating, how they used to spend Sundays binge-watching shows, how he still sometimes texts her even if she hasn't replied in months—I shift in my seat.

I fix my gaze on the flickering candle on the table, racking my brain for a way to steer the discussion away from his ex. But it's no use. Malik has disappeared down a rabbit hole in memory lane and is not coming back. His eyes mist over as he continues to reminisce, and I pat his hand while he sniffles, unsure if I should offer him more bread or a tissue.

When our server approaches, asking if we're interested in dessert, I decline even if the chocolate cake sounded promising. I'm ready to leave.

"I guess this wasn't what you signed up for," Malik says once the server returns with the check.

I shrug. "We've all been there. Break-ups aren't easy."

He nods, blowing his nose loudly—turned out tissues were the way to go. "You're right. Sorry for dumping all this on you. I thought I was ready to date again, but clearly, I'm not."

I give him a sympathetic smile. "It's okay. Healing takes time. Focus on taking care of yourself, and the rest will fall into place."

Ahha, how collected I am when advising others. I'm a pot calling the kettle black.

I wish Malik a good life, and, as I wait for my cab, I wonder if I'm a magnet for walking red flags.

My car arrives, and I climb into the back seat, scoffing. Two dates, two disasters. At this rate, I'm wondering if the dating app gives out loyalty points for not-so-meet-cutes. Five points: a pint of ice cream (it's better to spoon something that won't talk back). Ten points: a bottle of moonshine (only a borderline illegal drink could blur your memory enough). Twenty points: a coupon for therapy (because, let's be honest, you need it at this stage). Fifty points: a plush pillow embroidered with *At Least You Tried* (soft enough to cry into). And the grand prize at one hundred points: a lifetime subscription to streaming services (because sometimes, the only commitment you need is to continue watching).

I've only accumulated two points so far, but I might still indulge in a carton of ice cream.

* * *

Despite my resolution to give dating apps a fair chance and win at the numbers game, tonight, I'm putting zero effort into it, already bracing myself for disappointment. I throw on a pair of jeans and don't even bother showering again before heading out. I'm meeting guy number three, Tyler, at a casual burger joint— no need to get all dolled up.

At 8 p.m. sharp, I walk into the upscale pub. The walls are covered in chalkboard menus listing craft beers and specialty burgers with quirky names. The atmosphere is lively and loud with chatter and clinking glasses.

Tyler is easy to find. He's leaning against the bar, arms crossed over his chest, looking every bit the fitness junkie from his photos. I can't tell his hair color since it's shaved in a short buzz cut. His snug black T-shirt shows off his lean, muscular frame. If I had to assign him a vibe, I'd say ex-military. I try to remember what his bio said, but can't.

We grab a table in the corner, and small talk rears its awkward head. Tyler asks me about work, hobbies, and we joke about our mutual dislike for people who think the entire subway car needs to hear their call.

I'm still laughing when Tyler freezes, eyes fixed on something over my shoulder. "Did you see that?"

I turn, following his gaze. "What?" I ask, scanning the bar for anything unusual.

Tyler nods toward the ceiling, where a small security camera sits tucked into the corner. "The camera," he hisses. "They're watching us. All of us, all the time."

I laugh, thinking he's joking, but he leans in, lowering his voice. "They've been hiding things from us for decades. Take the moon landing, for instance..." His eyes widen with a sort of feverish excitement.

I blink as a nervous laugh escapes my lips. "The w—what?"

Turns out, Tyler's dead serious. He explains in great detail how the government staged the first man walking on the moon. That NASA is part of a global conspiracy. And how the media have brainwashed everyone. His hands wave as he describes hidden truths and shadow organizations.

I take a big bite of my burger, chewing slowly to buy myself time. I don't know how to reply. "Um, that's... an interesting perspective. But I'm pretty sure Neil Armstrong walked on the moon."

Tyler's eyes narrow. "That's what they want you to think." He's not having any of my "facts." He's too deep into his rant now, explaining how he's been researching "the truth" for years and how I need to wake up.

His burger sits untouched, while he launches into a full-on tirade about how everything we've ever been told is a lie. I discreetly check my phone under the table, wondering how fast I can get out of Dodge as Tyler's blue eyes dart around like he's worried someone might overhear.

When he tells me vaccines are a cover for injecting tracking devices, I lean in, lowering my voice to match his intensity. "Is the guy in the blue cap watching us?"

Tyler's head snaps toward the man, who's just eating his burger in peace. He tenses, scanning the bar with practiced paranoia, his eyes narrowing on every person who glances our way.

"This place is crawling with them," Tyler whispers, as though sharing state secrets.

I nod, throwing a cautious glance over my shoulder. "We should split up, throw them off."

Tyler shoots me a look of admiration. "You're right."

I sit back on my stool, keeping quiet. There's only so much bullshit I can spin before I laugh.

He slips two twenties onto the table. "I don't use cards. Not safe. Too easy to track."

"Wait." I frown. "How come you're on a dating app, then?"

"Tyler's not my real name. I would've told you, eventually."

Note to self: switch to an app with verified identities.

Not-Tyler gives me a regretful stare. "Sorry this didn't work out. But I can't be with you. You're on their radar."

"No, I understand."

"I knew you would." He stands up and adds, "Don't follow me out for ten minutes."

He gives me one last look, then slips out, disappearing into the night. I wait a bit before raising my beer bottle in a silent toast. Cheers to all the sane people who decided not to match with me and to the dating-app algorithm that thinks I deserve this.

* * *

By the time Friday evening rolls around, I'm dreading my last date. But it's also the start of the weekend, which means the odds of Dylan and Olivia spending time together are high. Especially since Dylan, Tristan, Nina, and I are all having dinner at Adrian's place tomorrow to meet Rowena's fake fiancé. If Dylan can't be with his girlfriend on Saturday night, he'll want to see her tonight. Here or at her place, I don't know. But I'm not taking the chance of being a third wheel again if they're staying here. I'd rather be out meeting another weirdo than watching them get cozy on my couch.

I leave the house before Dylan is back—extra points for avoiding another mortification. A short walk later, I venture inside a fancy French bistro that has opened a couple of blocks away. I suggested this place to my date since I've been hearing great things about it and I was curious to try it out. Once, I would've come with Nina and Rowena for a girls' night out. Sadly, those days are gone.

As the warm, inviting scent of fancy cheese and warm baguette wraps around me, a small pang of mourning for my youth tugs at my chest. Nina is living with her boyfriend and they'll probably get engaged soon. Rowena is having a baby and getting married—okay, that situation isn't by the book, but it's still a big step. And me, I'm getting older but just never wiser.

My friends are moving on with their lives while I'm stuck meeting internet weirdos, hoping to overcome a teenage crush. Everyone else is boarding a train to somewhere exciting but I'm alone on the platform, clutching a ticket to nowhere. For years, I've pinned too much on the idea of Dylan. He's been my "will happen one day"—the excuse I used to avoid taking risks or trying to build something real with anyone else. He was an imaginary safety net. But safety nets don't catch you when you're standing still. They're for people brave enough to leap, and I've been too scared to jump.

Now everyone else's lives are moving on without me. I've spent years letting this one-sided crush seep into everything, coloring how I live, how I love, and how I don't. It has to stop. The thought of starting over terrifies me, but so does the idea of staying exactly where I am, trapped in a cycle of waiting for something that might never happen.

If online dating doesn't work out, I'll find something else. Maybe I'll join obscure hobby clubs, like competitive origami. Or try a singles-only trivia night and dominate all the Taylor Swift categories. Or throw myself into singles hiking groups, pretending I love sweating uphill. I'm already pretending to be a happy early raiser; what's one more layer of misery?

At least the restaurant I picked looks nice. The flickering candlelight and soft background noise of conversations create an intimate atmosphere. Still, as I ask the hostess for my table, I wonder if I should stop going on dinner dates and meet new guys for drinks. Give me a faster, easier escape. Assuming I'll ever have the courage to set up new dates. If tonight's another bust, I won't have the fortitude—I'd rather join a bowling league.

As the hostess guides me through the maze of tables, my eyes land on Lucas, seated by the main window. He's meticulously groomed, his short, gel-slicked hair sitting rigidly in place like it wouldn't dare defy him. His broad shoulders strain against the seams of his too-tight button-up, the fabric pulled taut over a chest that seems more swollen than natural. The rolled-up sleeves reveal thick, veined forearms that look like they've seen more dumbbells than daylight. When he spots me, his brown eyes narrow briefly, scanning like I'm a cut of steak he's deciding whether to throw on the grill. Did he look like that in his photo? He seemed much less... muscular? Inflated?

He stands to greet me, offering a warm smile that at least seems genuine. "Hunter, nice to meet you." He pulls out my chair in a smooth, chivalrous motion.

So far so good on the attitude, but I can't help being on edge, searching for red flags instead of concentrating on the positives. Should I ask him right away if he believes there are aliens hidden in Area 51 or when his last break-up was and if he still texts his ex?

The hostess hands us our menus, and we fall into the standard first-date script—where we're from, how we ended up in New York, how we like the city.

Lucas's answers are smooth, making me wonder how many first dates he's been on. His responses have a rehearsed quality that leaves me wary. Still, I keep up with my lines, nodding at the right intervals, but there's a part of me already wondering how much longer this will last. He suggests a wine from the list, and I go along, deciding to reserve judgment for later.

Just then, the hostess reappears, escorting a couple to the table next to ours. I glance over—and my stomach drops. Because, of course, the universe can't resist throwing a pie in my face.

It's Dylan and Olivia.

15

DYLAN

Inside the restaurant, candlelight flickers across burgundy tablecloths, casting a warm glow against the exposed brick walls. Muted conversations and the clink of silverware echo around the room as Olivia and I follow the hostess to our table. The vibe could be described as romantic—or suffocating, depending on your mood. Honestly, it'd be perfect for a date if I weren't this on edge.

Taking space from Olivia hasn't helped me chill or get more into this new relationship, nor has lying awake in bed every single night of the past week listening in for when Hunter would return from her dates. It was never too late. Does it mean the one-on-ones went poorly? And why does the supposition cheer me up?

Anyway. She's out with another dude tonight. I only caught a whiff of her perfume as I came back home, but she was already gone.

Olivia grabs my hand as we follow the hostess. "Wines from Bourgogne are supposed to be the best in the world." She points at the chalkboard behind the bar with the day's special and suggested wine pairings. "I bet they have a great selection here."

I'm about to respond we should order a bottle when the back of my scalp prickles. My attention shifts as I glance around, wondering what the heck happened.

Then I see her.

Hunter.

My stomach clenches, hit with the force of a sucker punch. Of course. Of all the restaurants in this city, she's here. She has her back half turned away from me and hasn't seen me. Only the curve of her profile is visible from behind, but her date is right in my face. The guy looks like a puffed-up jerk who thrives on pushing people around. I turn my head. One glance is plenty; I've no desire to get the full picture.

I'm still half-hoping the hostess will deviate at the last second and steer us in a different direction, but, to my horror, she heads straight for the empty table next to Hunter and the guy who must curl his biceps while staring at his reflection the entire time.

"Here we are," the hostess chirps, oblivious to the storm brewing in my gut.

"Thank you," I say because *fuck me* doesn't sound like an appropriate response.

Hunter, who was smiling at something Mr. Self-Impressed yapped, glances up at hearing my voice, eyes locking with mine. I freeze. The smile dies on her face as her mouth goes slack—not that the shocked expression does anything to diminish how stunning she is.

She looks different tonight. Her lids are shadowed in smoky-gray and her dark hair, instead of the usual natural waves, is straight, falling in a curtain of black silk over her shoulders. I notice all this in an instant, and it doesn't help the been-punched-in-the-gut sensation in my stomach.

Does she feel it too? That immediate shift in the air?

Her hair might be sleek, but her obsidian gaze is wild for a hot second. Before her features quickly shift, going blank and polite, as if we're nothing more than passing acquaintances.

Olivia tenses beside me. She's half-smiling, the expression uncertain as she tries to figure out why I've stiffened.

"Hi," she says brightly, her tone a little too cheerful as she glances between Hunter, her date, and me.

Hunter straightens in her chair, offering a tight smile. "Dylan. Olivia."

"Hunter." I give her a nod, then turn to her date. "Hey, man. We haven't been introduced. Dylan." I offer him my hand.

"Lucas." He grins, flashing straight white teeth worthy of a QVC host ready to convince you to buy a Facial-Flex. "And how do you know Hunter?" He stands and extends a hand, which I take, squeezing a little harder than necessary.

"I'm her roommate."

Olivia shifts on her feet, tucking a strand of hair behind her ear, her gaze bouncing between all of us. She forces a polite smile, but her lips are pressed a little too tight, her eyes lingering on me, waiting for an explanation as if this were my fault. "Olivia." She offers her hand, forcing me to let go of Luc-ASS. "Nice to meet you." Her voice sounds strained as she glances over at Hunter. "Hunter, nice to see you again."

Hunter nods, but her smile doesn't reach her eyes. "Yeah, so good to see you."

The awkward silence stretches, thick and uncomfortable. Olivia's not speaking, but I can still hear the question: *Why didn't you mention she'd be here?*

I shrug, hoping Olivia will surmise this wasn't planned. In fact, the impromptu run-in goes against the plan. Tonight was supposed to give me clarity on my feelings for Olivia, keeping my sexy roommate out of the picture. But here we are.

We sit down, Olivia still eyeing me expectantly—presumably waiting for an answer to the silent question she hasn't asked, but that's burning behind those slightly pissed amber eyes. Her smile has dimmed a touch, and the shift in energy as the hostess hands us menus is palpable.

I flip open the menu, and panic washes over me. It's all in French. Not a single recognizable word leaps out at me. I only see a tangled mess of words that mock me from the page. English is hard enough most days, but French? Forget it. I try to read the first item, but my brain hits a wall. None of the letters string together into anything familiar. I've got no foothold, no starting point. Just a page full of alien characters designed to make me feel like an idiot.

But that's the least of my problems right now.

As soon as the hostess is gone, Olivia leans in closer, whispering, "I didn't realize this place was so popular."

"And I didn't know she was coming here." I keep my voice low as I respond to her passive-aggressive insinuation. "It's a coincidence."

Olivia's lips purse. "Right."

I hold Olivia's stare for a second before my gaze wanders back to Hunter's table. She's laughing at something Lucas said. But it's not the usual throaty giggling I've come to recognize and be drawn to; it sounds more forced. Hunter is sitting with a stiff spine and her fingers toy with the edge of her napkin, twisting it in her lap.

Olivia clears her throat, demanding my attention. "Should we share an appetizer?" she asks, glancing at me over the edge of the menu.

Her tone has brightened as if she's decided not to let the proximity with my roommate ruin her evening. But something flickers underneath. Doubt? Jealousy? I can't blame her. If our places were reversed, and my girlfriend was living with some hot dude who I suddenly saw everywhere, I'd react the same way.

I hesitate, the squiggly French words swimming on the page. "Why don't you choose? French isn't exactly my forte. I don't understand half the things on here."

She raises an eyebrow, as if it's a joke. "Just read the English translation underneath."

"Yeah, sure." I nod too quickly.

I glance down again, pretending to skim the page, but the translation is written so small it might as well not exist. I could tell Olivia the truth: that I have dyslexia, that reading anything this dense is near impossible for me. But I don't. Protecting this part of myself has become second nature. A reflex I can't unlearn.

"See anything you like?"

"It all looks great," I deflect. "I'm okay with whatever you prefer."

"Yeah, whatever." Olivia's nostrils flare, but she lets it drop, flipping through the menu. Meanwhile, my attention drifts inevitably back to our neighbors.

Hunter's voice cuts through the murmur of the restaurant. "You said you're in finance, right? How do you like it?"

"Yeah, it's great. It requires a sharp mind." I keep my eyes on the leather-bound menu that's being crushed in my hands. "Not to say what you do isn't... interesting, of course."

A flicker of annoyance rises in my chest. What a douche answer.

I dare a sideways peek. Hunter's smile tightens ever so slightly.

I clench my jaw, staring back hard at the list of main courses. The only word I can make out is filet—sounds good to me.

"How was your week?" Olivia asks, also still looking at her menu.

I blink. "Uh... long. Yours?"

I half-listen to her reply, every word from the conversation next door echoing louder in my brain than anything my girlfriend is saying.

"Engineering consulting is interesting, yeah. It's all about problem-solving," Hunter explains, to stay upbeat, but I know that tone. She's fighting to keep the conversation polite.

"Dylan?" Olivia's voice pulls me back, and I realize she's been talking this whole time.

"Sorry, what did you say?" I force myself to meet her eyes.

"I asked if you wanted to start with wine or cocktails."

"Wine's good. Did you find a Bourgogne you'd like to try?" I ask as Lucas's voice floats over again.

"Right, problem-solving." He chuckles dismissively. "Many people don't get what engineering consulting is. It's not real engineering, is it? More like overseeing projects and making sure the actual engineers know what they're doing, right?"

He talks as if Hunter's work is a joke when her job is every bit as demanding as his. I grit my teeth, fighting the urge to turn and correct him even as an angry retort burns at the back of my throat. But Hunter can handle herself. She doesn't need me butting in.

"I was thinking the Chablis," Olivia says. "If it's not too expensive."

"No, we're good, whatever you want."

"Are you sure you don't even want to have a look at the list?"

"No." It'd be probably as useless as the menu. "Surprise me." I turn slightly to gauge Hunter's reaction to Lucas's last comment.

She's forcing a smile, but her eyes are narrowing. "We do a bit of everything, yes. Design, project management, troubleshooting. It's all hands-on."

Before Lucas can respond, a server appears at their table with a practiced smile. "Are we ready to order?"

Hunter's shoulders relax a little as if she was relieved by the interruption. I tear my eyes away, forcing myself to focus back on Olivia, who's been perusing the menu in silence, presumably waiting for me to engage. I realize I haven't started a single conversation.

"What looks good to you?" A weak opener, but it's all I've got right now.

Olivia glances up from the menu, her eyes flicking between me and the table beside us. I can't tell if she's suspicious. "I was thinking about the duck confit."

"Yeah, that sounds... yummy." I'm not sure what a confit is; my culinary expertise stops at baked goods.

In my peripheral, I trace the server leaving Hunter's table. *Don't look, Dylan.* I sustain Olivia's gaze, willing myself to stay present.

"I'm going for the filet." If they were handing out Oscars for the most painful small talk, I'd be the winner.

Mercifully, that's when the same server who interrupted Hunter and Lucas appears at our table.

She rattles off the specials in a rehearsed cadence, but I don't pay attention—half the words are obscure French culinary terms, anyway. Why did I ever pick this stupid restaurant? It seemed the kind of place Olivia would approve of. Hunter, too, apparently. Unless her date suggested it.

I order the filet, and Olivia takes the duck whatever.

"Anything to drink?" the server asks.

"We'll take the Chablis." Olivia folds the menu, handing it over. "And we'd like to start with the *escargot*, please."

See? Another word I ignore the meaning of.

The server nods, scribbling down the order before disappearing again. The beat of silence that follows is filled by Lucas's dick talking.

"Hmm. Anyway, what you do is cute. I always pictured engineering as more... I don't know... men's work. Lots of tools and blueprints. But I'm sure what you do is important too, in its own way. You must be good with people."

I glance toward their table, catching Hunter's posture stiffening as she takes a sip of water. She's not smiling anymore.

"You'd be surprised how much technical work goes into it." Her voice is taut, but controlled. "But yeah, we deal with people, too. And deadlines. And budgets."

Lucas smirks as if he's in on some joke no one else finds funny. "Ah, numbers can be tricky. Good thing they've invented spreadsheets, huh?"

Did he seriously say that? Pity they still haven't invented brain-to-mouth filters to cure his verbal diarrhea. This guy's a complete jerk. But Hunter, always composed, doesn't flinch. "I have a minor in mathematics. But sure, spreadsheets help."

Olivia taps her fingernails against the side of her empty wine glass, the sharp clicks drawing my attention back to her. "Did you want to do something together tomorrow?"

"Uh, sure."

"We could check out the new Harlem Renaissance and Transatlantic Modernism exhibit tomorrow night at The Met. It's supposed to be incredible—showcasing artists who redefined modern art."

I tune out Lucas's laugh and another one of his obnoxious answers. "A math minor. Wow, color me impressed."

Stay focused, Dylan. "Uh, actually, I can't tomorrow night," I say, scratching my jaw. "I've got dinner with my friends."

Olivia gapes at me. "*Girl*friends aren't invited?"

I sigh, knowing my next few sentences are a potential mine-field. "It's not like that... but it's complicated. We're meeting the fiancé of my sister's pregnant best friend, Rowena. I barely got asked along myself. Winnie wouldn't be comfortable if I brought along someone she doesn't know."

Olivia's smile tightens. She glares at Hunter, probably doing the math that my roommate is invited and part of the inner circle, and she gives a short, clipped nod. "Sure. Of course. If I knew you already had plans for Saturday, I could've made my own with my friends."

I'm sweating cold. "S-sorry, work's been a shit-show this week. I—it was inconsiderate of me."

"It's okay. I forget stuff all the time, too." Her tone is light, but there's no mistaking the offended edge in her words.

The server arriving with the wine saves me again. She sets the bottle down on the table, uncorking it with a flourish. Unfortunately, this leaves me free to hear another one of Lucas's pearls.

"I'm glad women can contribute to fields that used to be over their heads."

"Over our heads?"

I pretend to follow the server's maneuvers to study how Hunter is taking this last gem. Her expression is tight, her hands now folded in her lap, and Lucas, oblivious, shrugs with a smug grin. "Oh, come on. It's great to see women getting involved in more technical stuff. Even if it's more in a supporting role."

Hunter crosses her arms, her lips thinning into a tight line. "I'm a lead consultant on most of my projects."

"Right, right. You must be great at organizing everyone else. Guys need that sometimes. We can be all over the place. Good thing someone's around keeping things tidy."

I stare at the pale-gold liquid the server just poured and take a long sip.

"This is great." I drop the glass, struggling to smile. "Thanks for picking it."

"Glad you like it." Olivia clinks her glass with mine. "Hey, do you want to hang out during the day tomorrow since you're busy at night?"

"Tidy?" Hunter asks in a bitter tone.

"Yeah, I'm free all day." Paying attention to two conversations at once is maddening.

Lucas laughs, missing the rising frustration in Hunter's voice. "Yeah. You know, women are naturally better at organizing things. Like keeping the house in order. Or a project."

"Dylan?" Olivia's inflection sharpens. "Are you okay?"

I didn't even realize I was crushing the stem of my wine glass. "Yeah, yeah. We can go to the Transit Renaissance thing at MoMA."

"You mean the Transatlantic Modernism exhibit at The Met?"

"Yeah, the one."

"Platter of *escargot* for two." The server comes back with our appetizers.

I gape at the plate she's set between us, my stomach doing an uneasy flip because, there, sitting in little pools of creamed herbs, are... snails. I glance up at Olivia, who's already reaching for one, unfazed.

Did she order a snail appetizer? Guess that's my punishment for thinking I could bluff my way past a learning disability. I watch Olivia in a sort of fascinated revulsion as she easily extracts the slimy creature from its shell with a small fork. She doesn't eat it, though, and looks at me instead. Does she expect me to partake?

With a sigh, I grab the tiny fork and stab at a shell, the slick mollusk sliding free with a sickening squelch. My stomach turns.

The rubbery thing wobbles as I raise it to my mouth, steeling myself. *Just swallow. Get it over with. Don't think about it.*

I pop it in my mouth, the chewy texture hitting me like a punch. Garlic butter coats my tongue, but it's not enough to mask the gummy horror I'm trying hard not to gag on. I bite down, each gnaw worse than the last. This is a nightmare.

At least having my mouth full saves me from having to talk. I chew slowly, pretending to enjoy the "delicacy," but my ears are tuned in to Lucas's voice. He's talking again, still missing the quiet, simmering anger from Hunter.

His tone has taken on a slimy, suggestive edge—slimier than what's currently in my mouth. "Oh, I'm sure you're great at a lot of things. You've got that whole 'boss lady' vibe going on. You're used to telling guys what to do, huh? That's hot."

"Excuse me?" Hunter hisses.

"Did you like the *escargot*?" Olivia asks.

I grimace as I will myself to swallow the thing. "They're something. Maybe not for me." I gulp down wine to wash the awful taste away.

Olivia chuckles. "Well, I can't finish them on my own."

There are like a dozen of the suckers on the plate. I hope she doesn't expect me to eat half of them. Still, dutifully, I grab another one.

I'm fumbling with the snail, trying not to think about what I'm eating, when Hunter scoffs next to me. Instinctively, I glance over as Lucas leans in closer, his voice dropping. "It's not often you meet a woman who can be both smart and still... take care of a man's needs. You're the full package. Brains, looks... bet you're even a little feisty between the sheets."

Hunter's face hardens, and her voice cuts like a blade. "You're the full package, too. Arrogant, condescending, and now, gross."

"Hey, I'm paying you a compliment. You can be tough at work and still know how to relax after hours, right? I bet you're a lot more fun when you're not calling the shots."

Hunter drops her napkin on the table. "Well, I'm calling the shots now and I'm leaving."

I want to whoop in relief that this ordeal will be over for both of us.

Hunter stands, her chair scraping against the floor as she moves to leave. But Lucas grabs her wrist to drag her back down.

Seeing his filthy hand on her perfect skin is the breaking point—I snap. My lips pull tight, baring my teeth as my legs push my chair away from the table. I'm already halfway standing before I even realize what I'm doing.

16

HUNTER

I throw in the towel on this date—literally by dropping my napkin on my still-empty plate. But as I stand to leave, Lucas shows cobra-like reflexes, grabbing my wrist from across the table to prevent me from standing. His clammy palm closes around my flesh, gripping too tightly. It feels like I have an actual snake coiled over my wrist instead of a human hand.

I yank my arm away, but he holds fast, his fingers digging into my skin.

"Let me go," I hiss.

But Lucas doesn't budge. As an irrational panic is about to set in, Dylan surges from the table next to ours, his presence dominating the scene.

"Let her go," Dylan orders, deathly calm.

Lucas ignores his request. "Look, buddy, we're in the middle of—"

Dylan's expression remains mild as he clamps his hand on Lucas's shoulder, the grip firm enough to silence him. "First off, I'm not your *buddy*. And whatever you think you were in the middle of? That's done."

The two men stare each other down, our bodies locked in this bizarre chain where Dylan's gripping Lucas, and Lucas still has his disgusting fingers around my wrist. We're like some twisted version of a team-building exercise, except no one's bonding, and everyone wants out of the circle.

Dylan cuts an impressive figure in his tailored suit. He has this "Clark Kent moments before ducking into a phone booth to become Superman" vibe to him. He emanates a quiet strength, an untapped well of energy waiting to be unleashed. His broad shoulders fill out his jacket in a way that suggests he could rip through the fabric if the situation called for it. Lucas, instead, looks like he's poured himself into an off-the-rack suit that strains against his protein-shake muscles.

The contrast between them is stark. Dylan exudes a calm, dominant authority, while Lucas radiates the desperate bravado of a schoolyard bully who's just figured out he's picked on the wrong kid. Under Dylan's steady glare, my date seems to shrink, as if realizing he isn't facing an ordinary man, but a force of nature barely contained by a civilized attire.

It's easy to imagine Dylan's tie coming off, his shirt ripping, revealing a big 'S' underneath. Judging by the way Lucas's face reddens, but his lips stop moving, he's clearly hoping this particular Superman keeps his alter ego in place.

After a few more beats of silence, Lucas decides he can't win the fight and releases my wrist, leaving a reddish mark where his fingers had been. Finally free, I massage my skin. Dylan's eyes follow the gesture, zeroing in on the faint bruise. His expression darkens, and he glares with such controlled fury that Lucas recoils in his chair, making it scrape on the floor as he stands up, chuckling while he backs away.

"Hey man, no need to make a scene." Lucas raises his hands. "It was all a misunderstanding. And I was leaving, anyway."

Dylan doesn't break eye contact with Lucas, his body still tense, not even when Lucas makes one last attempt at maintaining some semblance of dignity, tossing a careless comment my way.

"She's not worth the trouble, man."

Dylan's jaw goes so tight I fear a vortex might whip around him after all and reveal him in his superhero suit as he wipes the floor with Lucas. But Dylan doesn't move. His stance remains rigid and controlled, his eyes burning with quiet fury. But his silence still speaks louder than any words could. Lucas shrivels under the weight of it, giving Dylan a wide berth as he circles our table and bolts for the exit.

Once Lucas is gone, Dylan's gaze shifts back to me, his concern softening the hard edges of his expression. "Are you okay?" he asks, his voice gentle.

I'm mortified, but I manage a nod. "Yeah, I'm okay. Thanks for..." For what? Thanks for rescuing me from the latest gem I found on a dating app? Thanks for ruining your own date to save me from my disastrous one?

Speaking of his date, I spot Olivia behind Dylan, and she looks absolutely *not* okay. Her face is a storm of emotions: hurt, confusion, and most of all, anger. She's sitting rigid, her hand clenched around the edge of the table as if she's struggling to hold back her rage.

I try to convey this to Dylan, widening my eyes and tilting my head in Olivia's direction. But Dylan, bless his oblivious heart, is still looking at me, missing my nonverbal cues.

Just as I'm about to verbalize the impending girlfriend crisis, Olivia stands up, throwing her napkin on the table, nostrils flaring, as she addresses Dylan.

"I'll leave as well." Her voice rises with every word. "Since you are more interested in her night than ours."

Dylan spins around, registering Olivia's presence and her less-than-pleased demeanor. "Olivia, wait," he starts, his hands raised in a placating gesture. "I had to step in."

But Olivia is having none of it. She grabs her purse, her knuckles white from the tight grip. "Really, Dylan? Because from where I'm sitting, it looks like you care more about *her* date than ours."

The accusation hangs in the air, heavy and loaded. Dylan opens his mouth to respond, but Olivia doesn't give him the chance.

"Save it. I've had enough bullshit for one night." She stomps out of the restaurant, her heels clicking sharply against the floor with each furious step.

Dylan calls after her, his voice tinged with desperation. "Olivia, please. Let me explain."

She doesn't even falter. Olivia heads straight for the exit, not sparing him a second glance. And just like that, she's gone, leaving Dylan gaping and stunned.

He stays rooted on the spot. Then, as if snapping out of a trance, he turns to me, his expression apologetic.

"Hunter, I'm so sorry, but I have to..." He gestures toward the door.

I jerk my chin in the same direction. "Go," I tell him, mustering a weak smile. "And thanks again for everything."

He gives me a quick, grateful nod before rushing out after Olivia, shouting for her to wait, to let him explain. My wrist aches where Lucas grabbed me, but what hurts the most is watching Dylan run after his girlfriend.

And then, I'm alone. Sitting deflated at my table, my pulse still racing from the confrontation. I slump as the weight of the night settles into my bones. Everything feels heavier now: the room, my body, the not-quite-silence of the restaurant. I'm too drained to contemplate how I'll face Dylan after this. Or the mess our cohabitation is turning out to be.

Soon, the adrenaline wears off, leaving me even more exhausted. I'm about to drop my head in my hands when the server arrives with our main courses, balancing the plates with an awkward smile. The rich aroma that would have been enticing under normal circumstances now turns my stomach.

"Could you please box everything?" My voice sounds distant even to my own ears. "And bring the check. Thanks."

She nods, whisking the plates away, and returns a short while later with my boxed meal and *two* leather folders.

I expect her to hand me one, but she doesn't, shifting uncomfortably on her feet.

"I'm sorry, miss." She hesitates. "But will you be settling the bill for the table next door as well? They've left, and you all seem to know each other..."

If the situation didn't suck so much, it might be funny. Isn't it hilarious? Having to foot Dylan's bill is the cherry on top of an already calamitous evening.

"I'll pay for both," I tell the server.

She hands me the leather folders. I open the first, and my jaw drops as I scan the items. Twenty-six dollars for a platter of snails, plus tips and taxes.

It's a metaphor for my life. Unwanted, bitter, and far more costly than I bargained for. And then there's the eighty-dollar bottle of wine they ordered...

I contemplate the receipts in stunned disbelief. How fitting to be left alone, with no man, no love, no direction, and not one, but two printed reminders of how pathetic my life is.

I swipe my credit card and sign on the dotted line, my hand moving on autopilot. As I rise from my seat, I glance at the bottle of wine still sitting nearly full on Dylan and Olivia's forlorn table.

Without thinking, I grab it, tucking it under my arm. If I'm going to wallow in misery tonight, I might as well have a decent drink to keep me company.

The warm summer air hits my face as I emerge onto the bustling New York street. The city's alive around me, people laughing and chatting as they pass by, but I feel disconnected from it all.

Clutching the wine as a tragic consolation prize, I raise my hand to flag down a cab because even a few blocks' walk home seems like too much. One slows, then speeds up the second the driver spots the bottle under my arm. *Seriously?* I try again. The next one doesn't even hesitate, just zooms right past like I'm holding a grenade. *Perfect.*

After the third cab swerves out of reach, it hits me how people must see me from outside, walking down the street with an open bottle of wine. No one's stopping for me.

Great. I'm officially "that girl." You know, the hot mess you avoid eye contact with because she looks like she's going to drink herself into a stupor on a sidewalk.

I sigh, resigning myself to walk home. Please, don't let me get arrested for public drinking. With my recent luck, a cop is bound to stop me any second, and then I'll be explaining how I'm not starring in a rom-com, and there's no hidden camera crew ready to film my "everything will be okay" moment. I'm just someone who got dumped—no, wait, that isn't the right word. Gaslighted by one man and platonically rescued and then ditched by the other? Yes. I'm the loser who had to pick up the tab for two men who definitely aren't dating me.

And spending the night in jail would sound more promising than having to share an apartment with Dylan. *Dear officer, could you also write me up for tragic life decisions while you're at it?*

17

DYLAN

I stumble on the uneven sidewalk as I march down the dimly lit street, heading back to the restaurant—alone. The muggy summer air is not entirely responsible for the icy trickle of sweat down my spine. Each step feels heavier than the last, weighed down by the guilt settling in my gut after my failed attempt at reconciling with Olivia. Her words keep echoing in my head.

"You were never really there, Dylan. You've been distracted all night, paying more attention to your roommate than me."

She's right, of course. I rationalize it, telling myself I was being a good friend, looking out for Hunter when that sleazeball was getting handsy. Anyone would have done the same.

If Nina were in the same situation, I'd have intervened, too.

For the first time, a true wave of gratitude that she's dating Tristan hits me. At least my sister will never have to sit across the table from a jerk like Lucas.

But even as I try to convince myself of my brotherly disposition toward Hunter, the nagging ache in my gut won't let up. The truth is, the instant I saw Lucas reach for Hunter's wrist, something inside me snapped. It wasn't friendly concern—it was a visceral, possessive anger that took me by surprise. I keep picturing that faint-pink line on her skin where his fingers had been, and it sends a fresh wave of rage rippling through me.

But that's not the only thing that haunts me. Alarmingly, the memory of Hunter laughing at his jokes before he revealed himself for what he was, gnaws at me even worse.

As I round the corner, the restaurant comes into view, its flashing neon sign a beacon in the night. My steps slow as I brace for an unpleasant interaction. They must've thought we did a dine and dash—no matter that the dining part stopped at the snails. Going back in will be humbling, but it's still better than facing my thoughts. I don't want to examine why Hunter's interactions with her date bothered me so much. I'm not ready to confront what it might mean. Let's focus on fixing one screw-up at a time. First off, the bill I forgot to pay in my hurry to chase after Olivia. I steel myself and push inside.

The warm aroma of garlic and herbs envelops me. I should be hungry, having had a single snail for dinner, but I'm not. All I want is to leave. I scan the candlelit space, hoping to slip up to the bar, pay the bill, and make a quick exit unnoticed.

I approach the bartender, a burly guy with a salt-and-pepper beard. "Hey, um, I was here earlier, and I... uhm, had an emergency... and I forgot to settle my bill."

He raises an eyebrow, giving me a once-over. "Forgot?"

Heat crawls up the back of my neck. This isn't like me. I'm the responsible one, the guy who always has his shit together. I'm a people pleaser, run a tight ship, and avoid confrontation as much as I can. The humiliation of coming back here, tail tucked between my legs, to confess I skipped out on a bill is like swallowing glass. "Yeah, my girlfriend and I had a bit of a disagreement, and I guess I just... left in a hurry."

The bartender's expression softens a fraction. He nods toward a server passing by. "Yo, Mia. This guy says he dashed on his bill earlier." I wish he wouldn't yell about my business for everyone to hear. "That ring any bells?"

Mia, the server who attended to us, stops in her tracks. She looks me up and down, recognition dawning on her face. "Oh, yeah. I remember you. You were with that blonde, right? The one who was shooting daggers at the couple next to you all night?"

I wince. "That's us."

"No worries, hon." Mia waves a dismissive hand. "Your bill's been taken care of."

I blink, sure I must have misheard. "I'm sorry, what?"

"The woman at the next table, the one with the dark hair and the jerk date? She covered your check."

The floor tilts beneath my feet. Hunter paid for my dinner with Olivia. Of course she did. Because apparently, tonight wasn't cringe-worthy enough.

I mumble my thanks to Mia and the bartender, then make a beeline for the exit, my face burning. Out on the sidewalk, I suck in the sultry summer air to clear my head.

It's no big deal. I'll give Hunter her money back. No harm, no foul. Then why is my gut twisting with an odd tangle of embarrassment and frustration?

I start walking, wondering how slowly I have to go to find her already asleep. I don't have it in me to talk to Hunter tonight.

One stretch of sidewalk blurs into another, until I'm at my new building, fumbling with my keys and riding up in the elevator.

I unlock the front door, releasing a wave of cool air that tightens the skin on my arms as I step into the stillness on the other side. I kick off my shoes, not bothering to line them up in a neat row like I usually do.

The apartment's layout has finally settled into my mind as I make my way to my room. All is quiet except for the AC vents. I'm halfway down the hall when I notice a thin strip of light spilling out from under Hunter's door.

She's still awake.

I stall, frozen with my hand reaching toward her door. I could knock. Go inside and... what? Thank her for covering the bill? Confess the confusing tangle of feelings I've been grappling with all night?

I let my arm drop.

No. I can't. Not now, when my thoughts are so muddled, when I'm still reeling from the fight with Olivia and from realizing how much Hunter affects me. It wouldn't be fair to either of us.

Instead, I force myself to keep moving. I pass her bedroom, ignoring the tug in my chest, and slip into my room, closing the door behind me.

In the semi-darkness, I strip off my suit, letting it fall to the floor in an uncharacteristic heap. I'll deal with everything in the morning, starting with the fallout with Olivia. I was a true jerk to her tonight; even the server noticed. My girlfriend should be my priority.

But for now, I need to sleep. A few hours of oblivion before reality hits and reminds me that everything in my life just got a lot more complicated.

I crawl into bed, the sheets cool against my skin. My last thought before exhaustion claims me is of Hunter's face, the slight fear in her eyes when that jerk grabbed her, and that pink line around her wrist. My dreams are going to be pretty violent tonight.

* * *

I wake up to the harsh morning light after barely sleeping. My brain is still tangled in the events of last night. I need something to take my mind off it all. Before I know it, I'm in the kitchen, preheating the oven.

With the temperature set, I pull out flour and chocolate chips and grab a mixing bowl. The simple, repetitive motions of measuring and stirring ground me—scoop, roll, place, repeat. The mindless rhythm allows my thoughts to unspool. As the cookies start browning in the oven, the warm scent of chocolate and butter fills the kitchen, and for once, it's almost as if everything is under control. I let the comforting smell wash over me as I ladle another ball of dough onto the second baking sheet.

The oven timer dings, shrill in the kitchen's quiet. I slide a new batch of cookies in, the heat blasting against my face as I seal the door. Leaning back against the counter, I close my eyes, letting my head thump backward on the cabinets.

Just breathe, Dylan. It can't get any worse.

That's when footsteps jolt me from my spiraling thoughts. I jerk up, and my heart becomes a fist in my throat as I find Hunter standing in the doorway, all sleep-rumpled and cuddly in her pajamas.

Our eyes lock, and last night presses into the space between us, awkward and scraping. I want to break the silence, make a joke—make it alright—but my mouth has forgotten how to form words as I drink her in.

She's beautiful in the morning light, her dark hair mussed, her eyes still hazy with sleep. Beautiful and achingly forbidden. Then she says, "Hey," and I'm ready to drop to my knees.

18

HUNTER

The clang of pots and pans jars me awake, the noise cutting sharp against the quiet of early morning as the sweet, buttery scent of freshly baked cookies fills the air. I groan, rolling over in my bed. The embarrassment of last night slams against my sleep-huddled brain the instant I'm conscious. Memories of the restaurant debacle replay in vivid clarity, every mortifying detail sharp as a knife. The urge to hide in my room forever is overpowering, but I can't spend the entire weekend sequestered with no food, water, or use of the bathroom. My stomach rumbles in response to the mouth-watering aroma. Of course, Dylan is baking cookies. Because the universe is a bastard and truly hates me.

I sigh in resignation. I'll have to face my roommate eventually, and it might as well be now, especially if baked goods are involved. Shuffling out of bed, I give myself a mini-makeover to look presentable but not like I tried, and trudge down the hallway. As I reach the kitchen threshold, I freeze, stunned by the sight before me.

Dylan is leaning against the counter, head thrown back

against a cabinet, eyes closed. He's pulling off the disheveled, just-rolled-out-of-bed-after-a-night-of-hot-sex look. His golden hair juts out in wild, unruly tufts. A smudge of dough clings to his chiseled chin, and there's a white fingerprint on his left cheek. The kitchen is just as messy. Flour dusts the counters, and dough sticks to various surfaces. Bowls and spatulas clutter the sink, along with a whisk that's coated in a gooey mix of butter and sugar. The rich aroma of melted chocolate and vanilla mingles with the warmth of the oven, its fan whirring steadily along the muted sounds of the city outside.

I barely register the clutter as my focus hones back on Dylan.

Despite the ridiculous pink apron over his white tee and sweatpants, he looks... absurdly sexy. Way too sexy to behold first thing in the morning. My lady parts give an internal swoon against my will. Damn him. Why does he have to resemble a Calvin Klein ad even in an apron and sweats? And he's like that naturally, no makeovers needed. It's not fair.

His eyes fly open and meet mine. He doesn't speak, just looks, winding me up to a tension so tight I'm afraid I'll snap right in half. I've no idea what's going through his mind.

"Hey."

"Hey, yourself." Dylan's eyes skim over me with a soft concern that makes my pulse quicken. They linger on my wrist as if to check all markings are gone—thankfully, they are—then drift back to my face. "How are you doing?"

I avert my gaze, busying myself with the coffee pot. "I'm so sorry about last night. For ruining your date."

Dylan straightens, his smile faltering. "I ruined my date, not you. And are you okay after... you know... everything...?"

Of course, he'd worry about me instead of himself. His genuine concern only makes things worse. It's most likely pity.

I nod quickly, forcing a smile. "I'm fine, really. The date was a disaster, but nothing a little ice cream couldn't fix." *And half a bottle of your Chablis*, I add in my head.

I pour us each a mug of coffee, using it as an excuse to avoid his worried, blue-green eyes. "Seriously though, thanks for coming to my rescue last night. I feel awful about the whole thing." I hand him his mug, finally meeting his gaze.

Dylan shakes his head, his blond fringe falling into his eyes. "No, I'm sorry I walked out and left you with my bill; I feel terrible." He wipes his hands on the shouldn't-be-sexy pink apron, and reaches for his phone. "How much do I owe you? I'll Venmo you the money."

Not able to sustain eye contact with him for prolonged amounts of time without melting, I look away. "Oh, no, it's nothing." I wrap my hands around my steaming mug and inhale deeply, praying the rich scent will overpower the hollow ache carving me out from the inside. If only caffeine could erase heartbreak as easily as it jolts me awake. Having to pay for his bill was humiliating, but somehow, getting the money back stings even worse.

But Dylan isn't having it. He insists, his eyebrows drawn together in concentration as he taps away on his phone. "Hunt, let me make it right. Just tell me the amount."

I sigh, knowing he won't let it go. I reluctantly give him the figure, trying not to wince at the exorbitant cost of his dinner date. At once, my phone pings with the Venmo notification. I hold it up, mustering a smile. "Got it. Thanks." I take a sip of my coffee, scalding my tongue. "So, um, did you patch things up with Olivia? After you ran after her." I'm not even sure what I want his answer to be.

Dylan's shoulders slump, and he runs a hand through his tousled hair. "No, she left. Still pretty upset."

I nod, glancing around the kitchen, taking in again the mess of flour and cookie dough. "Is that why you're stress-baking so early? To whip up an apology?"

He cute-frowns, realization dawning on his face. "I hadn't thought of that, but it's a great idea. Homemade cookies would be the perfect peace offering."

I resist the instinct to bang my head against a cabinet. Why did I have to suggest that and serve him the ideal romantic gesture on a silver platter? I picture Olivia melting at the sight of him on her doorstep, cookies in hand, all transgressions forgiven.

The oven timer dings, startling me. I move aside as Dylan slides on a pair of oven mitts, looking unfairly adorable in his flour-dusted apron, and carefully removes a tray of golden-brown chocolate chip cookies. The sweet scent of browned sugar and warm dough fills the air, making my mouth water despite my mental spiral of bitter regret.

He sets the tray on the counter, and I admire the perfectly round cookies, doing my best to ignore the sinking pit in my stomach. Leave it to Dylan to excel at everything, even baking. When Olivia sees them—and *him*—she'll forget about breakfast altogether and devour the chef instead. Guess that leaves me with just the crumbs...

With a spatula, Dylan lifts a cookie from the tray, plates it, and offers it to me, grinning. "Care to be my guinea pig?"

I hesitate, but the temptation of a warm, gooey cookie proves too strong to resist. I accept it with a nod, taking a tentative bite. The flavors explode on my tongue—rich chocolate, buttery dough, and a hint of salt. I can't prevent the moan that escapes my lips.

Dylan's grin widens, eyes sparkling with satisfaction. "Think Olivia will forgive me after tasting these?"

I swallow the bite, along with the lump in my throat. With

cookies this good, Olivia will perform acrobatics in bed and beg him to father her future children. I wince.

Dylan's brow furrows, concern etching his features. "Is something wrong with the cookies?"

Mentally, I reply, *With the cookies? No. With my life? Everything.* But aloud, I force a smile and shake my head. "No, they're delicious. Olivia will forgive you."

He stares at me, his expression unreadable. I squirm under the scrutiny, wondering not for the first time what he's thinking when he looks at me like that. But then he nods, satisfied, and places another cookie on my plate.

"I should bring these to Olivia as a surprise breakfast." He reaches for a Tupperware. "Might spend today with her, try to smooth things over."

A knife is plunged into my chest, and every little thing that comes out of this man's mouth twists the blade, creating more damage. I nod against the devastation, my smile never faltering. "Good idea."

"But I'll be back in time for dinner at Rowena's. I'm curious to meet her fake fiancé. He's a legend in the finance world," Dylan adds, his tone brightening. "Want to share a taxi?"

The thought of being confined with Dylan in the back of a cab is both dreadful and exciting, but I agree anyway. "Sure, sounds good."

He packs the rest of the cookies and goes to his room to change. He's back five minutes later in jeans and a T-shirt. As he grabs his keys, my gaze drifts to his backside. Mmm, more biteable than the cookie I'm finishing. With a last wave, he's out the door, off to win back Olivia's heart.

Sighing, I take another bite of my cookie, savoring the sugary fattiness. But as I dust my hands on my PJ bottoms, I survey the disaster zone that is our kitchen and marvel at how seamlessly I've transitioned from picking up Dylan's restaurant bill to sweeping away the broken eggshells. I'll send him the cleaning charge *and* a therapy invoice this time. And he can Venmo me both.

19

DYLAN

It's already late afternoon by the time I come back home. This morning, Olivia forgave me the moment I showed up on her doorstep with the apology cookies. We had a nice breakfast together, visited the exhibition she'd been raving about, and afterward, grabbed lunch near Central Park. It was a lovely day, but it still left me unsatisfied.

Maybe it was the sense of everything being so perfectly pleasant, yet lacking that undercurrent of *something*. I didn't feel that magnetic pull couples in love are supposed to share, the inexplicable urge to bridge any distance between us, as if gravity itself was bending to keep us close.

It's not been love at first sight with Olivia, but I'm not in lust with her, either. Between us is more niceness all along. I don't want to grab her wrists and pin her against a wall to kiss her. I'm not even sure I enjoy spending time with her that much. Today, I never caught myself holding my breath, waiting for her to say something unexpected that would make me laugh. Or wanting to reach for her hand because I *needed* to touch her.

Instead, being with her gives me this nagging sensation of

wrongness I can't put my finger on. Which is ridiculous, considering I had a perfect-on-paper day with an equally perfect woman.

As I kick off my shoes in the entry hall, my eyes dart to the kitchen, and I do a double take. It's spotless, without a single dirty dish or speck of flour in sight. I groan, remembering the mess I left behind this morning in my rush to get to Olivia's. And Hunter had to clean after me—*again*. Holy shit. The bill at the restaurant last night, and now this. I'm the worst roommate ever.

Guilt gnaws at my insides as I head down the hall to Hunter's room. Her door is half-open, so I knock, pushing it ajar. She's seated at her desk, engrossed in her laptop, but she turns when she hears me enter.

"Oh, hi," she greets me, her dark eyes meeting mine. And that gaze lands straight at the base of my spine. My tailbone is being electrocuted.

I lean against the doorframe, an apologetic expression on my face. "On a scale of one to ten, how much do you hate me for how I left the kitchen?"

To my surprise, a smile tugs at her lips instead of the scowl I'm expecting. "Oh, you mean your avant-garde flour installation?" she quips. "I didn't have to scrape it. MoMA called, and they picked it up."

I chuckle, shaking my head. "I can't believe you cleaned up my baking catastrophe. Sure you don't hate me, not even a little?"

Her eyes narrow playfully. "Don't worry, you're still behind the neighbor who leaves trash in the hallway overnight on my hit list."

I laugh as relief washes over me at her lighthearted response. "I would like the record to show that I'm really sorry. It won't happen again." I run a hand through my hair. "I've been stressed lately, but I promise this isn't me."

"Well, at least the stress-relief cookies were delicious." Hunter's lips quirk. "But maybe next time, try to keep more of the ingredients in the bowl."

I touch two fingers to my forehead and give her a mock military salute. "Will do. Is it okay if I hop in the shower?"

Hunter nods, gesturing to her laptop. "Yeah, go ahead. I've already showered and only need to change."

With a grateful smile, I head to the bathroom, the tension in my shoulders easing for the first time all week. As the warm water pelts my back, I clear a circle in the fogged-up glass and catch myself grinning like an idiot.

The hot jet is amazing, and I whistle for the rest of the shower until I step out, towel off, and pad to my bedroom. I call Hunter on the way, yelling that the bathroom is free if she needs it. In my room, I change into a fresh pair of jeans and a polo shirt. As I style my hair in the closet mirror, I find I'm looking forward to dinner at Rowena's new place tonight. Except for Adrian, it'll be good to be just us, our close group of friends. The people around who I feel most comfortable. When I don't have to try so hard and can be myself.

Refreshed and ready, I knock on Hunter's now-closed door. "Hey, are you good to go? The car I booked should arrive soon."

The door swings open, and the sight of Hunter on the other side turns my lungs into concrete. She's dressed in a light-blue button-down shirt, the fabric tied at her waist, revealing a tantalizing sliver of skin and that fucking belly ring. The sleeves are rolled up, exposing her delicate wrists adorned with simple gold bracelets. My gaze travels down to her white linen shorts, skimming the tops of her toned thighs, giving her an effortlessly cool vibe. Her dark hair tumbles in lush, beachy waves around her shoulders, and even though she's not wearing any noticeable makeup, she looks stunning.

"Err..." *Speak, Dylan, speak.* "You look... definitely ready," I manage, mentally kicking myself for the lame quip.

Hunter glances down at her outfit, a hint of uncertainty in her onyx-black eyes. "Is there something wrong with what I'm wearing?"

"No, not at all," I assure her, nodding with conviction. "You look perfect. I mean, your clothes are perfect. For dinner. At Rowena's." I'm rambling, but I can't stop myself.

Hunter's lips curve into an amused smile. "Okay, great. Let's head out, then."

We exit the apartment together and find our ride already waiting for us downstairs. As we slide into the back seat, I'm enveloped by Hunter's intoxicating perfume. It consumes me in wisps of shadows and secrets, mysterious and magnetic. A whispered invitation, curling into my thoughts like smoke under the moonlight.

I try to focus on the passing city scenery, but my gaze keeps drifting to Hunter's lithe thighs, tantalizingly bare in those shorts and too close for comfort in the confined space.

The cab ride is nothing short of sweet torture, and I'm relieved when we pull up to Adrian's building. As Hunter and I step out onto the sidewalk, I spot Tristan and Nina emerging from their own taxi.

"Hey, guys," Nina calls out, waving. "Ready for an interesting evening?"

"That's one way to put it." Tristan chuckles, slipping his arm around Nina's waist.

I smile at them, glad of having a buffer of people between me and my hot roommate.

Inside the building, the doorman informs us we have to ride all the way to the top. I'd expect nothing less of Adrian West, the Wall Street legend.

The penthouse lives up to the stereotype as well. It's an apartment that belongs in a magazine, all clean lines and understated luxury. Everything about it screams "expensive," but I try not to let it intimidate me.

Hunter's laugh rings through the entryway, warm and genuine as she hugs Rowena, reclaiming my focus. It's a sound I've heard a thousand times, yet tonight, it hits me differently.

When the ladies are done hugging each other, the official introductions begin. I offer Adrian a firm handshake, making sure my smile reaches my eyes. "Great to meet you, man." I put the right amount of friendliness in my tone.

Adrian matches my grip, his smile easy and confident, and his eyes flashing with... relief? The guy must've been nervous about "meeting the friends." "Likewise," he responds, and we exchange a few more pleasantries before Rowena ushers us into the living room.

As I follow the group, my gaze shifts to Hunter again. She's walking ahead of me, her hair catching the suffused light. A lock of it is falling over her eyes and the sudden, inexplicable impulse to brush it behind her ear almost overpowers me. I clench my fists at my sides to stop my hands from doing something stupid.

We all settle at the table. Rowena is next to Adrian, Nina by Tristan's side, and Hunter and I get inevitably pushed together. *It's okay, not a big deal*, I tell myself, even as her inebriating scent hits me again.

Rowena and Adrian are playing the perfect hosts, making sure everyone's comfortable. I catch Adrian watching Rowena in a way that's hard to decipher—something between admiration and uncertainty. I wonder what the deal is with them. Their engagement is fake, yet there's an undeniable connection between them, one neither of them seems to have figured out.

When Adrian asks how we all met, I have an excuse to turn

my full focus on Hunter as she dives into the story of their disastrous Halloween meet-spook. Her voice is animated, eyes sparkling, and I can't stop watching her. I'm caught in the way her lips move, or how she gestures with her hands, those fucking golden bracelets catching the light and making me want to rip things—her clothes, more specifically.

"We met in college," she's saying. "On a tragic Halloween night where we all ended up ditched by our dates, soaked in a diner, and wearing the same Elle Woods costume." She sighs, looking at Nina and Rowena. "It was love at first sight."

"I think I saw a picture." Adrian grins at Rowena with an expression not too dissimilar from the goofy stupor affecting me earlier in the shower. "Nice costumes."

"We all used to live together," Nina adds. "Until, well, recent events."

Rowena gets uncomfortable for the first time tonight, probably wanting to avoid the topic of her fake engagement, aka the elephant in the room no one has mentioned yet. "You mean since you moved in with that guy?" She points at Tristan. "And Dylan leaped at the chance to turn my old bedroom into a home office, right?"

I grin at this. "Guilty as charged. And the company's not bad either." I check Hunter's reaction, but she's not looking my way; she seems very interested in her salad.

To distract myself, I toss a breadcrumb at Tristan. He laughs, deflecting it. I'm about to throw another breadcrumb when Adrian, without missing a beat, catches the one that flew his way and tosses it right back at me. I laugh, pretending to be outraged as I clutch my chest dramatically.

"Man, you've got some arm there. Did you play any sports?" I am genuinely curious now. The guy's reflexes are impressive.

Adrian grins, leaning back in his chair, looking more relaxed than he has all evening. "Varsity baseball, but I gave that up in college because I didn't have time for athletics." He glances at Rowena, and something unspoken and private travels in that look. They share a deeper understanding, a secret language the rest of us don't speak.

"Rowena told me you two played basketball in the NCAA?" Adrian adds, shifting the conversation to safer ground.

"Yeah, we did." I shoot a quick smile at Tristan, who nods in agreement. "It was a crazy time. We ended up winning the national championship our senior year..."

Nina groans. "Not the highlights of the final again, please."

We ignore her and give Adrian a blow-by-blow of our epic victory.

After that, dinner flows effortlessly. Adrian fits in seamlessly, his dry wit and easy-going nature a perfect complement to our seasoned banter.

As the conversation winds down, we finish the wine, lingering over the remains of the dessert. The atmosphere is relaxed and familiar despite the newness of Adrian. He and Rowena exchange a quiet glance, and it strikes me how comfortable they are with each other. They seem to have found a balance that's still elusive for me in my new house setting. If they can make it work as platonic roommates after knowing each other for three weeks, Hunter and I should be smashing the cohabitation after... Wait, how long have we known each other? I do the mental math and, fuck me, it's been over ten years. How did I never notice her before?

I turn to her. She's laughing at something Nina said. Her lips curved in that easy, radiant smile that never fails to disarm me. The sight stirs a deep warmth within me, unsettling yet grounding.

Platonic, my ass.

I look away, focusing instead on the candle flickering in the center of the table. What is going on with me? I stuff my mouth with the last bite of cake and try to forget about it.

When dinner wraps up, we gather our things and head toward the front door, a pleasant buzz in the air.

Rowena walks us out onto the landing, closing the door behind her. Tension coils in her gaze as if she's bracing for something. She glances back at the door before leaning in slightly, her voice dropping presumably so it won't carry to Adrian.

"What do you think?" Her tone is tentative but eager.

A brief silence follows as we all exchange glances, and then a general murmur of praise for Adrian makes the rounds.

Rowena beams, reassured by our reaction, at least until my sister gives her a quick hug, whispering something in her ear the rest of us can't hear.

Rowena nods, the smile on her face losing some of its brightness as she hugs Nina back. "Promise?"

With that, Rowena walks us to the elevator.

No one speaks until the doors slide shut and we begin our descent. Tristan is the first to break the silence. "Well, that was... not what I expected."

Nina nods, her brow furrowed. "Yeah, same here. Adrian seems like a genuinely nice guy. It's just..."

"Strange," Hunter finishes for her, her arms crossed loosely over her chest. "Seeing them together like that. It's almost too natural, you know? Like they've been doing this for years."

I glance at her pensive face. "I felt that too," I admit. "But Rowena seems okay. Better than okay. Whatever this is, it's working for her."

Tristan leans back against the elevator wall, his expression thoughtful. "Yeah, and Adrian didn't strike me as the shark everyone describes him to be."

"He was more of a teddy bear," Hunter jokes, "ready for some cuddles."

Tristan smirks. "The way he was looking at her, I'm sure he wouldn't mind getting *cuddles*."

The elevator falls into a contemplative quiet as we each mull over the implications. I think back to the way Adrian watched Rowena throughout the night, the small, almost imperceptible gestures that spoke volumes.

"Guys, for all we know, it's still fake. I hope she doesn't catch one-sided feelings," Nina brings us back to earth. "But we'll be here for her, no matter what. If things get complicated, she has us."

"Absolutely," I agree, glancing around at my friends. "We'll stand by her."

The elevator chimes as the doors glide open, revealing the lobby. We step out into the warmth, the city lights twinkling above us. Despite the cautious optimism, I can tell we're all relieved after meeting Adrian.

The night seems less heavy now, more hopeful. We say goodbye and Nina and Tristan hop into a passing cab, while Hunter and I wait for the car I ordered on my app.

We stand on the curb in comfortable silence. Hunter is looking up at the sky, her expression thoughtful.

"What are you thinking about?"

She turns to me, a small, mysterious smile on her lips. "Just... life."

It's a vague answer, but I don't push.

The cab arrives, and we settle into the tight back seat. It's not as confining as earlier, but there's still an awareness of her being beside me, her presence a steady whizz in the background of my thoughts.

"Tonight was good." She breaks the silence. "I'm glad Winnie is doing okay. That he is a decent guy. She deserves that after Liam."

I nod, turning to look at her. "Yeah, she does."

Her eyes meet mine, dark and unfathomable, and everything else fades. Her gaze is guarded, almost as if she were keeping a secret. And before I can grasp it, she looks away, her attention returning to the window.

We say little after that, the silence between us stretching but not uncomfortable. As the cab nears our apartment, a strange reluctance settles over me. I don't want the closeness to end.

But the car pulls to a stop, and we get out. As we reach our floor, I catch Hunter's eye again, and there's that pull, that tug, subtle but persistent.

At our door, we fumble for who should unlock it. I have my keys in my pocket and I'm faster fishing them out than Hunter, who has to search into a giant handbag that must contain all the objects in the world. It's weird, the familiarity of getting into the same apartment, removing our shoes in the entryway, and then going down the hall to two separate bedrooms.

"Goodnight." Her voice is almost shy, and it makes something tighten in my chest.

"Goodnight," I reply, watching as she disappears into her room, the door closing with a quiet click.

I stand there, staring at the closed door—realizing with terrifying clarity, I want her to open it again, for me.

20

DYLAN

I have to break up with Olivia. The singular thought swirls in my head, taking over my entire mental space as I sit in the office on Monday morning, staring at the blinking cursor on my laptop screen, the open spreadsheet a blur of numbers and data.

It's not that Olivia isn't great. She's sweet, kind, a woman you'd want to bring home to meet your parents. But as much as I've tried to convince myself otherwise, there's no spark, no excitement when we're together. It's like trying to force two mismatched puzzle pieces to fit.

And then there's Hunter. My roommate. My sister's best friend. The woman I can't stop thinking about. A romantic involvement with her would be beyond complicated. If things went south, not only would it make living together awkward as hell, but it could also blow up my entire social circle. And yet.

I sigh, passing a hand over my face. One problem at a time. First, I need to end things with Olivia. Grabbing my phone, I dictate a text before I lose my nerve.

DYLAN

Hey, can I come over tonight?

Her reply comes a minute later.

OLIVIA

Sure, I'd love to see you. Let me know the time

Guilt twists in my gut, but I'm doing the right thing. For both of us.

I give her message a thumbs up and set down my phone, drumming my fingers on the desk. How do I explain the lack of a spark to her without making it sound like it's her fault?

It's not you, it's me is a punchline for *it* is *you*. Even if in this case, it's true, it's not her. It's me. But she wouldn't believe me.

No matter how I do it, now that I've decided, I can stand up straight again. For the first time in days, I'm able to focus on work. The charts and graphs that have been harder to read lately make more sense. I attack my inbox with a vengeance, the emails that had been piling up all morning quickly dealt with.

Tonight won't be fun, but it's the right call. And after, I'll figure out what, or who, I really want.

* * *

Early that evening, I shut my laptop and stand to leave while the office is still full. I'm taking off earlier than usual because I don't know, it seems like bad etiquette to make someone wait on you all night to break up with them. Olivia will hate me all the same, but the least I can do is to be polite about it.

A weird sort of detachment washes over me as I grab my jacket and backpack. But my palms are sticky and my pulse is too elevated for someone who's been sitting at a desk all day. Everything in me wants to smooth the waters as if my job were to ensure nobody felt a ripple. Confrontation has always felt like stepping into a ring I was never trained for. Ever since being put on the spot in school left me scarred, I'd rather fade into the background, and maintain the peace, but this time... I can't. People call me nice. Sometimes, I wonder if that's a euphemism for pushover. I'm sorry that Olivia will be the one to see me grow a spine.

By the time I'm outside, I almost invent an excuse to go home and avoid what's coming. But even the gentlest tide has to turn.

I flag down a cab, sinking into the back seat. I rattle off Olivia's address to the driver and close my eyes to contain the anxiety gnawing at my gut. She won't see this coming. She thinks I'm dropping by to hang out. But I have to rip off the Band-Aid—the sooner, the better. The driver is talking about something—traffic or the weather—but I barely register his words as we zip through the blurry city lights.

When the car pulls up outside Olivia's building, I pay the fare and step out. I compose her buzzer number and wait, tapping my foot on the sidewalk, the concrete sticking to my sole in the heat.

Olivia's voice crackles through a minute later. "Who is it?"

"Dylan?" Wasn't she expecting me?

"Oh, right. Come on up." She sounds weird, surprised but also as if she was already crying?

Has she guessed why I'm here?

Perplexed, I push through the main door and cross the lobby, opting for the stairs since Olivia lives on the second floor. The distant, muffled sounds of a TV playing greet me as I reach her hallway and walk down it. I pause outside her door, steeling myself for what I have to do. My hand lifts to knock, but I hesitate. Before I muster the courage, a distraught Olivia flings the door open, ushering me in. Her face is splotchy and tear-streaked, her normally coiffed hair disheveled. Behind her, I glimpse her usually tidy apartment in disarray, clothes strewn everywhere.

"Dylan, I'm so sorry," she chokes out between sobs. "I completely forgot you were coming over. It's just—" She stops, fluffing her hands in front of her face, hyperventilating. "Theo died," she whimpers. "And the funeral is in two days. I have to go home and—"

Her words dissolve into incoherent blubbering as she ushers me inside. My heart sinks as I take in the open suitcase on the couch, half-filled with hastily folded clothes. The speech I'd rehearsed on the way over turns to ashes on my tongue.

"Oh, Liv, I'm so sorry." I'm the world's biggest hypocrite.

The part of me that hates standing up for myself is relieved our talk will have to be postponed, but the rest of me is simmering frustration—I wanted this to be over tonight.

But between the two of us, Olivia's having a rougher night than I am. I'm uncomfortable, sure, but Olivia's in a different league of upset.

"Who was Theo?"

"My best friend."

Fuuuuuck. "I'm so sorry," I repeat, at a loss for what else to say. "Was he sick?"

"Nooo," she bawls. "A car ran him over."

She spins in a tight circle, her hands shooting up to her temples. "One second, he was there, and then," she puffs. "And then this!" Her voice cracks, turning into a strangled screech that makes me flinch.

Olivia stops mid-step, clutching her chest as if she can physically hold her heart together. "He didn't deserve this—" She breaks off into a high-pitched wail, doubling over and gasping for air.

I take a hesitant step forward. "Liv, just sit down for a second and—"

"No!" she shrieks, spinning to face me, her face twisted with anguish. "Don't tell me to sit! Don't tell me to breathe! I can't—I can't even talk about it, okay? I just can't! I have to go; please stop asking questions."

"Okay, whatever you need."

She paces, arms flailing as she explains between hiccups. "I won't be back for the Fourth of July. You probably wanted to do something together, but I just—I need to be with my family at this difficult time."

I fight back a wince. Even before deciding to break things off, I had zero plans to spend the holiday with Olivia. Nina, Tristan, Hunter, Rowena, and I are headed to my parents' place in Mystic, Connecticut, for a big family weekend—grilling burgers, setting off sparklers, and lounging on pool floats with cold drinks. Days soaking up the sun, the smell of barbecue in the air. Nights lit up with fireflies and fireworks. A mental image where, once again, Olivia doesn't fit.

But of course, I can't say any of that. Not now. I nod, guilt twisting tighter in my chest as she sobs and packs in frantic bursts. I try to make sense of it. If Theo was her best friend, why is her family so involved? She's from a small town. Maybe it's one of those tight-knit communities where neighbors are practically family. I want to ask, but she's begged me not to. Also, I'm a little scared to probe. She seems riled up enough.

How do I help her? Do I hug her? Pat her shoulder? Both strike me as insensitive considering what I came here to do. But standing in her living room like a statue, tongue-tied and useless, seems equally heartless.

The seconds stretch out, filled only with the sounds of Olivia's sniffles and the zipper of her suitcase. I've never felt more adrift between what I should do—support her unconditionally without throwing another wrench into her night, and what I want to do—break up with her.

Olivia whirls around, her amber eyes wide and pleading. "We could escape somewhere the weekend after the fourth? Since we can't spend the holiday together?"

I stand slack-jawed and scrambling for something to say, but my skull is filled only with critters scraping their claws against the bone; all the words have left. I'm here to cut her loose. I don't want to string her along now that I know we won't work out as a couple. I can't make plans with her. But how do I explain that without telling her I'm breaking up with her? Because I can't pull the trigger when she's reeling from a loss and looking at me like I'm her savior.

"Um, sure, maybe." I nod mechanically.

I hate the side of me who's relieved the confrontation is postponed. He's not getting this win. I'll talk to her, soon. After the funeral, once things settle. Do this right. But for now, I paint on a smile and pretend everything's fine.

"Do you want to book something? The funeral is going to be agony, and I could use a break." She gestures at the four walls surrounding us as if they were responsible for Theo's death. "Away from here."

I can't break up with her tonight, but I should definitely avoid making promises. How? The critters resume their frenzied scrambling inside my skull. I need an excuse that sounds thoughtful, or at least halfway decent. A snippet of a conversation from Saturday night at Adrian and Rowena's pops into my head, giving me a perfect out. "Actually, that weekend might be tough for me. It's Rowena's engagement party, out in the Hamptons."

Olivia's eyes light up, her grief flickering in the background. "Oh, Rowena, the friend you went to see Saturday night?" The lingering accusation of *and didn't invite me* still strong behind her casual tone. "I'd love to go together."

Crap. That backfired spectacularly. I fumble for any reason to tell her no. But I'm drawing a total blank. "Uh... mmm... It's a small party for just close friends and family. I'd have to check if it's okay to bring someone else." I keep vague, giving her an indefinite answer carried on a wave of guilt and cowardice. Outside, I'm trying to keep neutral. Inside, I'm Kate Winslet at the beginning of *Titanic*—screaming.

Olivia launches herself at me as if I'd given her a solid yes, her lips finding mine in a fierce kiss. I go through the motions, but the contact is hollow. No spark, no warmth, just a gnawing void where something bright should be blossoming.

She steps back, gives me a teary smile, and hoists her suitcase. We walk out together. On the curb, she hugs me tightly before sliding into a waiting cab. At least I did the right thing by not offering to take her to the airport—too romantic. Would've given the wrong signal.

As the taxi merges into traffic and disappears, I let out a gusty sigh. I royally screwed up. But at least I'm getting a reprieve— a week without having to pretend or force non-existent feelings.

The thought of heading home to Mystic, of long, sunny days spent with the people I love most, wraps around me like a warm hug. The salty tang of the sea air, Mom's peach cobbler, shooting hoops in the backyard with Tristan... Hunter in a bikini. I censor the image before my brain can pull up memories from the last time she visited Nina at my parents' place.

On second thought, my so-called "reprieve" sounds more like torture. Four days of Hunter in swimsuits, and me stuck in romantic limbo, playing the role of the platonic friend... Now I've turned into another character from *Titanic*: Captain Smith, fucking iceberg alert in hand and still ordering more speed.

21

HUNTER

I'm sandwiched in the back of Dylan's pickup between Nina and Rowena, my skin sticking to the leather seats as sweat beads down my spine. The seatbelt digs into my shoulder, an unrelenting pressure as we wind along the coastal road toward Mystic.

I keep my arms pinned to my sides, careful not to brush against anyone. Easier said than done in such close quarters. I glance sideways at Nina; she's hijacked the car's Bluetooth and is dictating the road-trip playlist. While on my other side, Rowena has her eyes closed, one hand resting on her still-flat stomach. Despite the cramped discomfort, I'm glad it's just the five of us packed into the car like sardines.

I've become a person who celebrates funerals, or finds them convenient at least. But with Olivia sidetracked, the electric wire clamped to my spine that would zap me with 200 volts of current every time I imagined her tagging along this weekend has been cut. Horrible, I know. What does that say about me?

I'm not even sure if Dylan had invited Olivia or not; he didn't say, and I didn't ask. But either way, her absence is a small reprieve, temporary packed car ride be damned. Four whole days

without wondering if she'll be showing up in my life unexpectedly—at my apartment, in a restaurant, or wherever it is she and
Dylan hang out.

The miles roll on, the road unwinding ahead of us in a line of
coastal scenery accompanied by the steady sound of waves.
Finally, the Thompsons' house comes into view, and a new kind
of excitement kicks in. I'm ready to leave the car—and thoughts
of Olivia—far behind.

The sun hangs high in the sky, the afternoon heat shimmering off the pavement, and even if I can't see it yet, I hear the
pool calling my name. I tumble out of the pickup in my haste to
escape, tilting my face up to the sun as I stretch my cramped
limbs. The air smells of freshly cut grass and salt from the
nearby sea.

"Well, look what the cat dragged in," Mr. Thompson booms
from the porch, a wide grin splitting his face.

Mrs. Thompson appears beside him, hands on her hips. "Get
in, the lot of you," she calls, waving us forward. "I've got
lemonade and cookies waiting."

We grab our suitcases and troop to the porch, greeting the
Thompsons as we pass them.

Dylan bumps my shoulder as we head toward the kitchen, a
conspiratorial smile on his face. "Now you can tell me if my
mom's cookies are better than mine."

I roll my eyes, smirking. "You're fishing for compliments,
Thompson."

"Me?" Dylan brings a hand to his chest as if wounded.
"Never."

He winks before turning and pushing the kitchen door open,
the cool air rushing out to meet us. It's a walk-in fridge compared
to the temperature we left in the front yard. But that wink has a
traitorous warmth boiling through me that has nothing to do

with the summer heat and doesn't care about the blast of air conditioning.

As we all settle around the island, Rowena perches on one stool, her hand still pressed to her stomach, while Nina leans against the counter, eyeing the snack spread. I pull up another stool and position myself in front of Dylan, giving him my shoulders. My scalp prickles like crazy, but it's a lesser discomfort than having to meet his eyes while I'm still flushed from a stupid, meaningless wink.

Mrs. Thompson hovers nearby, smiling as she passes the cookie plate. But her brow furrows with concern as she stops in front of Rowena.

She places a gentle hand on my friend's shoulder. "You alright, dear?"

I check on my friend. Winnie looks a little green around the gills.

Rowena offers a wan smile. "Just a bit of morning sickness. The car ride didn't help, but the pills I'm taking manage the nausea pretty well."

Mrs. Thompson's eyes widen, her mouth forming a perfect 'O'. "Morning sickness? Are you... are you... expecting?"

Nina shoots her mom a sheepish look. "I hadn't told them yet, Winnie."

"Oh, congratulations, sweetheart." Mrs. Thompson envelops Rowena in a warm hug, her face alight with joy. "Do you want a glass of water? Milk?"

"Milk might be better."

Mrs. Thompson gives Rowena a cookie and then pours her a glass of milk from the fridge. "Here, this should help settle your stomach."

"Hey, do I get milk and cookies too, even if I'm not pregnant?" Dylan jokes behind me. And hearing his voice that close reconnects the electric wire fused to my spine, sending jolts through every nerve.

Mrs. Thompson levels her son with a look; Nina is next. "You two, come with me."

As they disappear into the other room, Mr. Thompson takes out more mugs and keeps passing around the plate with the cookies. "I don't see why we all can't enjoy a snack while they sort out whatever it is they're up to." He chuckles, setting everything on the table.

I eagerly accept a still-warm cookie. The first bite is pure bliss —buttery, sweet, and utterly divine. But as good as these are, they don't come with the sight of Dylan, tousled and flour-dusted, grinning in that heart-wrecking way that ruins my entire existence. So really, they're missing depth.

Just as I'm polishing off the last crumbs, Mrs. Thompson returns with her children in tow. A brittle silence settles over the room following their entrance. Mrs. Thompson's expression is carefully neutral. Dylan looks like he's seen a ghost, his face pale and eyes wide. And Nina is grinning from cheek to cheek.

The stark contrast in their reactions makes my lower back grow tight. What could have provoked such opposite responses?

Mr. Thompson clears his throat, his gaze flickering between his wife and kids. "Alright, what's going on?"

"Well, given the new... circumstances." Mrs. Thompson wrings her fingers together as she looks at Rowena. "We can't have a pregnant woman sleeping in the basement as planned."

I frown, confusion swirling in my mind. The Thompsons have always had an extra room with a single bed that converts into a double; it's where Rowena and I have bunked during previous visits. And true, everyone calls the spare *Tristan's* room. But with him and Nina sharing now, no one should be sleeping in the basement.

As if reading my thoughts, Mrs. Thompson continues, "When Nina and Tristan got together, we converted Tristan's room into a home office for me. Dylan's room has a single bed, so..." She pauses, her gaze shifting to me. "Rowena will have to take Dylan's bed."

My heart stutters, a sense of foreboding creeping up my spine, especially since Dylan is looking everywhere but at me.

Mrs. Thompson offers me an apologetic smile. "Hunter, would you mind sharing the sofa bed in the basement with Dylan? You're already roommates; it's not that different, is it?"

Oh, but it is. It's entirely different.

I stare at Dylan, my pulse racing, but he's still studiously staring at the floor, his ears tinged pink. Realization dawns on me; his earlier expression of terror was about the prospect of sharing a bed with me. A sharp, unwelcome pang pierces my chest. He must be mortified at the thought of having to explain all this to Olivia.

"I can stay at a hotel in town," I blurt out.

A chorus of protests erupts around me.

Mr. Thompson shakes his head. "You won't find anything decent last minute on July third."

Nina reaches out, squeezing my arm. "And it wouldn't be the same without you here, Hunter."

Rowena shifts uncomfortably on her stool. "I can sleep in the basement..."

But Mrs. Thompson cuts her off with a firm, "Absolutely not. You need a proper bed, dear."

I sense the moment Dylan's eyes lift to my face, and like a compass finding true north, I turn to him. The intensity of his gaze on me is a collision of galaxies. Time compresses and stretches simultaneously as I wait for him to speak.

Dylan offers me a small, tentative smile. "I don't mind sharing, Hunter. Really."

My pulse speeds faster than machine-gun fire. I know he's being polite, that he's probably still appalled. I should let him off the hook. But I don't want to inconvenience the Thompsons, or put them on the spot, not after they've so graciously welcomed us into their home.

I nod, forcing a smile. "Okay, sure. It's only for a couple of nights, right?" More four nights.

The room breaks into cheers and relieved sighs. Mr. Thompson claps his hands together. "Alright then, now that's settled, who's ready to fire up the grill?"

As the men head outside, chattering about barbecue techniques and the perfect burger, Mrs. Thompson and Nina follow them to the backyard, offering to help with the preparations.

Rowena stays with me in the kitchen. She still looks pale, her shoulders slumped. I reach out, gently touching her arm. "Hey, you okay?"

She meets my gaze, her eyes filled with uncertainty. "I don't know. Are you?"

"I... I don't know either."

I hesitate, wondering what she guessed about my bad mood and what worries her. Is she missing Adrian, worrying about the baby, or just anxious about the future? But I get a sense that she, same as me, would prefer not to discuss it. We share a small, understanding smile, and without another word, we each reach for a cookie. Because sometimes, words aren't necessary when sweets and denial are on the menu. Nothing says "emotional avoidance" like literally sugarcoating our problems.

22

DYLAN

Smoke from the grill has sneaked into the house and clings to the night air as we all file in from the backyard after having a cozy dinner under the stars. With five of us camping at my parents', it's a long line to use the spare bathroom upstairs. But eventually, the house falls silent, and only Hunter and I are left. We head down to the basement together. She's quiet, and so am I. The echo of our footsteps down the narrow stairs mingles with the buzz of crickets and the occasional hoot of an owl.

The basement isn't fancy, but it's comfy. The ancient sagging couch takes up most of the space, especially now that my mom has pulled out the mattress underneath the seat and made the bed. My ancient gaming console, on which Tristan and I have played infinite games, has been pushed to one side together with the big, old TV.

The walls are a muted beige, dotted with faded family photos, and shelves filled with board games that, thanks to my mom's obsessive tidying, don't have a flake of dust on them. Behind the meticulously organized boxes of holiday decorations and extra toiletries, cleaning supplies, light bulbs, and other household essentials hides Dad's not-so-secret stash of junk food. A large, industrial dehumidifier hums in the corner, valiantly chugging to combat the inherent dampness.

Hunter and I stand on opposite sides of the bed, an awkward tension hanging between us. She's wearing a scant pair of pink cotton shorts and a white tank top. My mouth goes dry as I take her in. The PJ bottoms hug her hips and thighs, leaving her legs almost completely bare. And the thin tank top clings to her curves, hinting at the lacy pink bra underneath. It's a small mercy that she kept her bra on, but not much of one. The delicate straps peeking out from under the tank top tease me, drawing my eyes to her smooth shoulders.

I try my best not to stare, but it's a losing battle. My gaze travels down her slender arms to her navel, where, under the thin fabric, the outline of that damned belly button stud is unmistakable.

"You're stuck with me again," I joke to ease the strange tension.

Hunter's darker-than-night eyes meet mine, inscrutable and alluring. After a long moment, the corners of her full lips twitch. "Could be worse," she says as a shadow of something unreadable swirls in her dark gaze, setting my pulse racing.

I chuckle nervously and rub the back of my neck. "Wow, being classified as 'not the worst' is doing wonders for my ego."

Hunter rolls her eyes, but her smile grows. "Don't let it go to your head, Thompson."

She climbs onto the bed, the mattress dipping under her weight, and the old springs squeaking in protest. I join her, causing even more creaks. Every slight movement elicits a symphony of metallic whines, making it impossible to shift without announcing it to the entire house.

I experimentally wiggle my hips, and the bed lets out a loud groan.

Hunter's eyes go wide, and she covers her face with both hands, laughing. "Dylan, stop." She peeks at me through her fingers. "If anyone's upstairs, they're going to think we're... you know." Her voice trails off, her cheeks blooming with color as she drops her hands, looking both mortified and amused.

A slow grin spreads across my face and, instead of heeding her warning, I bounce rhythmically, making the springs protest even louder. "That we're testing the structural integrity of this fine piece of furniture?"

The sound is comically obscene, like a cheesy soundtrack from a low-budget porno.

Hunter buries her face into the pillow, her long hair flopping down to hide her burning cheeks.

"Stop." She sounds mortified but her shoulders are shaking with the effort to contain her laughter.

I do a few more bounces and settle. In the quiet, Hunter lifts half her face, one eye spying me. Her hair is still falling across it, and I'm once again hit with the powerful urge to tuck those silky strands behind her ear, to tip her chin up and taste her smiling lips...

No. Nope. I can't think like that. Even if the relationship has run its course, I'm still technically with Olivia. I might've decided to break it off with her, but until I do it, I won't cross that line. I'm not that kind of guy. And I'm not even positive Hunter would want me to. That she shares even a fraction of the restlessness I can't escape since moving in with her. She's probably more sensible than me and has "dating your roommate" double-underlined in red in her not-to-do list. As should I.

"Alright, alright, I'll behave."

I flop back against the pillows with an exaggerated sigh—and the couch promptly protests again.

We both start laughing, causing even more squeaks. Gradually, our laughter fades into a comfortable silence, and we settle down to get some sleep. I flip off the lights, plunging the basement into thick darkness punctuated only by the faint moonlight glow filtering in through the narrow hopper windows. The shadows turn the room smaller, more intimate.

I want so badly to tell Hunter about my decision to end things with Olivia—test how she'd react. But I bite my tongue. It wouldn't be right, not yet. First, I need to have that difficult conversation with Liv.

Until then, I'll have to content myself with stolen glances at the stunning woman lying next to me, close enough to touch but still maddeningly off-limits. I know this weekend is going to be sweet torture, but I wouldn't trade it for anything. Because when I'm with Hunter, everything feels... right. Like this is where I'm meant to be.

Even if, for now, "right" means platonically sharing the world's squeakiest sofa bed. A closeness that borders on agony.

I squeeze my eyes shut, willing myself to ignore the heat radiating off Hunter's skin, the subtle scent of her shampoo wafting over to me.

"Night, Thompson," she murmurs, her voice already thick with impending sleep.

"Night, Brolin." The words catch in my throat.

I never knew how much effort it took to keep still. Beside me, Hunter vibrates with the same effort. After a while, I dare to turn my head and peek at her. The moon filtering through the windows casts everything in a silvery glow, including the planes of Hunter's face. She looks ethereal, too beautiful to be real. But she's not sleeping either; her posture is too rigid. I swallow hard and force myself to look away.

Minutes tick by, but sleep remains elusive. The basement is stifling, the air heavy despite the dehumidifier. We don't have air conditioning down here, and while the temperature is several degrees lower than the main house, the natural cooling is not enough to fend off the oppressive July heat. I toss and turn to find a cool spot on the sheets. Beside me, Hunter does the same, our movements making the springs creak in protest.

"Sorry," she whispers, sounding more amused than contrite.

I chuckle. "If this bed had a voice, I bet it'd be saying, 'Can you two take this somewhere else?'"

"Like the floor? I could take it up on that offer."

Silence descends again, but it's more alert than comfortable now. I'm hyper-aware of every breath she takes, every rustle of the sheets. It's maddening and exhilarating all at once.

Unable to stand it any longer, I sit up. "I'm gonna open the windows." I hop off the couch. "See if it gets better."

It does. The night air is blessedly cool against my sweaty face as I crack open all the hopper windows. Mercifully, a breeze coming in from the ocean makes the heat more bearable.

I crawl back into bed, careful not to jostle her. Hunter smiles up at me and gives me a double thumbs-up. "Great problem-solving skills, Thompson."

I grin. "I have my moments."

If only she knew the problem I want to solve is how to keep my hands off her for the rest of this unbearably sultry night—and possibly all the nights after.

She shifts, the thin sheet sliding down her torso. Soon, she stills, her breathing becoming even. Asleep, I think, with a pang of something dangerously close to longing.

Closing my eyes, I will myself to drift off to thoughts of anything but the incredible woman beside me.

Eventually, mercifully, I do.

* * *

I'm in the shower, steam billowing around me. The water sluices over my skin, hot and perfect. But not as perfect as the woman in my arms.

Hunter presses against me, all soft curves and slick skin. She tilts her face up to mine, her eyes dark with want, and I lower my head to capture her lips in a searing kiss. She opens for me instantly, igniting a fire low in my belly.

My hands skim down her sides, over the flare of her hips, to grip her thighs. I hoist her up, and she wraps her legs around my waist, a guttural moan escaping her as I press her back against the cool tiles.

"Dylan," she breathes, and the sound of my name on her lips undoes me. I need to be closer, to taste every inch of her.

I lean in, trailing open-mouthed kisses along the column of her throat, reveling in the little gasps and sighs I draw from her. Lower, lower, until I reach the gentle swell of her breast. She arches into me, a wordless plea for more.

Smiling against her skin, I oblige. She writhes in my arms, nails digging deliciously into my shoulders.

Lost in sensation, it takes me a second to realize the water pelting my face is no longer warm, but icy cold. Startled, my eyes fly open—and I'm back in the basement, panting, wet, and disoriented. Water rains down on me from somewhere.

For one confused moment, I think the house must be on fire and the ceiling sprinklers have gone off. My heart races as I sit up, blinking rapidly to clear my vision.

But as my eyes adjust to the semi-darkness, I turn toward the open windows where the water keeps gushing in. The garden sprinklers must've come on during the night and the spray is catching the moonlight and sparkling like a thousand tiny diamonds as it arcs through the openings, soaking everything in its path.

Beside me, Hunter stirs, sputtering. "What the hell?" She pushes sodden hair out of her face, blinking up at the windows in groggy confusion. With her hair wet and plastered to her forehead, she looks too much like the dream I was having.

Thankfully, the sprinklers are gracing me with a *literal* cold shower, and my brain cools quickly enough from the fantasy of Hunter in my arms and jolts me into action. I vault over the couch and over a startled, still half-asleep Hunter to get to the hoppers.

The mattress squishes under my weight as I leap, water splattering against my legs. I fumble with the windows, my hands slipping on the wet handles, and snarl curses at the waterfall until I slam all of them shut.

I push the wet hair away from my forehead. Water drips from it, running in rivulets down my face and neck.

As I turn, I find Hunter standing awkwardly, bathed in moonlight, her clothes soaked through and clinging even more to her body than before. The sight makes it hard for my lungs to hold on to air. The moonlight turns the water droplets on her skin into a glistening sheen, highlighting the dip of her collarbone, and the swell of her breasts.

She's an ethereal vision, wet and shimmering, and a jolt of longing shoots through me so powerful, it almost brings me to my knees. The image of her like this will stay with me forever, haunting me to my grave.

She's the most beautiful woman I've ever seen.

We stand there, dripping and staring at each other, still shocked. Then, out of nowhere, Hunter starts to laugh. It's a sweet, infectious sound that lands straight in my gut, wrapping tight. She playfully shoves my shoulder. "Are you always this much trouble?"

I start laughing with her; the whole situation is so bizarre, it's surreal. Here we are, soaked to the bone, shivering in the middle of the night, stuck in my parents' basement together.

As our laughter dies down, Hunter wraps her arms around herself, still shuddering. She glances at her suitcase, which she unfortunately left open right under the windows. The contents are drenched, a soggy mess of clothes and books, the once-crisp pages now crumpled and limp.

"Oh no," she groans, gingerly picking up a waterlogged novel. "I was looking forward to reading this."

My heart twists at the disappointment in her voice. I hate seeing her upset, even over something as small as a ruined book. I want to fix it, to make everything better for her.

By some stroke of luck, my suitcase ended up on the far side of the room, safe from the sprinkler's wrath. I grab one of my basketball shirts. "Here." I hold it out to her. "It's dry, at least."

"Thanks," Hunter says, her voice hoarse. "Can you please close your eyes while I change?"

I nod and shut my eyes tight as I hear the rustling of fabric. Wet clothes smack against the hardwood floor and my imagination spirals, filling in the vivid details I can't see. The snap of her bra unclasping nearly undoes me.

Each shuffle and whisper of movement send electric currents through my body. Knowing that Hunter is mere feet away, wearing only damp panties, makes me unhinged. Raw nerve endings sizzle and my brain synapses misfire in all directions. I squeeze my eyes even tighter against the overwhelming temptation to peek.

Behind my eyelids, tantalizing images of Hunter flash and

meld with memories of my dreams, the real and imagined blurring together. An eternity passes before her voice breaks the charged silence.

"Okay, you can open your eyes now."

I blink and the sight before me is even more devastating than my fantasies.

She's haloed in the faint light filtering in from the windows, my old basketball shirt swallowing her. Her damp hair is finger-combed away from her face, her skin dewy and fresh. She looks soft, vulnerable. Utterly unattainable.

"Thanks." Her eyes crinkle with a smile. "Much better now. Your shirt might be a keeper. It's super comfy."

She does a little twirl, and I tighten my fists. I want to pull her to me, bury my face in her neck, and breathe her in. I want to press her body against mine, to explore every curve and hollow...

With a hard mental push, I shove the thought away and muster a smile. "It looks good on you. Better than it ever did on me."

She laughs, the sound warming me from the inside out. "I don't know about that. I bet you looked pretty good in your basketball days."

"Unfortunately, those days are gone," I joke, falling into the easy banter that has always defined our relationship.

"Fishing for a compliment? Because I won't tell you that you still look more fit than any guy I know... even the under thirty..."

I smile. "As long as you won't tell me, my ego will be kept in check."

I swallow against the constriction in my throat, barely resisting the primal urge to close the distance between us. To wrap her in my arms and never let go.

Seeing her in my clothes, surrounded by my scent, sends a possessive thrill through me. I want to see her in nothing but my shirt, the fabric skimming her thighs, her hair mussed from my fingers...

I choke back the inappropriate thoughts. "Do you want to go back to sleep, or are we done for the night?"

Hunter tentatively touches the couch, her fingers sinking into the damp cushions. "It's still pretty wet. We can't sleep on it."

I nod dumbly and glance at my watch. "It's almost five. How about we surprise everyone with homemade brownies for breakfast?"

Her face lights up, a grin tugging at her lips. "If your brownies are as good as your chocolate chip cookies, I'm totally down. I need to... uh... just check something real quick."

Hunter rummages through her suitcase, searching for dry underwear, I realize with horror. She tries to be discreet, but I catch a tantalizing glimpse of lace peeking out from her fingers. My breath hitches.

She stands, hiding her hands behind her back. "I'll wait for you in the kitchen." She leaves me to change out of my own soaked clothes.

As she climbs the stairs, I stare at her legs, transfixed by the smooth expanse of skin disappearing under the hem of my shirt. Once she's out of sight, I drag a hand down my face, frustrated and overwhelmed.

The image of Hunter in my shirt, her damp hair clinging to her neck, is seared into my brain. And the rustle of fabric as she undressed echoes in my head, stoking the fire burning under my skin.

I change and try to focus on something else, needing a minute before I join her in the kitchen. I grab a towel from the laundry room to mop up the puddles on the floor. But my mind keeps wandering, imagining Hunter peeling off her wet clothes, exposing inch after tantalizing inch of smooth skin...

"Get it together, man," I mutter to myself, wringing out the soaked towel with more force than necessary.

I'm tired, I reason. It's been a long day, and the unexpected wake-up call has me all out of sorts.

But like never before, I desperately wish I were more of a jerk, that I'd broken things off with Olivia before this trip, funeral or not. The timing couldn't be worse, but every fiber of my being yearns to test the waters with Hunter, consequences and complications be damned.

23

HUNTER

The citrusy tang of lemonade lingers on my tongue as I lean back in the chaise longue, the condensation from the glass chilling my fingers. Bright sunbeams dance across the pool's surface, glinting like scattered diamonds. Nina, Rowena, and I are soaking up in the half-shade of a giant white umbrella, our skins glistening with a sheen of sun lotion in the thick, July heat.

Soft beats pulse from portable speakers connected to Dylan's phone, mingling with the rustle of leaves in the faint breeze. While us gals lazy it out, the guys are hauling the ratty, old—now also soggy—couch through the basement egress door. They're shirtless.

As they emerge, Dylan's golden hair catches the light, the flex of his back muscles mesmerizing. Beside him, Tristan grunts with the effort, biceps bulging.

"Damn." Rowena lowers her sunglasses. "I know one's your boyfriend and the other's your brother, but holy hell. How are we supposed to look anywhere else right now?"

Nina laughs, propping herself up on her elbows for a better

view. "Oh, don't hold back on my account. I'm enjoying the show."

Her appreciative hum blends with the music as we watch the men navigate the couch across the lawn. Sweat glistens along the ridges of Tristan's abs and over Dylan's shoulders, broad and sculpted from years on the basketball court.

I take a long sip of lemonade, the ice clinking against my teeth. I hiss at the stab of pain, wishing ice could chill more than just my incisors. If only I could put a cold compress on my raging crush. I should tear my eyes away; ogling Dylan's bare, sweaty chest is doing nothing to cure me. Especially not as the guys drop the couch and face us—it's a muscle onslaught.

Dylan flashes an easy smile our way as he calls out, "Hey, any of you lovely ladies want to give us a hand?"

"We wish we could," Nina yells back, "but we don't want to."

Dylan huffs out a laugh and bends to grab the couch again, those delectable shoulder muscles rippling. I hide my shameless gawking behind my sunglasses.

Rowena smiles playfully. "If Tristan ever loses his job, he can always get a role in the next *Magic Mike*."

Nina jokingly groans. "The jerk even wore a backward baseball cap when he knows we'll have to wait all day to—"

Rowena finishes the phrase for her, "To make tender, caring, sweet love?"

Nina scoffs. "After that display, what I plan to do with Tristan ain't going to be sweet." She turns to Rowena with a mischievous grin. "I bet your fiancé is just as ripped, huh?"

At the mention of Adrian, a cloud sweeps over Rowena's face, her gaze becoming distant. "He's not my fiancé, so I won't be *ripping* the benefits—pun intended."

I study my friend closely. Rowena tries to act carefree, but she's been downcast for the entire journey. Even more broody than me, which is saying something.

"What about you?" Nina nudges my foot with her toe. "Seeing anything you like?"

On reflex, my gaze darts back to Dylan. The guys have dropped the couch on the grass, and he's stretching out, bathed in sunlight. His blond locks gleam like molten gold, catching every ray, and his body—oh, his body. Muscles flex as he lifts his arms above his head, the smooth skin of his torso gleaming with sweat. It looks as if the god of the sun himself has come down to Earth to haul furniture.

If ancient poets had ever witnessed this, Apollo would've had some serious competition in the worship department. Every inch of Dylan ripples with strength, each movement a reminder that some people were built to make the rest of the population suffer.

And suffer I do; my mouth goes dry at the sight. I take a hasty swig of lemonade, the cold tartness a reality check. He's taken. And even if he weren't with Olivia, he has never shown an interest in me in eleven years. We're friends. Roommates. Platonic as can be.

Nina pokes my foot again. "No comment, Miss Brolin?"

I try to play it cool, shrugging nonchalantly. "Just thinking that none of my disastrous dates from last week must've looked that good without a shirt. I should add 'must be an ex-basketball player' to my desiderata on my profile."

Nina shushes me as the guys approach, their footsteps muffled by the grass. "Shh, don't let them hear you talk about basketball or they'll delight us with some college glory days anecdotes."

I make a zipper motion over my lips as they arrive. Tristan catches my gesture, raising a mock suspicious eyebrow at his girl-friend. "Keeping secrets, are we?"

Nina provokes him teasingly. "I can't tell you everything, babe. I've got to keep a little mystery alive."

Tristan's response is wordless. He lies on top of her, sliding his sweaty body over hers in a move that's at once gross, playful, and sensual. "Is this mysterious enough for you?"

Nina screeches, her hands flailing in mock protest. "Ew, you're disgusting." But the struggling lasts about two seconds before she pulls him down for a passionate kiss, her fingers tangling in his damp hair.

I glance away, feeling like I'm intruding on a private moment. My gaze lands on Dylan, who's watching the display with a look that's equal parts fondness and exasperation.

Until, at the lack of restraint from his best friend and sister, Dylan scoffs and upends their chaise with a casual shove. Nina and Tristan tumble into the pool in a tangle of limbs, water splashing everywhere, the scent of chlorine rising in the warm air.

They emerge laughing, Tristan pushing his hair back from his face, his cap floating away. "Thanks, man. I needed to cool off." Then he grabs Nina again, and their lips meet in a kiss that's even more heated than before.

"If you two get into any more PDA, I'll grab the hose, I swear."

Nina and Tristan ignore him, lost in their own world.

Dylan looks away, shaking his head. He rights the now-empty chaise and sits, the plastic creaking under his weight as he stretches his long legs out in front of him. "About the couch situation." He turns to me and I'm glad I'm wearing sunglasses as a shield of sorts because being the sole focus of his blue-green gaze is overwhelming, like staring straight into the sun. The heat of it washes over me, my skin prickling with awareness. If Dylan is Apollo, the sun god, in our little Greek mythology drama, I'm Icarus. I might want to fly to the sun, but the only thing that's going to happen to me if I do is that my wings will melt and I'll splatter to the ground, shattering my heart.

"What about it?" I ask, ignoring the pounding organ in my chest. "Will it dry in time for tonight?"

"Even if it dries, the old guy doesn't have another night left in him." He grins. "It's smelling a bit too moldy for my taste."

I return the smile. "Ah, he had a valiant death, then. Serving his purpose until the end."

"A true hero," Dylan agrees solemnly. "But that leaves us with a problem. All the shops are closed today; we can't get a replacement."

I raise an eyebrow. "What's the plan then?"

He shrugs, the movement causing the muscles in his shoulders to ripple in a way that's entirely too distracting. "You can take the couch in the living room. I'll blow up an air mattress and stay on the floor. At least we'll have air conditioning. Silver linings, right?"

"Air conditioning sounds way better than spontaneous garden sprinklers."

Dylan is about to reply when Nina and Tristan creep out of the pool behind him, wicked grins on their faces. Before he can react, they each grab one of his arms and yank him backward into the water.

The splash is enormous, and almost gets me and Rowena, too. Dylan emerges a second later, sputtering and shaking his head like a wet dog. Droplets fly everywhere, catching the sunlight and splintering into tiny rainbow crystals.

"Oh, it's on," he declares, his eyes narrowing playfully at the giggling couple.

With a roar, Dylan lunges for Tristan, trapping him in a headlock and dunking him under the water.

Tristan comes up laughing, his hands raised in mock surrender. "I yield, I yield."

But Dylan isn't done. He turns to Nina. "And you, dear sister. You think you can escape unscathed?"

Nina squeals, to swim away, but her brother is too fast. He captures her waist and hoists her over his shoulder, spinning her around as she beats her fists against his back. Tristan comes to a heroic rescue, and together, they overwhelm Dylan.

"Hey, you'd yielded," he protests with Tristan.

"Sorry, bro. All's fair in love and water fights."

Dylan splashes him and turns to Rowena and me. "You two joining in, or are you too chicken?"

Rowena sets her lemonade down and stands. The sun catches on her chestnut hair, turning it to burnished copper as she saunters to the edge of the pool. With a playful grin, she drops backward onto a floatie, the plastic squeaking under her weight. She sighs as the cool water laps against her sides. Rowena wiggles her butt, adjusting her position, and leans back, tilting her face toward the sky. All her worries seem to melt away.

I hesitate. The idea of being near a wet, shirtless Dylan is both tempting and terrifying. But the heat is oppressive, and the water looks inviting... also, I don't want to be a party pooper.

Dylan is watching me and cocks his head in invitation or in a challenge, I'm not sure.

Oh, what the hell. I stand by the pool's edge and dip a toe in. The water is colder than I expected. I could ease myself in gradually but I'd take forever, so I dive in. The contrast in temperature against my overheated skin makes me gasp as I resurface, goosebumps erupting all over my body despite the warmth of the day.

But after the initial shock, I swim below the surface again, letting the coolness envelop me as I float back up.

When I open my eyes, I realize I've drifted closer to Dylan

than I intended. He's watching me, an unreadable expression on his face.

I panic and paddle backward, putting distance between us. Safer. I develop a radar system tuned into his location and always position myself at the opposite edge. The safety buffer holds until Tristan dive-bombs into the pool right next to me, sending a wave crashing over my head.

I sputter, flailing my arms to regain my balance. My hand connects with something solid and warm, and I grab on instinctively.

I blink water out of my eyes and find my fingers wrapped around Dylan's bicep, the firm muscle flexing under my touch. Heat sears through me, and I drop my hand as if burned, walking and paddling backward.

"Sorry, I—" My apology is cut short as my foot slips on the pool floor. I go under. Water rushes into my mouth, and then powerful arms are around me, hauling me up.

I break the surface, coughing and gasping, as I find myself plastered against Dylan's torso. Our legs tangle as we tread water, his hands gripping my waist to steady me, my palms flattening on his chest. Even in the cool embrace of the pool, his touch scorches my skin.

For a suspended moment, we're frozen, our bodies molded together. I feel every inch of him, hard and unyielding against my softness. His heartbeat thunders under my palm, matching the frantic pace of my own.

Our eyes lock, and a live wire replaces my veins again, the current setting every nerve ending alight. I can't breathe, can't think. There's only Dylan, the heat of his gaze, the pressure of his hands.

Just as I'm about to fry in the pool with all the electricity coursing through me, the music cuts off, leaving a ringing silence in its place. Dylan's phone, abandoned on a lounge chair, chimes with a new message. A robotic voice reads it out on the speakers' system.

"Message from Olivia: Miss you, babe. Wish you were here with me."

The words slice through me colder than a blade of ice. Dylan jerks away as if stung, his face shuttering. He clears his throat, looking anywhere but at me.

"I should... I need to—"

I paste on a tight smile and gesture toward Dylan's phone. "Yeah, you'd better go respond to that," I say lightly as sourness fills my stomach.

Dylan nods, avoiding my gaze as he climbs the metal ladder. I hate myself a little for not being able to tear my eyes away from the muscular planes of his back as he strides over to his phone, water sluicing down his sun-kissed skin, tracing paths I want to follow with my fingers—also with my tongue, if I'm being honest.

He grabs a towel and starts drying off, putting an end to the show and to the synchronized body-lock performance we were having underwater.

I'm left bobbing backward, my skin still tingling from his touch, as reality crashes over me colder and more unforgiving than the water. Nothing like getting a wake-up call in the form of your crush's gorgeous girlfriend declaring her undying love on the Dolby surround system. I bite the inside of my cheek, half-laughing at myself. I'm beyond tragic.

My arms are heavy as lead as I lift out of the pool, weighed down by disappointment. Nina and Tristan are still playing around, too wrapped up in each other to notice the drama unfolding. Rowena shoots me a knowing look from her floatie. I deliberately turn away, not ready to face her pity or curiosity.

"Well, at least tonight I won't have to worry about sharing a mattress with Mr. Committed," I grit out quietly, grabbing my towel. "Silver linings, right, Dylan? The air conditioning won't be the only thing keeping things frosty."

Dylan, already halfway to the house, doesn't hear me. Just as well. The disaster would be complete if he picked up on my hopelessly one-sided feelings.

I flop down on my chaise, letting the sun bake away the lingering chill. It's fine. Super. So what if the guy I'm halfway in love with is head over heels for someone else? I'll get over it. It won't take another eleven years either.

24

DYLAN

The air mattress squeaks under me as I shift my weight, trying in vain to find a comfortable position. Sleep eludes me once again despite the late hour and how much I'm begging my racing mind to settle. It's not the unfamiliar surroundings of my parents' living room keeping me up. It's her. Hunter. She's slumped on the couch across from me, her breathing soft and steady.

And I'm lying wide awake. A moron who can't stop replaying the accidental snuggle-in-the-deep-end debacle in the pool earlier, when our bodies tangled under the cool water. The way her curves molded against my chest, the electric slide of her bare skin on mine, the slight pierce of her belly button piercing scraping against my stomach; it's as if every touch was tattooed on me, available to revisit whenever I feel like torturing myself. Heat unfurls over me, skull to toes, just thinking about it.

I flip onto my back with a low groan. I'm going to be dead on my feet tomorrow if I don't get some shut-eye. But every time I close my lids, there she is. Tempting me. Taunting me.

A muffled sound breaks the silence. At first, I think it's an animal outside, but then it comes again. A stifled moan, from the direction of the couch. My pulse quickens and my imagination runs wild. Is Hunter having a dream? The sexy kind, from the breathy way that noise escapes her?

Fuck. I must've racked up some serious bad-luck points somewhere. I've been fighting the attraction to her all damn night, and now I have to listen to her make those sounds in her sleep?

Another whine floats over, and frustration crashes through me. I'm reaching for the pillow, ready to pull it over my face to block her out, when a whimper reaches my ears.

I freeze.

Because it's not a sound of pleasure, but of pain. An agonized cry that sends a spike of alarm through my chest.

Concern floods me, instantly replacing the frustration. I prop myself up on my elbows, squinting through the darkness at Hunter's form on the couch. Her body is tense, curled in on itself. She shifts, another whimper escaping her.

"Hunter?" I call out. "You okay?"

No response. I sit up fully, push the bedsheet aside, and kneel beside the couch. Her face is scrunched in discomfort, even in the dim light. I try again, a little louder this time. "Hunter?"

She stirs, her eyelids fluttering open. Her gaze is unfocused. "Sorry." Her voice is thick with pain. "I didn't mean to wake you."

"What's going on?" My concern deepens as she grimaces. She doesn't look well. Her skin is pale despite the tan, and a sheen of sweat dots her forehead.

Hunter hesitates, looking embarrassed. She bites her lip, avoiding my gaze before admitting, "My period. It just... hit me out of nowhere. The pain's been building for the last hour."

I blink, not sure what to say at first. Nina's mentioned her feminine woes to me before, but this is different. More intense. Hunter's clearly in a lot of pain, beyond what must be normal.

"Can I help?" I offer, not sure how I can help, but wanting to do something, anything, to ease her suffering.

Hunter mutters something about painkillers, her words slurred. She's too uncomfortable to give more than a vague answer, her breathing shallow as another wave of pain hits her.

I spring into action, grabbing my phone to use as a flashlight and making my way to the kitchen. The medicine cabinet yields a bottle of ibuprofen, and I pour a glass of cold water to go with it. As I'm closing the fridge, my gaze lands on the plate of leftover brownies we made this morning. I remove the plastic wrap and pop two of them in the microwave, the rich smell of chocolate soon filling the air.

With the emergency supplies in hand, I return to the living room. Hunter is still curled up on the couch, her hands clutching her belly. She's trying to put on a brave face, but pain is etched in the tightness around her eyes, in the way her lips press together. I set the brownies down on the coffee table and kneel beside her, holding out the pills and water.

Hunter sits up slowly, a wince escaping as she moves. She takes the glass and medications from me. She tilts her head back, her throat working as she swallows the pills. It's strangely intimate to be with her in the dead of night, taking care of her. She glances at the brownies with a flicker of amusement. "What are these for?"

"Nina always craves chocolate when she's on her period. Figured it couldn't hurt." I give her a small smile. "Besides, it's better to take pills on a full stomach, right?"

Hunter returns the smile, but it's fleeting. Her face pales as she leans back, eyes squeezing shut.

"T-thanks for the thought, but I need a minute before I eat."

I settle on the floor beside her, my back resting against the couch near her legs as I quietly will the painkillers to act faster.

The silence stretches between us, broken only by Hunter's measured breaths. I glance over at her, taking in the stiffness in her body, the furrow between her brows.

"Is it always this bad?" The question slips out. It might be insensitive; she might not be comfortable talking about it. But I can't control the crave to learn everything about her.

Hunter hesitates, then nods. "Yeah. I have a couple of conditions that make it worse than normal."

I frown at that, concern welling up inside me. My knowledge of period pains is pretty basic, but the resignation in her voice makes it sound serious. "What conditions?"

Hunter lets out a groan, part pain, part exasperation. "You really want to talk about my reproductive health at two in the morning?"

My lips twitch despite the worry still churning in my gut. "I'm awake, and I've got nothing better to do."

Hunter looks at me, her expression impossible to decipher. She sighs, the sound heavy in the night's stillness. "PCOS and endometriosis. Both conditions cause my periods to be painful and unpredictable. That's why tonight came as a surprise."

I listen intently as she explains what they are. A hormonal disorder and a syndrome where tissue grows outside the uterus. She keeps her tone light and nonchalant, but the tautness in her shoulders and the way her fingers curl into the fabric of the couch are unmistakable. She's trying to downplay it, not to make a big deal out of it, but there must be more than she's letting on.

"Is it serious?" I'm unable to keep the concern from seeping into my voice.

Hunter tries to laugh it off. "It won't kill me if that's what you're asking." But then her expression sobers, and she adds quietly, "It could make it harder for me to have kids."

She says it matter-of-factly, but a quiet sadness underlines her tone and it hits me hard, the thought of her carrying that weight settling heavy in my chest.

Hunter catches my expression and waves it off, forcing a smile. "The worst part is the pain, not the potential future consequences. I've come to terms with the fact that I might not have kids naturally and have to try IVF or adopt." She glances at me sideways, clearly uncomfortable with the more personal turn the conversation has taken. "But enough about me and my dysfunctional uterus. Distract me. Change the topic."

I lean my head back against the cushion, staring up at the shadowed ceiling. "I have dyslexia."

The admission surprises me. Only a handful of people know about it. My family, of course. Tristan. My serious ex-girlfriend. The teachers and specialists I've worked with over the years. Kelly, my assistant, because I wouldn't survive the office otherwise. But no one else. It's not a topic I bring up often, not an issue I care to draw attention to. I've hidden it behind a wall of hard work and coping strategies for most of my life.

But in the dark, with Hunter, it comes naturally to share it. To let her see a piece of me I keep locked away.

"Before I was diagnosed as a kid, it was confusing." My voice echoes in the room's quiet. "I didn't understand why reading was so much harder for me than it was for the other kids in my class. Why I'd sit in front of my homework for hours while my friends could finish it in no time."

I remember the frustration, the shame of being different, being less than. "My teachers told me to 'try harder,' but no matter how hard I tried, the words wouldn't make sense. It made me feel stupid, even though I knew I wasn't. There was this teacher who noticed every tiny mistake. She'd call me out in front of the class, sighing loudly and shaking her head like I was a lost cause."

In the darkness, Hunter's hand finds mine, her fingers lacing with my own. She doesn't say anything, but I don't need her to. Her touch, her presence, says everything.

"After a while, I learned to be quiet, to fade into the background, not to draw her attention. I started going out of my way not to make waves. Even now, I avoid conflict on reflex—as if any wrong move will bring that same crushing spotlight back onto me.

"Once I got diagnosed, things got better. My parents were supportive. They hired tutors, specialists, and anyone they thought could help me overcome it. But it never went away. Dyslexia isn't something you can cure."

It's a part of me, as much as my blue eyes or my love for basketball. But I've learned to live with, to work around it. But the challenges are a constant. Telling Hunter, putting it into words, makes it real. It's a pressure valve releasing inside me—a secret shared, a burden halved.

Now that I've started, the words flow out. "Even now, reading isn't easy for me. It's exhausting. Over the years, I've developed coping mechanisms—memorizing what certain words look like instead of reading them, using audio tools to help with long reports at work, relying on my sharp memory to get through meetings."

Hunter listens quietly, her hand still in mine, a gentle reassurance.

"But at work, in my high-pressure job, I'm constantly terrified that someone will notice that I struggle to function at a high level, reading contracts, reports, and financial documents. It's one of my biggest fears." The admission leaves me exposed. "I've made it this far, but a part of me will always believe I'm an imposter."

Sitting in the quiet of the night, with Hunter beside me, I

realize how freeing it is to open up. For so long, I've carried this burden alone, hiding behind a façade of confidence and competence. But now, the mask slips a little, and I let her see the real me —the part that's scared, flawed, and still fighting to keep up.

Hunter squeezes my hand, her voice gentle when she speaks. "Dylan, what you've achieved, with dyslexia, is incredible. You're not an imposter. You're a fighter, and you're winning."

Her words wash over me, a balm to my insecurities. I turn to her. Only understanding shines in her eyes, acceptance, admiration even. It's a look that sends my pulse racing and makes me feel truly seen, perhaps for the first time.

Hunter sags back. "But gosh, Thompson, you're the worst at cheering up people."

"I disagree, Brolin; is that a smile on your face?"

Her lips part into a grin, and she looks at me with only one eye open. "Okay, I'm smiling, but only because it's been a while since someone made it okay for me to be a mess."

With me, she can be a mess whenever she wants, and I'll gladly carry whatever weight she can't. I hope one day, she'll let me.

25

HUNTER

Monday morning, I tiptoe around my apartment as the first slivers of light filter through the blinds. In the kitchen, the coffee pot gurgles and hisses right on schedule, the comforting aroma filling my nostrils as I pour the steaming liquid into my Thermos. It's early, too early, but I need to make up for lost time at work.

At least that's what I tell myself. That I'm not, once again, running away from my roommate. Or fleeing the memories of this past weekend with Dylan.

Sharing that dreadful sofa bed the first night, with the follow-up wet T-shirt contest. That moment in the pool the next day. And worst of all, the whispered confessions, raw and vulnerable, the second night. I push the thoughts aside. I can't afford to dwell on any of that, on him. Dylan isn't mine and never will be. The realization settles like a lead weight in my stomach as I screw the lid on my Thermos.

I gather my bag and keys, slipping out the door before Dylan emerges from his bedroom. Warm humidity slaps me in the face as I step outside, wilting my blouse. I hurry down to the stuffy metro station, wedging myself into the crowded car. As the train lurches forward, I grip the metal pole, my mind wandering despite my best efforts.

These past two weeks have been a blur of distractions and wasted time. Instead of focusing on my career, I went on disastrous date after disastrous date to forget about Dylan, only to have him consume my thoughts even more. And last week, I left work early on Wednesday to go to Connecticut for the long weekend, not even checking my emails once while I was away. My brain has been tuned 24/7 on the Dylan channel. But that ends now. It has to.

The metro screeches to a halt and I elbow my way out onto the platform. Striding into my building, I catch a break as the air conditioning envelops me. The heels of my sandals click decisively on the tiles as I walk over to my office, determined to regain control and focus on what matters—me, my goals.

I pause in my doorway, taking in the comforting sight of my organized space. The row of engineering manuals lining one shelf, my framed master's degree on the wall. My desk is empty except for my laptop docking station and a few tidy folders, a small oasis of calm.

Settling into my ergonomic chair, I power up my computer. No more distractions. No more Dylan. It's time to get back on track. I take a fortifying sip of coffee as my laptop whirs to life, ready to throw myself into work and leave the last few messy, confusing, nights behind.

As expected, after four and a half days of neglect, my inbox is overflowing with unread emails, the notifications popping up one after another in rapid succession.

I skim through the messages, triaging the most urgent items, when one subject line jumps out at me:

Carmichael Corp.: Project Revision Request

My pulse quickens as I click on the bold letters to open it, my eyes racing over the client's message.

"You've got to be kidding me," I mutter through clenched teeth as I reach the crux of the email. Carmichael Corp. is requesting significant changes to the design of their sustainable office complex—the challenging project I promised Daniel I could handle.

North Shore is my chance to make a name for myself, to prove that I have what it takes to lead a high-profile, ground-breaking building design from concept to completion. The goal is to achieve a LEED Platinum Certification, the gold standard for green building, by seamlessly integrating renewable energy, innovative materials, and eco-friendly technologies.

I've spent countless hours fine-tuning every detail, coordinating with the architects and tech specialists to complete the design: three sleek, modern towers connected by a light-filled central atrium. The roofs are fitted with solar panels, complemented by a geothermal heating system to decimate the carbon footprint. Triple-glazed windows and a closed-loop energy infrastructure will minimize waste, while rainwater harvesting will supply water to the toilets.

It's a delicate balancing act, each piece calibrated to work in harmony. And now, with the blueprints almost completed, they want to upend everything?

I lean back in my chair, exhaling slowly as I re-read the request. I haven't been giving this project my full attention as I should have, too caught up in the whirlwind of Dylan and our not-quite romance. Still, I've kept all the moving parts on track, even with the constant distraction. But this email changes everything.

They are asking for a major aesthetic shift: an expansion to the glass atrium connecting the three towers and the introduction of a vertical garden in the taller entrance hall. It isn't a bad idea; in fact, the biophilic design is intriguing, a way to bring the outdoors inside, to create a space that's alive and connected to nature. It's a feature that could make the complex stand out, generate buzz, and attract tenants for the parts they're leasing.

But it throws off the entire energy balance of the building. The original design relied on minimal sunlight exposure, on heavy insulation to keep the interior temperature stable. With a massive glass atrium, the summer heat gain will be enormous. It'll turn into a bona fide greenhouse, the sun pouring in, the temperature spiking.

The increased cooling demands will strain the geothermal system, driving up energy consumption and costs.

And then there's the vertical garden. It's a stunning concept: a living wall of green stretching up through the heart of the building. But all I can compute is the massive water demand. Constant irrigation, humidity control, the works. My original rainwater harvesting system was meant for basic needs—toilets and minimal landscaping. It can't handle this kind of load.

I lean forward, my elbows on my desk, my head in my hands. The planet doesn't need more water overconsumption, more strain on our resources. This vertical garden, as beautiful as it may be, is a step in the wrong direction.

I inhale deeply to calm my racing thoughts. The entire project is at risk. All my original calculations are worthless. If these changes are implemented, the building will consume way more energy than it was designed to.

I set up an emergency call with Carmichael Corp. and spend the time before they can get their team together jotting down a list of why the new atrium is a detrimental choice.

One hour later, tension buzzes under my skin as I wait for them to join the virtual meeting. When they do, I keep my voice calm as I surf through the initial greetings, eager to get to the core of the matter, which I explain in what I hope is a firm but professional tone.

"I understand your desire for a more striking design. But the alterations will have enormous implications. The glass atrium will drastically increase energy use, especially during the summer, and the vertical garden will require a new irrigation system. We'll need to adjust the entire water management plan."

But the client remains indifferent to my concerns. "Can't we just improve the efficiency?" they ask breezily.

"We could, but it's a major redesign."

The CEO looks to the guy on his left, who nods. "We were assured the impact would be manageable."

Cold sweat trickles between my shoulder blades. "I'm sorry, who told you that?"

Another suit whispers something to him. He nods, staring back at the camera. "A manager at your firm. A supervisor?"

It must be Mark. It couldn't be anyone else having the gall. He's the only one who constantly undermines me and who never gives me credit for my work. Anger flares in my chest as the pieces fall into place. My supervisor has moved from passive aggression to active sabotage.

"I see," I say, my voice tight. "Well, I'm afraid there may have been some miscommunication. As the lead engineer on this project, I can assure you that the new design will require significant adjustments."

The client hums noncommittally. "Well, we'll leave that to you to sort out. How soon can you come up with an alternative proposal?"

I smile tightly. "You'll have it by the end of the week." *Even if it means I have to kill myself with work.*

The call ends, and I blow air out of my cheeks. Mark has been working behind my back, encouraging the client to request these changes and downplaying the difficulties. He's positioning himself to step in when things go wrong. He must expect me to panic or to drop the ball on this.

My jaw tightens as I scroll through my inbox, but find no previous communications about these proposed changes. He never forwarded anything about the modifications he was discussing with my clients, knowing that springing them on me last minute would throw me off balance.

The temptation to stomp down the hall and confront Mark is strong, but I force myself to remain composed. I refuse to let his sabotage derail this project. I'll prove that I'm more than capable of working under pressure.

I crack my knuckles.

The water-management system needs a total overhaul: new calculations, new equipment, the works. All to keep some over-priced plants alive. My head throbs, but Carmichael Corp. isn't asking for my opinion; they're paying for results. And it's my job to deliver, no matter what unrealistic promises Mark made.

I sketch out a new design, integrating smart glass to manage sunlight—more performing than a simple glaze, and a more sophisticated irrigation system tied to rainwater and humidity recycling. It's not cheap, but it's the only way this atrium works. Hours slip by in a blur of research and sketches until the office is dark, and I'm the last one here.

By the time I finish the draft, exhaustion sets in, but so does satisfaction. This plan isn't just viable; it's a shot at meeting LEED standards despite the design revisions. More long nights await, but I've wrestled control back from Mark's sabotage.

This project isn't breaking me; if anything, it's making me sharper. Bring it on, Mark. I'm not going down without a fight. I close my laptop, stretching my arms overhead. My back aches, my brain hurts, and for the first time all day, I realize I haven't thought about Dylan once. Maybe after putting Mark in his place, I should send him a thank-you card.

26

DYLAN

On Monday night, I stand in front of Olivia's door, my heart pounding against my ribs. I stretch my neck and shoulders to loosen the tension coiled deep in the muscles.

You can do this, Dylan. Be kind but firm. Direct but not cruel. It's not her, it's you.

I repeat the words to myself like a mantra, to erase the memory of how it feels to be left on the outside, the sting of rejection. The thought of putting anyone through that is harrowing, but necessary.

I count to five. One of Olivia's neighbors walks by, eyeing me curiously.

"You okay, pal?"

"Yeah, yeah."

"Then why so nervous? Are you about to propose to the nice lady in 2B? She's a keeper."

I take in the bulky guy, wondering if he and Olivia are friends and if he'd beat me if he knew the real reason I'm here. "What? No, I... uh..." My tongue has turned into a wad of cotton in my mouth. Heat creeps up my neck as I fumble for words.

He gives me a mock military salute. "Don't sweat it, bro. Olivia is the nicest person I know."

I cringe while waving at him as if his words comforted me. As he passes on, I turn back to the door. Okay, it's now or never. I raise my fist and knock, my knuckles barely grazing the door before it flies open.

"Dylan." Olivia flings her arms around my neck, nearly knocking me off balance with the force of her hug. The cloying scent of her floral perfume floods my nose, too sweet and strong.

"Hey, Liv," I manage, my voice muffled against her shoulder.

"I'm so glad you came." She pulls back, her amber eyes shimmering. "Can we stay in tonight? I'm still too raw after this weekend."

"Sure, of course. Whatever you need." So much for being direct.

She leads me inside, her grip on my hand almost painful. "I'm barely holding myself together after... everything..."

"I'm sorry. Err... How close were you and Theo?"

"I told you, he was my best friend." She sniffles. "We grew up together; he's the only one I regretted leaving behind when I moved to New York. And now I'll never see him again. It's unbearable." She fluffs her hands in front of her face. "But Dylan, don't make me talk about him. It's too soon."

I nod, searching for the right words. "I didn't mean to upset you, only say again how sorry I am for your loss."

She hugs me. Her damp cheek presses against my collarbone, and guilt tightens around my chest like a vice, unrelenting and sharp. She looks up at me, her eyes glistening. "I'm so grateful to have you, Dylan. You're the only thing that kept me from falling apart this weekend."

Her voice quivers, and my resolve to extract myself from her life crumbles. I pat her back, my carefully rehearsed break-up speech evaporating. What kind of person would do this now, to someone in the middle of grieving? Even though I'm making a mess of this, I can't bring myself to beat her more while she's already down. To make her doubt her worth. I know how deep inadequacy stabs, and I wouldn't wish that sense of failure on my worst enemy.

Every word I rehearsed to let her down gently sounds callous. How can I break up with her now? It'd be like clubbing a baby seal on the head. I smile tightly. But I have to try; I'm making things worse by dragging on our relationship when it's going nowhere.

But as Olivia talks about her grief, my mind wanders to the worst-case scenarios of how this break-up could play out. Considering the dramatic state she was in last Monday, I imagine her sobbing on the floor, smashing picture frames, or throwing them at my head. Or worse, what if she interiorizes the rejection as her fault? I can't shake the memories of other people's reactions when I failed them. The anger, the disappointment, how small it left me, and I don't want Olivia to endure the same.

"...and our trip to the Hamptons next weekend is the only thing I'm looking forward to."

The silence that follows yanks me back to the present.

My stomach drops. The Hamptons? I'd completely forgotten about that. How can I possibly tell her I have no intention of taking her, that I've been meaning to end things with her for days?

She leads me to the couch, and I muster the courage to steer the conversation toward the inevitable. "Listen, Olivia, we need to talk..."

Her head jerks up, eyes wide, her face crumpling like I just told her the world is ending. "Oh no," she whispers, wringing her hands. "Did I do something? Have I been too much? Too emotional?" Her voice cracks as she folds her arms tightly across her chest. "I knew I was being too needy and now you want nothing to do with me."

"Liv, stop." I reach out, resting my hands gently on her shoulders. "You didn't do anything wrong, okay?"

She throws herself at me, hugging me tight. "Oh, thank goodness, for a moment there, I thought you were about to break up with me. I don't think I could've taken it."

"Liv." I pull her off me.

"Listen, Dylan, I want to be a supportive girlfriend and hear whatever it is that's troubling you. Hell knows you've been so closed off lately." So I'm being chastised on top of being shut down. "And I'd hate you feeling like you can't talk to me. But..." She glances up, her expression almost pleading. "...not tonight, okay? I'm holding on by a thread."

"But I—"

"No, please." She presses her hand against her chest, her fingers trembling. "I want to be here for you. I really do. But tonight, I just need to curl up on the couch and cuddle." She exhales hard, her shoulders slumping as she looks away. "I know I'm being selfish, but I can't deal with other people's problems on top of mine right now..." Before I can retort, she asks, "Have you ever lost someone?"

"Oh, uh, not really. My grandparents all died when I was too little to remember them. But if any of my relatives were to pass, I'd be destroyed."

"I hope it doesn't happen to you for many, many years because it's devastating. I still feel like my heart has been ripped out of my chest."

And my cold-blooded plan is to stomp on it and finish crashing it. I nod, my resolve weakening with each word out of her mouth. My entire strategy of being kind yet direct evaporates in the face of her grief. No way she'd believe the break-up isn't about her now. About something she did.

Olivia pulls me down onto the couch, and I sink into the plush cushions. It's ridiculously comfortable and should be pure heaven. But I'd rather be sharing that lumpy, ratty sofa at my parents' place with Hunter like we did this past weekend. I'd prefer the old guy even creaky and soggy on his last day over being trapped on the world's most comfortable couch with a girl-friend I don't want, wishing I was anywhere else.

As the night wears on, Olivia leans into me more and more, asking me to hold her, nestling closer until I have no idea where to put my arms. Her warmth presses against me, more suffocating than a hot summer night, sticky and cloying.

Every time I adjust to create some personal space, she moves in closer, pressing her cheek against my chest, making it impos-sible for me to shift away without being obvious. I can't stand the thought of being cruel to her, but it's killing me not to do what needs to be done. The compression is suffocating. An invisible hand is squeezing my lungs, each inhale shallow and forced as if the air is being sucked out instead of in.

When she corners me at the end of the couch, I'm being liter-ally and figuratively imprisoned, with no room to maneuver as she cuddles into me more insistently. The pressure builds until I can't take it anymore.

"I, uh, I need to use the bathroom," I say, disentangling myself from her clutches.

In the bathroom, I splash cold water on my face to calm myself. What am I doing? I can't keep leading her on. Enough is enough. I have to man up and tell her the truth. Once again resolved to put an end to this farce, I get out of the bathroom.

But when I return, Olivia is holding a small black box, a sad smile on her face. "I wanted you to have these—we made them in

Theo's name. All profits from the sales go to a shelter to honor his memory. We gave these to everyone at the funeral." Olivia's voice catches as she sets the box in my hands, her fingers trembling. "He would've loved it."

As soon as I take the box, Olivia's composure shatters. She presses the back of her hand to her mouth, but it does nothing to muffle the guttural sob that escapes her. "I—I can't talk about him without... without falling apart. Every time I think about him, I can't breathe." Her voice cracks, and she covers her face with her hands, shaking her head violently. "Gosh, I'm such a mess."

I guess, *How about we stop seeing each other?* is not a great segue. Acting like a half-decent human, I undo the velvet ribbon and open the box. Inside are two white socks with black writing. One says, *Step Into Healing.* The other, *Toe-tally Here For You.*

I force a smile and accept the socks gracefully, while inside, I'm wondering if anyone has ever drowned in kindness—or a load of crap because right now, I've toe-tally stepped into a massive pile of it.

In the week following the second failed break-up attempt, Olivia and I mostly talk on the phone. I ask to see her every single day, but she's never available. Her friends have embarked on a mission to cheer her up and take her out every night. Apparently, my hours are too long and if she'd have to wait for me to get off work, she'd just go home and cry herself silly on the couch. She prefers to hang out with her girlfriends.

Still, as we talk, she keeps pushing for the Hamptons trip, asking if we'll be spending the night, hinting at how it'd be the perfect occasion to take our relationship to the next level. Aka she wants to have sex. Looks like in her mind, the waiting period is over. Her timing couldn't be worse. I have no intention of taking her to Rowena's party, but I can't tell her over the phone or break up in a text. I panic instead and invent a commitment in the city on Sunday as an excuse not to spend the night at the resort where Adrian and Rowena are hosting their engagement party.

I tell her I'm volunteering at a summer soup kitchen. They're short on hands, and I committed months ago. If Theo used to volunteer—why else would socks profits go to a shelter?—she won't ask me to skip. And she doesn't. I also make her promise we'll see each other on Friday night, the day before the party, so I can break up with her before we even go. She promises. So at least there's that.

With the overnight-stay bullet dodged, I still sign up to serve meals to the homeless. If I'm going to lie, I might as well commit and actually go—cleanse my conscience with a good deed. But as I fill in the volunteer form, I don't feel any less lousy.

The rest of the week slips by in a haze of frustration and anxiety. In my darkest moments, I draft break-up texts in my head: short, direct, apologetic. But every time I get close to dictating one out, I feel like the world's biggest jerk. Who does that? Who breaks up with someone over text after their best friend just died? The thought makes me queasy, so I put my phone down and tell myself I'll handle it face to face. But then another day slips by, and I'm still stuck in this fucking limbo.

At home, I almost never see Hunter. It's strange, how the apartment is emptier without her—off balance. I wistfully glance at her closed door more often than I care to admit.

With her, I never know where we stand. Are we friends? Then why is she avoiding me?

When I bump into her late on Thursday night, she tells me

she's had a work emergency and is putting in crazy extra hours. She's wearing that exhausted smile that people put on when they're barely holding it together, and I'm sure she's telling the truth. She isn't using work as an excuse to avoid me.

"Hey, you okay?" I double-check, noticing she's pulled tighter than a bowstring. "You look like you could use a week of sleep."

"More like a month." She chuckles. "But it's nothing I can't handle. I'm in survival mode. I just have to make it another day, until my presentation tomorrow."

"Yeah, but even superheroes need a break." I walk toward the kitchen. "Tell you what, take a seat. I'll make you something to eat."

"You don't have to do that, Dylan. I'm fine," she insists, but appreciation flickers in her eyes.

"I know I don't have to feed you, but I want to. You're running on fumes, and it's late. Have you had dinner?"

"Does a protein bar count?"

"No. And a midnight snack won't kill either of us."

She sits down with a sigh. "I won't argue with food at this point. What's on the menu, chef?"

"Grilled cheese sandwich," I reply with a grin. "Classic comfort food."

As we sit in comfortable silence, the kitchen filled only with the crunchy noise of teeth biting into toasted bread, I appreciate the ease of this simple moment. No pressure to fill the air with words, no awkward pauses. Just two people, sharing a sandwich when it's dark outside. There's something so... effortless about it. The world outside of these walls doesn't matter anymore, and all the noise in my head quiets down. I'd take a hundred of these quiet, late-night snacks with Hunter over any elaborate plans.

She eats the sandwich like she is starving and I wonder if she also skipped lunch. I don't ask. I don't want to mother her; the last thing I need is for our interaction to become even more platonic. When she stands up and tells me goodnight, I linger in the hall, staring at her door for the longest time.

* * *

Then Friday arrives and tonight, things with Olivia will finally be over. I've barely let out a sigh of relief at the thought when my phone pings with a text from her. The phone's virtual assistant reads it aloud to me, in her robotic, neutral voice.

"Message from Olivia: Babe, please call me when you have a minute. It's about tonight, please don't be mad."

I stare at the phone, a sense of dread creeping up my spine. It might be nothing, but with the bad karma I've been accumulating lately, it could be anything from her asking about dinner plans to another emotional gut punch that'll leave me tongue-tied and trapped. I rub my forehead, a headache already brewing. Only one way to find out what she wants. I press the call button.

27

HUNTER

I stride into the office on Friday morning with a giant smile plastered on my face. No, it's not because Dylan made me a sandwich at midnight yesterday. Grilled cheese doesn't hold that kind of power over me, no matter how ooey-gooey and delicious—the food and the chef. It was a nice gesture, sure, but he's just a nice guy being nice.

Dylan wasn't beaming at me extra brightly or holding eye contact for more than a purely friendly interaction would suggest. Nope, that was all in my head and not at all the reason I can't stop smiling.

No, I'm this excited only because I'm about to absolutely crush it at work today. I've been busting my butt all week on these revisions for the North Shore project, determined to wow the client with my brilliant problem-solving skills. Mark with his scheming and backstabbing won't know what hit him. This is my moment to shine.

I waltz into the Carmichael Corp. meeting, my mind clear and extra-caffeinated. Mark and Daniel are already seated at the sleek, glass conference table; I nod in their direction and shake hands with all the top executives who have come to hear my pitch.

Squaring my shoulders, I launch into my presentation, outlining the smart glass system designed to regulate the atrium's temperature without compromising the aesthetic. "By utilizing this innovative technology," I explain, "we can significantly reduce heat gain while maintaining the visual impact of the space."

I detail the vertical garden's automated irrigation and the sustainable materials sourced for the interior finishes. Mark shifts in his seat, but I continue undeterred. This is my element.

I get to the burning heart of the matter: the added costs the new atrium design will incur. Daniel leans forward, his brow furrowed, as I break down the numbers. No one likes to tell clients they're going over budget. "While these modifications do come with an increased upfront investment," I acknowledge, "the long-term savings on energy and maintenance will more than justify the expense."

I click on my last slide, a 3D rendering of the reimagined atrium glowing with green life. "This is more than an office complex," I declare, meeting the clients' gazes with unwavering conviction. "This is a chance to set a new standard for sustainable architecture in the corporate world. With the North Shore project, Carmichael Corp. can cement its position as an industry leader and innovator."

As I finish, a charged silence fills the room. I stare around.

Mark looks equal parts impressed and irritated. No doubt he'd been hoping for a different outcome. Daniel seems proud. But it's the client's reaction that counts the most.

The executive at the opposite head of the table clears his throat, his tie askew. "Ms. Brolin, while we appreciate your... enthusiasm, these additional costs are not insignificant." He taps his fingers against the gleaming tabletop, a subtle tell of his hesitation.

I'm ready for the pushback. "I understand your concern," I reply, my tone even and assured. "But if I may, these changes were proposed by Carmichael Corp. to add a wow factor. Unfortunately, adding such a visual impact has a cost. Of course, the initial design is still perfectly viable and in line with your budget." I pause, letting my words sink in. "The final decision rests with you."

The executives exchange glances, a silent conversation passing between them. I stand my ground, projecting an air of calm confidence even as my heart pounds under my blazer.

The head executive nods, a slow smile spreading across his face. "Well, Ms. Brolin, you drive a hard bargain. But you've made a compelling case. We're on board with the revised design and budget."

Relief and elation flood through me, but I keep my expression composed as we shake hands and exchange pleasantries until the executives from Carmichael Corp. leave the conference room.

Daniel and Mark linger behind, and I glimpse Mark's face. His earlier mocking pout has been replaced by a look of begrudging respect, tinged with a hint of surprise. A surge of satisfaction curses through me at proving him wrong.

Daniel approaches me, a satisfied grin on his face. "Hunter, that was outstanding work." His handshake is steady and slightly lingering as if he wants to reinforce the weight of his words. "You've shown incredible promise since you joined the firm, but this... this was next level."

The way he holds my gaze, resolute, yet warm, makes me realize he's finally seeing me as an equal. "Thank you, Daniel." I manage to keep my voice steady. "I'm glad we could find a solution that works for everyone."

"It's more than that," he insists. "The way you handled the client's concerns, how you made them see the value in the extra costs... I've never seen a junior engineer with that kind of finesse. Keep up the excellent work." He gives me a rare, almost fatherly nod before heading out.

As the door clicks shut after Daniel steps out, the atmosphere in the room shifts. Mark remains seated, his posture stiff, as if bracing for a confrontation.

The faint ticking of the wall clock punctuates the quiet until I speak up. "I know what you've been doing, Mark." Despite my simmering anger, my voice is calm and even—professional. "Working behind my back to sabotage the project."

He doesn't flinch, nor deny it. Instead, he links his fingers over his chest, a sneer curling his lips. "I'll admit, I didn't think you could handle the pressure." His tone drips with condescension. "But you proved me wrong. You showed you have balls."

I bristle at the backhanded compliment. "I shouldn't have to prove I have balls just because I lack a physical sack," I retort, my words sharp. "My competence has nothing to do with my gender."

Mark holds up his hands in mock surrender. "Hey, I'm giving credit where it's due. You solved the problem and got the client on board. That takes grit."

I lean forward, my eyes locked on his. "Let's get one thing clear. If you ever interfere with my work again, I won't be as gracious. I'll go straight to Daniel, and we'll see how much he appreciates your games."

For once, Mark is speechless. He stares at me, his jaw clenched, but says nothing.

I stand, smoothing my skirt. "Glad we understand each other." My tone is sweet, but my smile is razor-sharp.

As I walk out of the conference room, satisfaction and relief flood my system. This wasn't about impressing Daniel or the client; it was about showing myself what I'm capable of. I can handle anything this job throws at me, even a dirtbag supervisor like Mark.

On the way back to my office, I run into Clara, her face lit up like a Christmas tree. "Hunter," she exclaims, bouncing on her toes. "I heard about the meeting. You crushed it."

I grin, her enthusiasm infectious. "Wow, news travels fast, huh?"

"Are you kidding? Daniel's been singing your praises to anyone who'll listen. You're the office star."

I brush the compliment off. "It was nothing, just doing my job."

"Don't be modest. You're on fire, girl."

We fall into step together, and Clara's expression turns conspiratorial. "Speaking of being on fire, how's your dating life? Any good suitors?"

I grimace, the memory of countless terrible dates flashing through my mind. "Ugh, don't even ask. It's been a total disaster. I'm calling it quits, a failed mission."

Clara pats my arm sympathetically. "But you can't give up. You need a break, that's all. Hey, why don't we go out for drinks tonight? Celebrate your big win us gals, no guys involved?"

I hesitate, wondering if by saying yes, I'm giving up another grilled cheese sandwich. Then, I remember it's Friday night and Dylan will have plans with Olivia. The thought of going home to a quiet apartment and obsessing over him again while he's with her is unbearable.

"You know what? That sounds perfect." I grin at Clara. "Let's do it."

* * *

Hours later, I stumble down the hall of my floor, the world tilting pleasantly around me. The celebratory drink with Clara turned into several cocktails, the alcohol flowing a little too freely as we toasted my success. To be honest, I was simultaneously celebrating while also drowning my sorrows.

As I reach my door, I fumble with my keys, failing to slot them into the lock. They jangle loudly in the hallway's quiet.

I have to recalibrate my aim a few times before I succeed in opening the door. I wobble into the darkened apartment, unsteady on my heels. The room spins. I grope for the light switch, missing it twice before finally illuminating the space. The sudden brightness makes me squint, and I lose my balance, crashing sideways into the entrance console. It wobbles precariously, rattling.

"Shh," I hush it, pinballing over to the other wall and making even more noise.

I cringe, hoping I haven't woken Dylan.

"Hunter? Is that you?"

No such luck. Dylan's voice floats down the hallway, husky with sleep. He appears deliciously rumpled in a pair of basketball shorts and a T-shirt. His blond hair is mussed, and his dreamy eyes are half-amused, half-narrowed as he takes in my inebriated state.

"Hey, Dylan." I sway on my feet. "Sorry, did I wake you?"

"Nah, I was just heading to bed now." He chuckles, studying me. "You had a good night?"

I nod, instantly regretting the motion as the floor wobbles underneath me. "Yeah, celebrating a win at work. Maybe celebrated a little too hard."

Dylan's smile softens, his eyes warm as they meet mine. "The big project you were telling me about last night?"

"The one."

As I fight with the strap of my messenger bag to pull it over my head, I take in Dylan's face breaking into the brightest, goofiest smile.

"Congratulations, Brolin, you deserve it."

I go warm in several places, my alcohol-addled brain latching onto the way he called me by my surname as if he'd said babe.

Dylan takes a step closer, his hand reaching out to free me from the damn strap. He pulls it gently over my head and steadies me as I wobble again.

"Need help getting to bed?"

I laugh, the sound echoing in the quiet apartment. "You're so nice, Dylan. Like, the nicest guy ever."

"Thank you." Dylan grins, guiding me down the hallway toward my bedroom.

"Seriously, the nicest."

"Yeah, you mentioned," he teases, his hand warm on the small of my back.

We make it to my room, and I fall onto the bed, the world still spinning pleasantly. I'm struggling with my sandals, to kick them off; the thin straps are conspiring against me.

He watches me, amusement dancing in his eyes. "Does being nice include helping you with your shoes? Or is that crossing a line?"

I giggle. "Yes. Nice people help with shoes. It's in the rules of niceness."

Dylan's warm and rich laugh pulls my focus entirely to him as he kneels down, gently removing my shoes and setting them aside. His fingers barely brush my skin, but my head starts to spin faster.

As he stands back up, I throw my arms out wide and let myself fall backward onto the bed, grinning up at him. "Is this the part where you tuck me in and tell me a bedtime story?"

"A bedtime story?" Dylan smiles as he pulls a blanket over me. "Any requests?" he asks sarcastically.

"The one where he ditches the perfect princess and marries the nerd instead," I mumble, my eyes already drooping.

Dylan chuckles, his hand brushing my hair back from my face.

"I'm not sure I know that one."

"Of course you don't."

"And you might be too tired for a story, anyway."

I hum in agreement, sleep already pulling me under. "Yeah, I'm tireddddd..."

The last thing I'm aware of is the gentle click of the door as Dylan leaves.

And then I'm dreaming, lost in a world where nice guys help with shoes and tuck you in at night, and everything is warm and safe and perfect.

28

HUNTER

The next morning, I cringe before I even open my eyes, my head pounding like a jackhammer. But the physical pain is nothing compared to the emotional gut punch as hazy memories of last night flood back. Groaning, I press my face into the pillow.

What the hell did I blabber to Dylan? Something about him being the nicest nice guy, and then... a princess and a nerd? Oh gosh.

I made a complete fool of myself. My skull throbs in agreement, the beginnings of a hangover taking root. Not the look I was going for on a day I'll have to spend next to Olivia the Perfect. She probably sleeps a full twelve hours, wakes up humming a tune that makes flowers bloom, and has mice dressing her.

Meanwhile, my morning breath could qualify as an environmental disaster, a noxious cloud capable of wiping out entire ecosystems. I run my tongue over fuzzy teeth and wince. Did I even brush them last night? That I can't remember the answer is significant enough.

With a sigh, I crack one eye open, immediately assaulted by the too-bright sun streaming through the blinds. Coffee. I need coffee. But that would require me to show my face in the apartment and face Dylan.

If I hide long enough, he'll leave to go pick up Olivia, and I won't have to see them until the engagement party. I'm supposed to catch a separate ride with Nina and Tristan, anyway. Problem solved.

I've barely finished the thought when a knock sounds at my door. I freeze. Keep quiet and pretend I'm still asleep or woman up and face the music?

"Hunt? You okay?" Dylan's muffled voice filters through.

My stomach somersaults, but I manage a strangled, "Yeah, I'm good." I overcompensate, sounding too cheery to be believable. But I don't want him to worry on top of having had to put me to bed like a child. I try again, aiming for casual. "Just waking up."

"Mind if I come in for a second?"

I hum an affirmative, not trusting my voice. The door cracks open and Dylan leans against the threshold, all tousled blond hair and broad shoulders. A modern-day Prince Charming wrapped in a Greek god's body.

His eyes scan my face with a hint of amusement. "How's the head?"

I tug the comforter higher, realizing I'm still in yesterday's clothes. The fluffy barrier is my last line of defense, a plush fortress protecting me.

"I've had better mornings," I admit, trying for a wry smile. "What time is it?"

"Just past eleven, sleepyhead."

"Whoops, guess I'm living that rockstar lifestyle finally."

"What do rockstars prefer to cure a hangover? Greasy breakfast or painkillers?"

"Can you add a time machine to that list?"

"Unfortunately not, but I can throw in some bacon."

Fatty food and a cocktail of painkillers both sound like salvation, but the promise of crispy bacon wins out. "I'm sold. Breakfast, please."

Dylan nods, a smile playing at the corners of his mouth. "Coming right up. I'll get cooking."

He disappears down the hall, and I wait until I hear the clatter of pans before making my walk of shame to the bathroom. I crank the shower as hot as it'll go, letting the scorching spray wash away the remnants of last night's poor choices.

By the time I pad into the kitchen, hair still damp and wearing my favorite oversized comfort shirt, the room is filled with the most heavenly aroma. Sizzling bacon, melted butter, the earthy scent of scrambled eggs. Even the coffee smells richer than usual, more robust.

Dylan glances over his shoulder, pausing mid-scramble. For a split second, his smile falters, a glitch in his easy-going demeanor. But it's back in a flash as he gestures to the table with the spatula.

"Perfect timing. Breakfast is served."

He slides a plate in front of me, piled high with crispy bacon, fluffy scrambled eggs, and a buttered roll oozing with melted cheese. A steaming mug of coffee appears next, and I wrap my hands around it gratefully.

"You're a lifesaver." I inhale the rich aroma. "Thanks for this."

Dylan smirks as he settles across from me with his own plate. "Just carrying out my nice-guy duties."

I shoot him a mock glare. "Okay, now you're being mean."

"If I were being mean, there wouldn't be coffee."

"That's more survival instinct. I'm a terror without caffeine."

"Good to know coffee keeps you from becoming a supervillain."

There's no point fighting my smile. He might be taken, off-limits, but I still desperately long for him. This effortless morning banter is how I had imagined us falling in love before he moved in. Before I knew about Olivia. But I need to remind myself I'm not the one he's taking to the ball tonight, so I change topics.

"What's the plan for today?" I take a sip of coffee. "Do you know what time Nina and Tristan are coming to pick me up? How much time do I have to re-transform into a human being?"

Dylan's fork pauses halfway to his mouth. He sets it down, flashing me a lopsided, almost apologetic smile. "There's been a slight change of plan. You'll be riding with me."

The coffee mug nearly flies out of my hands as I choke on a sip, coughing as horror slams into me like a wrecking ball. Oh, hell no. Being stuck in the back seat while Dylan and his girl-friend make googly eyes at each other in the front for two hours? Playing the literal third wheel? Fuck, no.

"Alright?" Dylan frowns.

I wave him off, to catch my breath. "Fine, just... went down the wrong pipe."

As the initial shock of the awful driving arrangements settles, I rack my brain to find a way out of it. How can I decline without revealing why I don't want to go with him and Olivia?

Why did Nina cancel my ride? How could she do that to me? Well, probably because she isn't aware of the consequences. I've never confessed my true feelings for her brother to my best friend. And now I'm paying the price.

"Oh, um..." I keep my tone casual as I push my eggs around the plate. "Wouldn't Olivia prefer to have you all to herself? You know, quality couple time and all that?"

Dylan's brow furrows, and he hesitates before answering. "Olivia went to the Hamptons yesterday. She skipped work and her friends whisked her away for a long weekend." He says it with a grimace of regret as if spending a night apart from her left a gaping void in his world. *Gah.* "She's staying at their house for the weekend. She'll meet me at the party."

Another emotion I can't decipher flickers across his face—it's almost pain. But it's gone before I can analyze it further, but it leaves me unsettled. Is he holding something back? What?

"Oh." I blink, processing this new information. "Why aren't we all going together in one car, then?"

Dylan bounces his knees under the table, looking sheepish. "Well, I won't be staying the night at the resort. I signed up to volunteer at a soup kitchen on Sunday a while ago. I need to head back to the city after the party."

Of course he did. Cue the mental image of him feeding the homeless while looking like a real-life fairytale prince. Dylan, with all the charm of a storybook hero, ladling out steaming bowls of soup to the less fortunate, the picture of human perfection.

It is such a pity I am not the heroine in this story.

But at least the engagement party won't turn into a romantic Hamptons getaway for Dylan and Olivia. No moonlit walks on the beach for them. Or hot hotel sex.

Not that being back in New York will stop them from copulating. Maybe they'll do it in our apartment even—*cringe.*

All of a sudden, the idea of them having sex in the city doesn't sound much better than them doing it in the Hamptons. I'm not sure what's worse, but at least I won't be here to hear it. I definitely prefer their sexcapades to happen in a different zip code from where I'm sleeping.

29

DYLAN

The miles blur by in a shimmer of asphalt and sun haze as I coast along the highway toward the Hamptons, the summer heat radiating from the pavement. I shift gear, my fitted jacket pulling at my shoulders. Since I won't be staying at the resort tonight, I'm already dressed for the party.

Next to me, Hunter looks more comfortable. With a room booked for later, she's still in casual attire and will get changed at the hotel. Not that simple clothes make her any less appealing. My eyes dart briefly to her legs. To the pair of light-wash, ripped jean shorty-shorts that show too much skin to be good for my sanity, paired with a plain white V-neck T-shirt tucked loosely at the front.

No matter how resolutely I vow to keep my eyes on the road, at every stop, my gaze drifts toward her. To those mile-long legs that are lightly tanned, the denim frayed right to show off flawless, sun-kissed skin that catches the light, making me grip the steering wheel tighter. Her dark hair, now dry, tumbles down her shoulders, wild and un-styled—how I prefer it.

She kicks her shoes off, tucking her feet underneath her thighs on the seat.

"What is with this traffic? Aren't all the rich people supposed to go to the Hamptons in their private helicopters?"

"Adrian could have arranged helicopter rides for all the guests. Would you have preferred that?"

I peek sideways, and our eyes lock. Hunter looks away first.

"Nah, then we'd miss the thrill of being stuck behind this minivan going ten under the speed limit."

She says it with such a straight face, I laugh.

Hunter pulls her hair up into a messy bun, twisting it absently as she stares out the window. Now her long, lean neck is exposed, the stretch of smooth skin daring me to take a bite.

The motion also sends a faint citrusy smell my way that mingles with the scent of the car's cool leather. I breathe in her perfume, reminded of last night. Drunk Hunter was a perfect, chaotic whirlwind. Beautiful even while unsteady on her feet, slurring words, and rambling about how I was the "nicest guy" as I helped her into bed.

As I concentrate on the road ahead, I wonder if "nice" is what women want. Nice guys finish last, right? It's the bad boys who always get the girl. Suddenly, the title of "nice guy" is less a badge of honor and more a consolation prize. Kinda makes me the biggest loser. X TRuE

But then Hunter's bedtime story request from last night drifts back to me: *The one where he ditches the perfect princess and marries the nerd instead.* It sounded like a joke, something she threw out without much thought, especially after a few cocktails. But the more I replay it in my head, the more it feels like there was a hidden message buried under the alcohol haze.

Was it just another one of her offbeat comments, or was she

trying to tell me something? And why the hell does it keep looping in my brain? *She was trying to tell you something*

When she said the prince should ditch the princess. She didn't mean me and Olivia... did she? I shake my head, gripping the steering wheel tighter as the minivan in front of me slows down even more.

There's no way Hunter sees herself as the nerd of the story. She's about as far from nerdy as you can get. She's magnetic, sharp, and a hell of a lot sexier than she realizes. But if she did mean herself... then what does that make me? The prince stuck with the wrong girl? The nice guy fumbling around, trying to figure out who he's supposed to end up with?

Needing a distraction from the idea I might be the clueless prince in her narrative, or worse, not be her type, I suggest, "Hey, how about we play a game of 'would you rather' to pass the time?"

"Oh, fun." Hunter's eyes light up. "Okay, I'll go first. Would you rather have to sing everything you say or dance everywhere you go?"

Without missing a beat, I break into a falsetto, my voice playfully off-key. "I'd rather siiing my words than dance."

Hunter's bubbly laugh fills the car as she admits, "I'd choose to dance everywhere. At least I could keep it subtle."

"I'd love to see that." I grin, enjoying the lightness between us. "Alright, my turn. Would you rather be able to read minds but only hear negative thoughts, or teleport but only to places you don't want to go?"

She purses her lips, considering. "Hmm, I'd pick reading minds. Sure, negative thoughts might sting, but at least I'd know who to avoid."

"Good point," I agree, nodding. "Imagine you blink and you're in an airport security line on a holiday weekend. Or worse, you end up at the DMV during lunch hour."

"Aww. That's sadistic of you, Thompson." Hunter shifts to face me more fully, her seatbelt tugging across her chest. "Okay, next question. Would you rather live without coffee or never eat pizza again?"

I glance at her in mock horror. "Give up pizza? No way. Coffee keeps me functioning, but pizza... pizza is life. It keeps me happy."

"Guess you could convert to tea or drink a lot of sodas."

"Pizza makes you thirsty so that'd be perfect. Alright." I click my tongue. "Would you rather be stuck in traffic for two hours every day or have slow internet?"

Hunter's head falls back against the headrest as she thinks hard. "Ugh, traffic, I guess. I could listen to music or podcasts while I'm stuck. Slow internet would make me lose my mind."

We riff off each other, laughter filling the car as we toss around one ridiculous answer after another, until Hunter's tone shifts, her voice taking on a thoughtful edge as she asks, "Would you rather be happy or make someone else happy?"

Her gaze on the side of my face is a lick of flame.

The question hits a bit too close to home with my current situation with Olivia. "Oh, you know me, always the people pleaser. It's a terrible flaw."

My thoughts tangle like vines. Putting Olivia's temporary happiness before mine is what I've done so far. Choosing her well-being while she recovers from her grief. But now with Olivia, the relationship, the missed break-ups—I'm caught in a maze with no way out. Suffocating, like a shirt that's two sizes too small.

"But I guess you can't make someone else happy unless they're already happy themselves, you know?"

"Are you—are you happy?" Hunter asks, not looking at me.

How do I even answer that? *I am happy now, yes, because even if I'm stuck in traffic wearing uncomfortable clothes with a million degrees outside, I'm with you playing a silly game and suddenly, all my problems are miles away.*

"Miss Brolin, I'm afraid that inquiry violates the game's rules, and it's my turn, anyway." If she's wondering why I'm side-stepping the topic, she says nothing, and before she asks, I blurt out the first silly question that pops into my head. "Would you rather have Cheeto dust permanently on your fingers or cheese breath for the rest of your life?"

Hunter scrunches her nose, considering. "Cheeto dust."

"But you could cure the cheese breath with mints," I argue, grinning.

She gasps in mock outrage. "And you talk about rules. Terrible would-you-rather conditions are incurable, Dylan. In-cur-a-ble."

We share another two seconds of solid eye contact and then both burst out laughing.

As our laughter fades, a contemplative silence settles between us. I glance over, catching the way Hunter's gaze lingers on the passing scenery, her thoughts still tangled in something deeper.

She sighs, the sound barely audible over the honking of a nearby car whose driver must've had enough of the weekend jam. "Maybe relationships are like Cheetos. Messy, addictive, and they stain everything."

A quiet heaviness weaves into her words, a thread of something real and raw. It catches me off guard. A strange, tight pressure builds in my chest, and my ribs are suddenly too small for my lungs.

I want to tell her, to beg her to please stain everything I own with her light. But the words stick in my throat, trapped by the unfinished situation with Olivia.

I keep quiet, gaze ahead, and promise myself that I'll sort things out today. Because Hunter deserves more than my silence. And so do I.

* * *

The resort comes into view, a sprawling cluster of white buildings nestled against a backdrop of lush green and sand dunes. I pull up to the drop-off area, and the crunch of gravel beneath the tires echoes the sudden tightness in my chest.

Hunter gathers her things, shooting me a smile that's equal parts soft and uncertain as she opens the passenger door. "Thanks for the ride, Dylan. I'll see you later?"

"Yeah, definitely." I nod, attempting a reassuring grin even as my stomach turns hot and uneasy.

She steps out, the late-afternoon sun framing her figure, the breeze teasing strands of her dark hair across her face. She tucks them behind her ear and gives me a small, almost shy wave before heading inside.

I watch her go, the ache in my chest swelling, something painfully close to homesickness. This is it. No more excuses, no more delays. It's time to end things with Olivia, cleanly and honestly.

Resolved, I slide back into the driver's seat, ready to make a U-turn. But before I put the car into gear, my phone rings, Olivia's name flashing across the screen.

I frown, a sense of unease prickling along my spine as I accept the call through the car's Bluetooth. "Hey, Olivia. I was about to call you—"

"Where are you?"

"In Southampton. I was just dropping off my roommate at the resort and I'm driving to you next—"

"No, don't come back here," she cuts me off breezily. "The girls are giving me a lift. I'll be there in ten minutes tops."

"You're... on your way?" I try to keep the rising panic out of my voice.

"Yep. You can wait for me at the hotel."

"Are you sure you don't want me to pick you up."

"No, I'm on the road already. See you soon."

The line goes dead, the echo of her abrupt goodbye ringing in my ears. I stare at the dashboard, my plans crumbling around me again like a sandcastle against the tide.

With a sigh of resignation, I pull into a parking spot, killing the engine as I glance at the clock. If I move fast, I can still solve things. Break up with Olivia before the party starts, drop her back at her friends' place, and return before anyone notices I'm gone.

I'll be cutting it close, but it could work. And even if I'm a few minutes late, no one will care.

I climb out of the car, leaning against the sun-warmed metal as I wait. I've never smoked in my life, not even pot—bad for athletics. But if I ever saw myself lighting up a cigarette, this would be the time.

The rumble of an approaching engine pulls me from my thoughts as an open-top Jeep filled with chattering women swerves into the lot. Olivia and her friends.

My stomach sinks as they pull over, their laughter and excited chatter filling the air. This is it. The moment of truth.

I square my shoulders as Olivia spills out of the Jeep in a pastel sky-blue silk dress that floats around her legs. Her hair, sleek and glossy, catches the warm glow of the afternoon sun. She's a vision, her skin luminous under a shimmer of makeup, every inch the perfect, polished girlfriend.

She's objectively stunning. Dressed to impress. Any guy would be lucky to have her. Yet my heart doesn't so much as thump. Instead, a hollow disconnect settles inside me, an emptiness where excitement should be. It's a stark contrast to the way thinking about Hunter in her simple jeans and white tee sets a jackhammer loose in my chest.

Olivia waves to her friends, a bright smile lighting up her face as she hurries toward me. She leans in for a kiss, her lips landing against my cheek as I turn at the last second.

If she's offput by the gesture, she doesn't show it. She smiles brightly instead.

"I've been looking forward to this party all week," she gushes, eyes sparkling. "I spent all of today getting ready. Hair, nails, makeup, the works. I can't wait for a fun, silly night to get my mind off everything..."

She doesn't mention Theo by name, but her pretty mouth turns down at the corners, her lower lip wobbling. My stomach twists with guilt, but I need to break up with her. Only my tongue refuses to collaborate and becomes as heavy as lead. I try to imagine how I'd feel if the roles were reversed, spending all day primping for a date to get dumped on arrival. It'd be awful. Cruel, even.

But stringing her along to break it off *after* the party? That'd be worse.

I should do it now. (You should)

Come on, Dylan. Ignore her sadness. Tell her it's over. Do it. Just do it. You don't care if she's spent the day getting dolled up for you. Or if she's looking forward to tonight. And that she thinks you're ready to take the next step. Hand her a box of break-up socks with "You Deserve Someone Better" *written on the side and you'll be good.*

"Olivia, I've wanted to talk to you all week, and this is probably the worst moment, but can we take a moment before going in?"

"Oh, Dylan, you're so sweet. But don't worry." She cups my cheek. "You don't have to apologize."

I frown. Apologize for fucking what?

Before I even ask, she tells me. "I know you feel bad about not spending the night. That after everything I've been through, you wanted to give me a special weekend."

I so did not. *Just Dump Her She's g her Rock*

"But there'll be another chance." She grabs both my hands now as she stares into my eyes adoringly. Then she quickly stamps a kiss on my lips and pulls back. "But please let's go inside now because I only had a quick brunch before the spa appointment and I'm starving. I hope the hors d'oeuvres are already out."

Without leaving me room to reply, she turns on her heel and heads toward the resort.

I watch her go, wiping the sticky lip gloss from my mouth with the back of my hand and wondering if being the butt of every cosmic joke comes with a pair of socks that says, *On My Last Toe.*

30

HUNTER

I stand before the full-length mirror, scrutinizing my reflection. The simple, sleeveless sundress I've chosen for Rowena and Adrian's engagement party hugs my body, the thin fabric caressing my skin in the warm, summer breeze that drifts through the open window of my hotel room, carrying with it the saltiness of the ocean. I smooth my hands over the modest dress, second-guessing my decision to be understated. Perhaps I should have opted for something more eye-catching, more dramatic. A dress that would make Dylan's head turn. *You'll make his head turn anyway.*

No, I chide myself. Today is not about me or Dylan. It's a celebration of Rowena and Adrian. Even if their engagement is a ruse, I need to focus on being present for my friend, not on the tangled undercurrents of my emotions.

A bitter sting cuts my belly in half at the thought of seeing Dylan with Olivia, their togetherness a stark reminder of what I've lost—of what I never even had. Of what could have been, if they hadn't met a few days before he moved in with me.

I put a lid on the storm brewing in my chest. I can't change the past, but I can be there for Rowena today.

Grabbing my clutch, I exit my room and make my way through the hotel.

As I step into the garden where the engagement party is being held, I'm enveloped by the festive atmosphere. Out here, the mineral tang of the ocean breeze mixes with the fragrance of blooming flowers. The space is alive with the murmur of conversations and the melodious tinkle of champagne flutes being clinked together in toasts.

Rowena said Adrian had hired a planner for the event, but wow. I wasn't expecting this. The setting is breathtaking. Rows of pristine white tables are adorned with cascading bouquets, their delicate petals fluttering in the gentle wind. Beyond the garden, the ocean stretches out to the horizon, its turquoise waters sparkling in the sunlight. The sand dunes provide a picturesque backdrop, their golden hues a perfect complement to the clear blue sky.

Despite the beauty surrounding me, I can't shake the sensation of being out of place. The other guests are impeccably dressed, their attires far more glamorous than my simple sundress. I tug self-consciously at the hem, wishing I had chosen something more sophisticated.

My unease twists into icy dread when I spot Olivia entering the garden, Dylan by her side. She looks every bit as radiant as I feared she would, her sleek pale-blue dress floating behind her like she's Cinderella at the ball—minus the puffed-up skirt and sleeves. The fabric shimmers in the sunlight, casting a halo effect around her. Her golden hair falls in perfect waves, and her makeup is flawless, accentuating her natural beauty.

In comparison, I blend into the background, plain and unremarkable. Watching them make their way through the crowd, arms linked, is torture. But I can't look away. I trail their progress across the lawn until they disappear behind the bar.

*Do not worry about Olivia he doesn't
Love her NEVER DID

Desperate for a distraction, I scan the lawn to find Nina and Tristan. Relief washes over me at the sight of their familiar faces, and I hurry toward them, determined to pretend that Dylan and Olivia don't exist.

"Hunter." Nina pulls me into a hug. "You're gorgeous, babe."

I force a smile, ignoring the voice in my head that whispers the opposite. "Thanks, hon. You look amazing, too."

Nina beams, her eyes sparkling with joy as she leans into Tristan's side. He wraps an arm around her waist, pulling her close, and I can't stop a pang of envy at witnessing their easy affection.

I push the unkind feelings aside, reminding myself that today is about celebrating love, even if it's not my own. I plaster a smile on my face, determined to enjoy the party and not spoil anything for Rowena.

That becomes easier said than done when Dylan and Olivia reappear in my peripheral. She laughs at something he says, the sound so perfectly melodic, birds might harmonize in response.

They navigate through the crowd, heading straight toward us, and panic rises in my throat. I duck behind Nina as if her petite frame could shield me from this impending interaction, but it's too late. Dylan spots his sister and smiles, his grin widening as his eyes land on me, hiding behind Nina's skirt like a child.

I force myself to meet his gaze, even as the surrounding air thickens, amplifying my discomfort.

"Hey." He tilts his head.

I step out from behind Nina, smoothing my dress and trying to hold myself together. "Hey."

The fun ease I felt in the car with him a short hour ago now has traveled a galaxy away.

Olivia turns to me, her smile dazzling and her amber eyes

kind. "Hunter, it's wonderful to see you again. I'm sorry for my dramatic exit the other night; I didn't mean to be rude."

I nod, mumbling a half-greeting, half-apology in return, unable to match her enthusiasm. Rowena joins us shortly afterward, and Dylan promptly introduces his girlfriend.

Olivia steps forward, her movements graceful and poised. "Congratulations," she gushes, her eyes sweeping over Rowena. "You look stunning. That dress is divine."

Rowena beams, accepting the compliment with a polite smile.

Adrian arrives next, looking a bit like an overeager puppy dog as he slides by Rowena's side. He greets us and introduces himself to Olivia.

I guess *Livvie* is now officially part of our group. *I want to die.*

As the small talk continues, I do my best to fade into the background, to become an invisible spectator to their effortless interactions. Rowena catches my eye, her gaze probing, as if to gauge my reaction to seeing Dylan with Olivia.

I avert my eyes, wondering if my friends have picked up on my carefully guarded secret.

Too soon, Adrian whisks Rowena away to greet other guests, leaving me stranded again with Nina, Tristan, Dylan, and Olivia.

I search my surroundings for an escape route. The garden buzzes with energy as servers glide by, offering champagne flutes and canapés to the well-dressed crowd. Getting a little buzzed could be a way out of my current misery. But after last night's overindulgence, the mere thought of alcohol makes my stomach churn. I concentrate on the food instead, plucking a tiny quiche from a passing tray.

If I keep my mouth full, I won't have to join in the conversation and interact with the happy couple. I resort to tracking every move they make. How Dylan grabs a glass of champagne for her.

The way Olivia's hand brushes against his arm, a casual touch that screams intimacy. From that innocent gesture, my mind spirals, conjuring images of them together in private moments, their bodies intertwined, skin against skin. The jealousy that courses through me is toxic, a poison that threatens to consume me from the inside out.

I can't stand it anymore. I have to escape, to put some distance between myself and them.

"Excuse me," I mumble. "I need to make a quick call."

It's a lame pretext, and I don't wait for a response. I turn on my heel and walk away, not sure where I'm going. Anywhere is better than here.

As the evening progresses, I drift through the party like a ghost, keeping my distance from Dylan and Olivia. But no matter where I go, they are everywhere.

At sunset, the speeches begin, and I welcome the distraction, listening as Adrian talks about how lucky he feels to have Rowena in his life. His voice is steady, filled with a sincerity that surprises me, even though I know the engagement is a sham. Rowena joins Adrian on stage and, seemingly overwhelmed with emotion, she grabs the microphone and simply says, "What he just said."

The crowd bursts into applause, while I wonder if they're still faking it. I see the way Rowena looks at Adrian as if a switch has been flipped. Maybe love can sneak up on you like that when you least expect it. (PROBABLY NEVER REALLY BEEN IN LOVE I'VE LIKED GIRLS BEEN IN LUST)

Then the crowd chants for a kiss, and I lean toward the stage, waiting to see what they'll do. Rowena hesitates, but then she gives Adrian a tiny nod. He leans in and presses his lips to hers, and the cheer that arises around them is deafening.

I watch, frozen, as they kiss again, this time with more urgency, more fire. Something twists inside me—a mix of hope, jealousy, longing, and despair. Even though this isn't real for them, it looks authentic enough. If that's fake kissing, I'd take a fake kiss with Dylan any day.

After the speeches, dinner is announced, and the guests gather at the elegantly set tables indoors. I end up seated next to Dylan and Olivia, because of course. When it rains, it pours. *THAT'S LIFE*

The food is exquisite—a spread of gourmet dishes that would normally have my mouth watering—but tonight, I hardly focus on my plate.

The conversation flows around me. I attempt to engage, but all I want to do is escape someplace where I can breathe again.

By the time dessert is served, I'm emotionally spent, each interaction chipping away at my soul. The sweetness of the cake tastes cruel against the bitterness gnawing inside me.

I try to shake off the heaviness as the band starts to play. Guests drift toward the dance floor, and I debate whether to join them or sneak away. My decision is made for me when Nina appears by my side, linking our arms and pulling me onto the floor.

"Come on, Hunt." She grins. "Nobody puts Baby in a corner."

We sway together to the music, laughing and spinning, and for a few brief spins, I forget about everything else. But then Dylan and Olivia join us, and it all comes rushing back.

He catches my eye, and for a second, I see something in his expression—self-consciousness? Regret? But it's gone as quickly as it came, replaced by his usual serene smile as he twirls Olivia around.

By the time the evening winds down, I'm even more drained. I watch from the sidelines as Olivia rests her head on Dylan's shoulder, and the weight of everything becomes unbearable.

When the fireworks start, I slip away quietly, finding a secluded spot by the beach to catch the show from a distance.

Lights explode above us, and everyone else oohs and ahhs, but I feel numb.

The sky erupts into vibrant reds and golds, the colors offensively happy. I close my eyes, letting the sound of the waves wash over me and imagining a different ending to this night. One where it's me in Dylan's arms, me he's looking at with that smile that makes my heart thud.

But when I open my eyes, I'm still alone, and the fairytale fades away, leaving only the bitter truth in its wake.

31

DYLAN

I'LL BET YOU DO NOT

The night air hangs heavy with humidity, pressing against my skin like a damp cloth. Fireworks explode overhead, bursts of color illuminating Olivia's profile as she tilts her head to the sky. I've positioned us at the fringes of the crowd, preparing for the inevitable. As soon as the show ends, I'm ending our relationship.

Olivia sighs, her voice wistful. "Fireworks always remind me of Theo. He loved them so much. Isn't that weird?"

"Why? Most people love fireworks, don't they?" I hum noncommittally, determined not to get sidetracked again. No matter how many times she mentions Theo tonight, my heart is fortified, encased in steel. I won't let her sadness soften me, not this time. We are over.

Another firework bursts overhead, bathing us in electric-blue light. Olivia keeps her gaze fixed upward. "Yes, most people love fireworks. But dogs usually hate them, you know? They get scared and have to be kept inside." A faint, wistful smile curls her lips. "Not Theo, though. He used to run around the backyard barking at them, tail wagging a mile a minute. Pure joy."

I blink, certain I've misheard. "You mean, Theo is... *a dog*?"

The question comes out sharper than intended, my voice cracking in surprise.

Olivia turns to me, eyebrows raised. Her expression shifts from curiosity to something bordering on condescension as if she was looking at a particularly bone-headed monkey. Another firework bursts, gold and purple sparks raining down.

"Of course Theo was a dog." She talks as if explaining to a child. "The best dog ever." (THAT IS INSANE A FUCKING DOG) DOGS ARE A JOY BUT C'MON SO

Irritation prickles under my skin at her tone, at her acting as if I'm the unreasonable one. Then shock gives way to disbelief. "Hold on. You're telling me that all this time, you've been going on and on about your grief... for a dog?"

Olivia reels back as if I've slapped her. "Theo was like a brother to me, Dylan. We grew up together. He was my best friend." Her voice trembles, but holds an undercurrent of steel.

"But... but," I stammer, increasingly appalled, "you told me you had to go home for *a funeral*?"

"Yes. It was a beautiful memorial in our backyard. All the family gathered to celebrate his life." Olivia's tone is defensive, daring me to challenge her.

I can't help myself. "You held a memorial? For a dog?"

"Yes, I told you from the start."

"You told me your best friend had died, never mentioned it was *a dog*. I thought an actual person had died."

Olivia gasps, eyes narrowing. "Oh my gosh. You're one of those, aren't you?"

"One of what?"

"A simpleton who'd sneer at cherishing the memory of a soul that touched your life only because they walked on four legs instead of two."

I open my mouth to retort, but nothing comes out. I'm caught between anger, confusion, and the absurd urge to laugh.

"Olivia, you've been acting like you lost a close relative. An uncle, a grandparent, a beloved neighbor." I try to keep my voice level, but frustration seeps through. "I thought a member of your family had died."

"Theo *was* part of the family," Olivia yells, startling a nearby seagull into flight.

"Okay, okay. But what are you going to do when you lose an actual human relative?"

Olivia paces, feet kicking up sand. "I can't fucking believe this." She stops, fixing me with a stare that could freeze lava. "This isn't working for me, Dylan."

"What's not working?"

"This. Us." She gestures between our chests. "I could overlook you being distracted half the times we are together. Or that I always have to text you first. You have a demanding job and a life outside of me, I get it." She's flapping her hands like a mad person. "But I refuse to waste my time on a dog hater."

"I'm not a dog hater." I throw my arms up, exasperated. "I love dogs. But I have a realistic view of how much mourning is appropriate for a pet." (I'M NOT A DOG HATER ANIMALS ARE IMPORTANT BUT EVEN SO)

Olivia scoffs, folding her arms across her chest. "Oh, really? And what's the Dylan Thompson approved level of mourning, huh?"

I sigh, running a hand through my hair. "Look, when Frisky, my family's cat, died, I was sad. I cried. But we didn't build a shrine, or sing hymns about his favorite catnip, or spend weeks crying every time we saw a ball of yarn, convinced we heard his meow in the wind."

Olivia's eyes widen, her mouth falling open. "Are you mocking my grief?"

"No, I'm trying to put things in perspective."

"Perspective?" She laughs a harsh, humorless sound. "Here's

some perspective for you, Dylan. Theo was there for me through everything. When my parents divorced, when I got cut from the soccer team, when my first boyfriend dumped me. He never judged, and never gave unsolicited advice. He loved me, unconditionally. But of course, you wouldn't understand, being a cat person." (JeSus GIVE Me STRENGTH)

"What's that supposed to mean? Dogs aren't better than cats. And just because I grew up with a cat, it doesn't mean I hate dogs."

"No, you're right, dogs are *so* much better than cats," Olivia snickers. "And you have the same shitty personality as a cat."

"What?" I blink, taken aback. "How?"

Olivia ticks off points on her fingers. "Let's see. You're aloof, ungrateful, and self-serving. You only want affection on your terms. And you assume you're above everyone else."

I stare at her, my jaw clenched. "Frisky was none of those things. He was a great cat, and we all loved him. But we didn't host a funeral with grief-aiding party favors for him."

Olivia's eyes fill with tears as her bottom lip trembles. "If you're making fun of my grief socks, then you're a truly horrible person, Dylan Thompson. I want nothing to do with you ever again." (TOLD YOU YOU DON'T FINISH WITH HIR) ON PAGE 226

She spins on her heel, storming away toward the resort exit. I'm tempted to let her go, to call it a night and be done with this entire ridiculous relationship. But it's late, and despite everything, I don't want anything to happen to her.

Grumbling under my breath, I jog after her. She's already on the phone, her voice thick with tears as she pleads with her friends to come pick her up. "You're never going to believe what happened," she sobs. "It's always the harmless ones that turn out to be the biggest jerks."

I roll my eyes but keep following her until we reach the

parking lot. Olivia whirls around, glaring at me through her tears. "Leave me alone, Dylan."

"Trust me, I will. As soon as you're safe with your friends." I stuff my hands in my pockets, rocking back on my heels.

After that, we wait in the most awkward of silences. Olivia's shoulders are vibrating with indignation. Finally, the same top-off Jeep from earlier pulls into the lot. Olivia shoots me one last withering look. "Never contact me again."

I bite back a sarcastic *as if* and mumble low, "Not unless I need advice on how to mourn a hamster."

Olivia mounts the car, the angry glares of three other women in the seats boring into me. And then they're gone, tires screeching as they peel out of the parking lot.

Shaking my head, I make my way to my car. Sliding into the driver's seat, I close the door and lean my head back against the headrest. I sit staring at the interior roof. And then, I start to laugh.

It bubbles up from my chest, spilling out of me in great, heaving guffaws. I laugh until my sides ache and tears stream down my face. Because what else can I do? This whole night, this entire relationship has been one ludicrous misunderstanding after another.

As my laughter subsides, I wipe my eyes and start the car. One thing's for sure, I'll think twice before dating a dog person again.

32

HUNTER

I walk into the resort's breakfast hall, to shake off the exhaustion that's glued itself to my skin. I spot Nina sitting by the window alone, with her usual aura of *I'm up early and thriving*. Meanwhile, I've got dark circles that might as well be permanent accessories. At least the coffee smells strong.

Nina sees me and gestures to the seat next to her. I slide in, offering what I hope is a convincing grin. My mind's been on overdrive, and last night didn't help. I wonder if I should've stayed in bed this morning—maybe for the rest of my life.

After a few minutes, Rowena joins us, looking a little rumpled but still gorgeous. Her sundress flows around her and her skin glows, but she has bags under her eyes, too. "Hey," she greets us, her smile strained.

"How were things in the honeymoon suite last night?" Nina doesn't even give her time to take a sip of coffee before going on the offensive.

"Not a honeymoon suite," Rowena deflects with ease, but a catch in her tone contradicts her projected nonchalance. "You're about two months early."

"Oh, come on." Nina doesn't let it go. "That kiss last night? You and Adrian set the sky on fire!"

I nod enthusiastically to cover up the fact that I've fantasized a lot about Dylan kissing me like that. "Seriously, the fireworks had nothing on you two."

Rowena looks like she wants to vanish into her pancakes. She stuffs a forkful into her mouth probably more to avoid the conversation than for hunger, as if carbs could shield her from our questions. I should follow her lead and stuff my face.

"It was just for show," she mumbles between chews.

Nina raises an eyebrow, not buying it. "Riiiight. Because platonic fake-daters always kiss like they're reenacting the kiss-in-the-rain scene from *The Notebook*."

Rowena squirms in her seat. She has all my sympathy. I know what it's like to pretend nothing's wrong while your world is spinning. I've become an expert at it myself.

"Are you sure the farce isn't running away from you?" My question is more curious than accusatory. Is she losing control? Am I?

Rowena gives us that practiced shrug. But I've known her too long to be fooled by it. I've pulled that same move one too many times myself. "Look, guys, I appreciate the concern, but I've got this under control," she insists.

Before I can press more, she turns her attention to me. "Hey, you okay, Hunt? You seem a bit off today."

My turn to pick at my food. "I'm fine, just tired. I've been having trouble sleeping lately." Not a lie, but not the entire truth either. That'd be how I've been having trouble breathing around Dylan and Olivia.

Nina snorts. "Please. We all know it's because Dylan brought his new girlfriend last night. Probably has her over at your place often, too."

Thankfully, she only visited once, but Nina's words are still a punch to the gut. My fork freezes in mid-air. How does she know? I thought I was better at hiding my feelings.

"How did you—"

"Oh, come on, babe." Nina's voice softens. "It's obvious you're into my brother."

I suck in air between my teeth. I can't deny it, but I don't want to discuss my pathetic crush. "But he's clearly too blind to see what's right in front of him."

What's that? A hot, confused mess?

"Honestly, I give it two months tops," Nina declares, stabbing a sausage with unnecessary force. "Little Miss Perfect is not right for him. Even Tristan said so."

As soon as Nina ends her prophetic declaration, a long shadow appears over the table, and Adrian greets us with a smooth, "Morning, ladies." The sunlight dims slightly as if bowing in response to his presence. The deep, resonant tone of his voice rolls over the group, sending a ripple in the air. Rowena swallows.

Adrian asks if we mind if he takes a seat, and of course, we say not at all. He picks the spot next to Rowena and drops his plate and coffee mug on the table. His movements are smooth but purposeful, those of a man who knows how to command a room without even trying. Next, he pours an unbelievable amount of sugar into his coffee. He calmly steers the hot liquid, his silver spoon clinking rhythmically against the mug, the motion hypnotic.

I watch Adrian, taking in his thick raven-black hair, chiseled jaw that catches the light right, highlighting the faint scruff that he hasn't shaved off this morning, and his dark, deep-set eyes. He emanates a raw, primal sort of sex appeal, combined with an aura of money, power, and status. There's no way Rowena isn't falling for him. Even with his ridiculous sugar addiction, he's magnetic.

Tristan breaks the spell cast by Adrian, arriving a short while later. He stamps a kiss on Nina's head and tells her he has news. He steals a muffin from her plate and helps himself to a sip from her mug of coffee. Nina scowls at him, her eyes narrowing with a mixture of fondness and mild annoyance.

"It's an open buffet, you know," Nina scoffs. "You can go get your own breakfast."

The softness in her voice betrays how much she likes their constant banter. Tristan grins, the kind of smug smirk that means trouble, and shrugs, taking another bite of the muffin. "Okay, I'll go get some food first, and share the juicy gossip later."

He makes to stand up, but Nina stops him, her hand latching onto his arm. "No, no, no. You can have my pastries, my coffee, but you have to spill the gossip ASAP." She leans forward, her green eyes gleaming with unbridled curiosity.

Tristan's grin widens, satisfied. "Thought so."

Nina glowers at him again. "Your news better be good, Mr. Drama Queen." Her fingers drum impatiently on the table.

Tristan winks at her in response, and despite their having been a couple for months, now living together for one, Nina's cheeks still color.

They're so adorable I want to crawl under the table, curl into a fetal position, and cry.

Tristan shrugs, nonchalantly. "The gossip is great." He pauses for dramatic effect, his blue eyes sparkling with mischief. "Your brother is single again. Miss Perfect got the boot last night."

The words, so casual in their delivery, detonate like a grenade in my chest. I almost choke on a bite of my cinnamon bun, coughing heavily as I reach for my glass of orange juice. The citrus burns as it goes down, but it's nothing compared to the fire in my veins.

Dylan is single? How? When? Why? What happened? He and Olivia were the perfect couple yesterday. I have a million questions, but I'm stricken mute.

Nina has no trouble talking, though—even too much. She turns to me, a foxy grin spreading across her face. "We need a plan."

I play dumb, not wanting my infatuation for Dylan to be paraded in front of everyone, especially Tristan, his fucking best friend and also the worst gossip around. "A plan for what?" My voice stays impressively steady despite the flutter of nervous energy crawling up my spine at the idea of Dylan being single again.

Possibility and excitement wage war in my chest against confusion and disbelief. I take another sip of my orange juice, the cool liquid doing little to quench the burning thirst for answers.

Nina rolls her eyes, oblivious to my attempt at deflection. "A plan for you to seduce my brother, duh."

The word "seduce" hits me like a slap to the face, unexpected and way too public. The directness of her statement makes my cheeks heat, the flush creeping all the way to my ears. I hiss at Nina, "Shut up."

The eyes of the entire table fix on me, Tristan's included. The weight of his curiosity sharpens my embarrassment. Nina looks surprised. "Why?" she asks, then repeats, "You have to seduce Dylan before he starts dating someone else completely wrong for him."

I grit my teeth, to keep my voice low. "I'd rather not discuss my feelings for Dylan in front of *his best friend*."

Tristan raises his eyebrows, his mouth quirking into a smirk as he points at his chest with mock innocence. "*Moi?*"

Between gritted teeth, I reply, "Yes, you."

Nina hurries to reassure me. "Don't worry, there's a Chinese Wall in place." She turns to Tristan, her expression serious. "You won't repeat to Dylan anything you hear this morning, right?"

Tristan makes a cross-my-heart gesture. "I'm sworn to secrecy."

I grip my glass tighter than necessary, as though it could anchor my swirling thoughts, still unconvinced.

But Nina smiles wide again. "Now can we move on to the plan?"

I hesitate, doubt creeping in. "Is there any point? Dylan has known me for years and never made a move. Why should he suddenly realize he's into me now?"

Rowena counters, "But you've had a thing for Dylan for ages and never made a move either. You can't be sure how he feels."

Tristan low whistles. "Really, Hunt? You've been into my bro for years and never said anything?"

"He's *my* brother." Nina swats him. "And don't be a dick; can't you see she's head over heels in love and had to live with him for a month while he was dating someone else?"

"And here I thought I was the one with the big news." Tristan focuses his glacier-blue eyes on me. "You're seriously that into him, like in love?"

I reluctantly nod, unsure of what to feel. The possibility of Dylan loving me back is both tantalizingly close and impossibly far away. I press my nails into my palms to steady myself, but my pulse continues to race, fueled by a potent mix of hope and fear.

Nina jumps in, her eyes gleaming as she taps her fingers against her coffee mug. "You should take advantage of it being summer and parade around the house as little dressed as possible. Maybe even sabotage the air conditioning."

I nearly spit orange juice on her. And as I cough the liquid down, Rowena replies instead, her voice carrying a sharp edge. "She could strip naked in front of Dylan, but if he's not ready for a relationship or has his own holdbacks, he won't be seduced by her."

For the first time since arriving, Adrian speaks. He levels Rowena with a stare so scalding, I'm tempted to intercept it with my mug of lukewarm coffee to have it re-heated.

"He might not *act* on what he's feeling, but he'll be seduced alright." Adrian's voice is velvety and rough, and his dark eyes smolder with an intensity that shifts the mood in an instant, like a slow-burning match nearing a wick, making the air between him and Rowena ablaze with something raw and unspoken. They are having an entirely different conversation only they can understand.

Rowena blushes and looks away, her fingers fidgeting with her napkin. Adrian, cool as a cucumber, takes another sip of his over-sugared coffee, looking unaffected.

We all blink for a stunned, suspended moment at the end of Adrian's declaration until Nina jumps right back on topic, turning to Tristan with a mischievous grin. "You're Dylan's best friend. You should know what will seduce him."

Tristan raises his hands in mock surrender. "Whoa, it sounds like treason to divulge the man's secrets."

Nina pokes him in the ribs. "Come on, Montgomery. You'd better start talking."

"What's in it for me?" he asks playfully.

Nina whispers something in his ear, and Tristan's face turns sheepish. "I am a man of principle, but I have my limits. What do you ladies want to know?"

* * *

Half an hour later, my mind is spinning with newfound knowledge. Apparently, Dylan is into legs, and can't resist crew socks, messy buns, or off-the-shoulder tops—even better if it's his old basketball jersey. He likes women who are into video games. I can't play, but that's a plus, apparently. I should ask him to teach me and use the opportunity to be close to him. Nina assures me he'll be more than happy to mansplain to me all about boring video game stuff.

Basically, all I have to do now is put my hair up in a messy bun, steal Dylan's basketball jersey, and wear it off the shoulder with no bottom piece and only crew socks on while asking him to teach me how to play *Halo*.

The plan is simple, but at the thought of going through with it, a prickle of unease creeps up my spine. I feel ridiculous just thinking about parading my assets around the house.

Can I pull this off? Will Dylan see me in a new light, or will I make a fool of myself? The questions swirl in my mind, but despite the doubts, I won't let this opportunity slip through my fingers. Not again.

I glance around the table, taking in the faces of my friends. Nina is bouncing in her seat, her eyes sparkling with anticipation. Tristan leans back, his signature smug smirk on his lips. And then there's Adrian and Rowena, still lost in their own world of unspoken secrets.

It's now or never, I decide. I'm going to seize this chance and force Dylan to notice me.

33

DYLAN

The controller vibrates in my hands as my character narrowly avoids an enemy attack near a ravine on screen, nearly taken out by a low-level enemy I should've dodged with ease. My focus is so scattered the video game is barely holding my attention. I glance at the clock on the wall—6.37 p.m. Hunter should be home soon.

Today has been a surprisingly great Sunday. Volunteering at the soup kitchen this morning filled me with a sense of accomplishment. And spending an entire day without relationship drama and looming break-ups has been a welcome change of pace. And the evening should be even more promising. I'm equal parts nervous and excited to see Hunter.

No, I'm not planning to hit on her mere hours after ending things with Olivia. The last thing I want is for Hunter to assume I'm some kind of player, bouncing from one woman to the next faster than a New York minute. No, tonight is about having our first real, unburdened interaction as roommates and friends. No worrying about other people, crossed boundaries, or hurt feelings.

It'll be nice to relax and joke around with Hunter without

having to walk on eggshells. I can be myself. Maybe even flirt a little, see how she reacts.

My lips twitch into a grin. *Yeah, that should be interesting.*

The metallic jangle of a key turning in the lock yanks my attention to the front door. A quiet urgency unfurls within me, simmering, waiting. I twist around on the couch as Hunter drags her weekend bag across the threshold.

I'm speechless. Her dark hair is swept up in a messy bun, exposing the graceful curve of her neck. A few stray wisps frame her face, gifting her a careless kind of beauty. She's wearing the same shorts from our drive out to the Hamptons yesterday, revealing a criminal amount of smooth, tanned legs.

I nearly drop my game controller. Damn, she's a vision. The most gorgeous woman I've ever laid eyes on. I have to mentally stuff my fist in my mouth to keep from blurting that out.

Hunter looks up, catching me staring. A shy smile plays on her full lips. "Hey."

"Hey yourself," I manage, hoping I sound casual despite my thundering heart. "How was the drive back?"

She kicks the door shut with a groan. "Awful. We should've left early like Adrian and Rowena. But a day at the beach was too tempting." She drops her bag with a thud. "Then we hit rush-hour traffic. Took forever to get home."

"Well, I'm glad you made it back."

A pretty blush colors her cheeks. "Me too. It's good to be home." She toes off her sandals. "How was volunteering?"

"Rewarding." I grin. "Puts things in perspective, you know?"

Hunter nods, mirroring my smile. Then she grabs her bag and heads down the hall. "I'm gonna go change. Be right back."

As she disappears around the corner, I sink back into the couch cushions and blow my cheeks. I blink at the paused video game, the controller forgotten in my hands. The screen blurs into a hazy image while I wait until the quick snap of her bedroom door startles me back to clarity.

I shake my head like a dog after a bath, as if unruly feelings could fly off like droplets of water.

The effort proves useless when she reappears. Hunter has changed into an oversized T-shirt that slips off one shoulder, revealing a tantalizing expanse of smooth, olive skin. The shirt skims her thighs, and I can't tell if she's not wearing shorts underneath or only a tiny, tiny pair. Her legs are bare to mid-calf where her rolled-up white crew socks hit. She's walked straight out of my daydreams—effortlessly sexy in the most casual, domestic way.

I swallow as she pads over to the couch, trying to keep my eyes from roving over her body.

"What are you playing?" she asks, settling down beside me.

"*Shadowlands*," I manage, my voice miraculously steady.

Hunter tilts her head, intrigued. "Cool name. Is it fun?"

"Yeah?"

She scrunches her face in the cutest way. "That didn't sound convincing."

"No, no. It's a fun game, I promise."

Hunter smiles, making me sweat despite the cold temperature. Should I invest in a stronger deodorant? "Think you could teach me how to play?"

If she's into gaming, I'm toast.

"Yeah, sure."

We shift on the couch, getting comfortable. I hand Hunter the spare controller and will myself to focus. "*Shadowlands* is a story-based game, a quest. The first thing you have to do is choose your character class. That's gonna determine your abilities, your fighting style, magical powers, and weaknesses."

"Like in the new *Jumanji* movie?"

"Yeah, like that."

"If there's a character who can't eat cake, I don't want that one."

My lips twitch. "Noted."

We sift through the various avatars and Hunter settles on a sexy warrior elf. Of course. If she had pointy ears to go with those legs, I wouldn't be sitting on the couch; I'd be passed out on the floor.

As I walk her through the basics, and let her familiarize with the commands, I'm hyper-tuned into her presence beside me. The heat of her body, the scent of her, the way her knee bumps against mine as she attempts a complicated move on the screen. I'm talking and explaining, but my mind is short-circuiting.

The oversized T-shirt she's wearing is making me unhinged. It keeps slipping, baring more and more of her shoulder.

When I have to adjust her grip on the controller, sparks dance across my skin. I do my best to ignore the sensation, to stay cool, but everything sharpens into focus, the room closing in and opening up at the same time.

I'm sitting on the couch doing nothing but my pulse is racing faster than it ever did on the basketball court, even in the final seconds of my senior championship game.

We finish the practice drills and I ask Hunter if she has questions. She looks up at me from under those long, dark lashes and shakes her head, a small smile playing on her lips. My stomach bottoms out.

We start the game. Hunter's tongue pokes out the corner of her mouth as she concentrates, and it's so freaking adorable I can barely focus on my half of the screen. She giggles and I glance over to see her character stuck in a dead end, running endlessly against a wall.

Without thinking, I reach over and place my hand on hers,

guiding her through the sequence to free her avatar. My fingers linger on her skin for a beat too long. We both freeze. The world is holding its breath alongside me. I clear my throat awkwardly and pull back to refocus on the game.

As the sun drops out the windows, the living room remains lit only by the faint glow of the TV, but I'm not moving from this couch, not even to turn on the lights. I can't remember the last time I felt this at ease with anyone besides Tristan. It surprises me, how easy it is to be with Hunter.

She navigates through a tricky puzzle in an ancient ruin and a hidden door swings open. My jaw drops. "Hey, I've been trying to get through that secret passage for ages." I'm in awe of how smart she is.

Hunter grins at me, eyes sparkling. "Need me to show you how to pass the next part too?"

I bump her shoulder playfully. "Beginner's luck," I tease, but the touch sends another jolt through me.

Hunter's smile fades as she looks at me, her dark eyes wide and luminous in the half-light. My gaze drops to her mouth. She notices and those beautiful lips part in a gasp—the sound sets a fire to the base of my spine.

Gosh, it'd be so easy to toss the controller aside, to pull her to me and taste those lips...

But it's too soon. She doesn't even know about Olivia. Or does she? Is she aware we broke up? I have to tell her. The words fly out of my mouth. "Olivia and I broke up."

Hunter makes a face I can't decipher and pulls away. Uncertainty flickers across her features. I mentally chide myself, *way to kill the mood, dude.*

She gives me a small smile. "Tristan mentioned it at breakfast." She hesitates before asking, "Are you okay?"

"More than okay. I'm relieved."

Again, Hunter makes a cryptic face, but if I had to interpret, I'd say she doesn't seem too displeased by the notion. "Why relieved? I thought you two were happy together."

I rake a hand through my hair. "Nah, I realized almost right away that Olivia wasn't the right person for me. I wanted to break up with her, but then she had that funeral and it didn't seem like an appropriate time, you know?"

Hunter nods, a glimmer of understanding in her eyes.

I launch into the story of my failed attempts at breaking it off, down to the gory details of grief socks.

Hunter tries not to laugh at the mention of *Step Into Healing* and *Toe-tally Here For You*.

She purses her lips. "Those are hardcore motivational quotes." Then she turns somber. "What made you finally do it last night?"

I grin. "It was Olivia who dumped me. Apparently, I didn't display the proper amount of support for her grief over the loss of Theo... wait for it..." I pause for dramatic effect. "The dog."

Hunter's eyes widen. "Wait, Theo was *a dog*?"

I nod, and we both burst into laughter, unrestrained this time, the kind that makes your stomach hurt and eyes water. As our laughter settles, I turn to her with a curious smile. "You're not a dog person, are you?"

Hunter shrugs, eyes still watery but twinkling. "I like dogs, but I wouldn't give out grief socks for a Fido funeral." She claps a hand over her mouth. "Oh gosh, are we horrible people for laughing about this?"

I reach out and gently pull her hand away. "If we are, then you're my kind of horrible person."

"Said the dog hater."

We burst out laughing again.

When the chuckles fade, they leave a comfortable silence

between us. Hunter leans back against the couch, her fingers still loosely gripping the controller, her eyes shining from the afterglow of our shared amusement. The glow of the TV casts gentle shadows across her face, highlighting the curve of her smile. I want to kiss her so fiercely, but it's too soon, and for now, having her next to me is enough.

Hunter glances down at the controller in her hands, then over at me, a playful glint lighting up her expression again. She asks, "What's next? Want me to beat another puzzle for you?"

I grin, leaning in enough to make her breath hitch, our knees brushing again. "Alright, Brolin," I tell her, "but this time, I'm not going easy on you. If you get stuck against a wall, I'm going to let the dragon eat you."

Hunter sputters mock-indignantly, "That's not very chivalrous of you."

I smirk again, reminding her, "We established we're horrible people. As the villain, I can let the dragon eat the damsel."

She straightens up. "I'm not a damsel but a badass elf warrior. We'll see who the dragon eats."

I nod. "Game on, Brolin."

I push play on the console, the stakes of the challenge seeming much higher than a simple video game.

34

DYLAN

The air in the gym is saturated with the mingling scents of sweat, disinfectant, and rubbery linoleum. My shirt sticks to my back as I hover in a lazy defensive stance, not really focused on the one-on-one basketball game I'm playing with Tristan. He fakes right, sneakers squeaking, and I'm too slow to pivot. The ball arcs uncontested toward the hoop, and *swish*—another point for him.

Tristan snags the ball, eyeing me. "Dude, why'd you even invite me to play if you're gonna half-ass it and space out?"

I ignore his jab, blurting out the question that's been bouncing around my head. "How did you know with my sister that it was more than just physical attraction?"

His brows shoot up. "Way to pivot, Thirty-Three." He hurls the ball at me hard.

It thuds against my chest, forcing out a sharp exhale as I catch it with an "Oof." I lob it right back. "C'mon, be serious. I need your help."

Tristan tucks the ball under his arm against his side. "Are we talking hypotheticals or someone specific?"

"Someone specific." I avoid providing a name.

He cocks his head. "Does she happen to live with you?"

I stare at him in shock—have I been that obvious?—and manage a curt nod.

Bouncing the ball once, Tristan returns it to the rack in the corner. "This conversation requires a beer, man. And I've got a small confession to make..." He trails off, heading for the door.

I swipe at the sweat trickling down my temple. "What confession?"

Tristan glances back, catching my gesture. "Shower first, then we'll talk." He disappears into the locker room.

I blow the hair away from my forehead and follow him. I'm not sure I'm ready to voice what's been on my mind, but I need some perspective. Tristan figured out his feelings for my sister; he could help me untangle the confusing web of emotions Hunter stirs up in me.

* * *

"You did *what*?" I yell, almost spraying beer all over Tristan. A few heads turn our way, but I ignore them, focusing on my best friend with wide eyes.

The evening still clings to the day's heat as we sit at an outdoor table at our favorite pub. Tristan winces dismissively. "Oh, come on."

"Come *on*? Are you being serious right now?" I'm not sure if I'm more outraged or flattered by the discovery. Flattered, definitely.

Tristan leans back on the chair, his face a picture of nonchalance. "Dude, the poor woman has been in love with you for years. So I gave Hunter a few tips on how to... you know, poke the bear a little. Where's the harm in that?"

His words cut me off at the knees, leaving me unsteady. But

underneath the shock, hope is blooming in my chest, warm and giddy.

I rub my temples, to process. "Back up. Did you say Hunter is in love with me?"

Tristan nods, a smirk playing on his lips. "She's been carrying a torch for you from the moment she saw you, basking by the pool like the star of a sunscreen commercial, my golden boy."

I'm reeling. Shocked, but more than that... elated. The secret attraction I've been harboring for Hunter and forced myself to ignore, to push down—she feels the same way? More? How do I even feel? Am *I* in love?

"H-how long have you known this?" I ask.

Tristan shrugs. "Only a few days. The instant I told Nina at breakfast on Sunday that you'd broken up with Olivia, she said Hunter needed a plan to seduce you."

"She's trying to seduce me?"

"Yep," Tristan continues, "Nina is beyond happy, in case you've been wondering if she's going to go apeshit crazy on you like you did with us. She told me she's suspected Hunter's crush for years."

"And you discussed all this at breakfast in front of everyone?"

"No, this part came later."

I scowl, the pieces clicking into place. "So when you gave Hunter the playbook on how to *seduce* me, you didn't know she was in love with me."

Tristan shrugs with a smirk. "Puh-TAY-toh, puh-TAH-toh." A breeze coming in from the Hudson ruffles his dark hair.

The patio is alive with chatter and the sizzle of grilled meat, but I'm barely registering any of it.

"Hey, you shouldn't complain." Tristan gestures at me with his beer bottle. "If because of my actions, you've been seeing lots of Hunter's legs and bare shoulders and long necklines unencumbered by hair..."

A smile tugs at my lips as my mind puts on a slideshow of all the cute, sexy outfits Hunter's been wearing around the house. And the way she pulls her hair up in those messy buns I'm dying to pull loose...

It all started Sunday night. Makes sense now.

"And the socks." I groan at another memory. This time, I do bite down on my fist, then grab a chip from the basket and toss it at Tristan. "You told her everything, didn't you? Even about my thing for crew socks?"

Tristan dodges the projectile, grinning. "I guess the plan worked, then. You, my friend, are seduced."

He's not wrong.

Tristan leans forward. "Did it start last Sunday? Or before?"

My cheeks heat up. "Before," I admit, my voice low. "As soon as I moved in... even while I was with Olivia."

Shame twinges in my gut at the confession, but it's overshadowed by the exhilaration of voicing my feelings.

Tristan nods, understanding in his eyes. "Why haven't you acted on it yet, now that you're single?"

I muss the hair at my nape. "It's too soon after the break-up with Olivia. I don't want Hunter to think she's a rebound."

"What? From five-minute Olivia?"

"It was more like a month than minutes."

"About that," Tristan asks me pointedly. "Why did you try so hard with Olivia when it was obvious she wasn't right for you?"

I glance away, the dim light from the pub's patio reflecting off my beer bottle, casting a long shadow on the wooden table. I'm not entirely sure. "I think... I was on the rebound. I didn't want to be alone."

Tristan arches an eyebrow. "On the rebound? Your last serious relationship was two years ago."

I stare at my best friend. "I was on the rebound from losing you."

Tristan's eyes widen. "What? You haven't lost me."

"I know. But..." I trail off, to find the right words. "It's different now. I used to be your person, and now Nina is your number one. As it should be," I add quickly, not wanting him to think I still begrudge their relationship. "But with the dynamic shifting and me moving out of the apartment, I guess I felt left out. That's why I jumped into the thing with Olivia."

Tristan leans forward on the table and levels me with a stare. His blue eyes are intense and sincere. "Dylan, we're family. We'll always be family. Even having this conversation with you, I'm breaking a code. Nina made me promise not to say anything about Hunter to you."

I blink, surprised. "Why did you, then?"

"Because you're still my number one, too. Together with Nina. We're brothers, and that's never going to change."

My throat tightens at that. I nod, hoping he can see in my eyes what I can't put into words. I give him a fist bump and make a joke because that's what we do. "This is starting to sound too incestuous."

"Sorry, Thirty-Three." Tristan sits back, grinning. "I do feel a little guilty about spilling all your secrets to Hunter."

I groan, burying my face in my hands. "I still can't believe you told her about the socks."

"Which brings us back to the original question you asked." Tristan's tone turns serious again. "Is it physical attraction for Hunter, or does it run deeper?"

I pause, considering. My mind flashes to all the little moments with Hunter—the way she laughs at my jokes, the warmth in her eyes when she looks at me, the comfort of being around her. It's more than the allure of her long legs and bare shoulders.

"It runs deeper." The realization hits me with full force. "Definitely runs deeper."

Tristan leans forward, his eyes intent on mine. "What makes you say that?"

I take a swig of my beer, collecting my thoughts. "I just... can't wait to come home every night, knowing she'll be there. Being around her is easy, comfortable, right. I can be myself." I hesitate, then admit, "I even told her about my dyslexia. You know I tell no one about that."

Tristan's eyebrows shoot up. He knows the significance of that confession. A slow smirk spreads across his face. "Well, then. There's that." He pauses, then adds, "And of course... the legs."

I grin, my mind conjuring up the image of the smooth expanse of Hunter's toned thighs under those tiny shorts. "And then there are the legs," I agree, my voice husky.

Tristan chuckles, shaking his head. "What are you still doing here, man? Why don't you go home and kiss the woman already?"

I mull the question, a wide grin breaking across my face. The beer in my hand is cold, but inside, I'm all warmth, giddy excitement bubbling up at the realization that I'm allowing myself to want this, to pursue it.

"Maybe Hunter needs a bit of harmless seduction back," I muse, the wheels already turning in my head.

Tristan scoffs. "She seemed pretty cooked to me; she doesn't need more seducing, buddy."

"Fair, but she deserves a little payback." I smile, still incredulous. "You have no idea, Eleven, the torture these last few days have been. The shorts she's been putting on... becoming shorter and shorter. Maybe she needs a taste of her own medicine. We need to come up with a counter-seduction plan."

"Not sure I can give you the inside scoop." Tristan shrugs. "I don't know Hunter as well as I do you."

I smirk, an idea forming. "True. But you know who we both know really well? My sister. And those two do everything together; they have most of the same tastes. We can brainstorm and reverse-engineer what makes Hunter tick based on what we know about Nina. And I've been living with Hunter for a month. I can fill in the gaps."

Tristan's eyes light up, a grin spreading across his face. He nods, lifting his beer in a toast. "Alright, Thirty-Three. Let's do this."

I clink my bottle against his, excitement thrumming through my veins. *Game on.*

35

HUNTER

The muffled notes of "Don't Blame Me" greet me as I trudge up to my apartment door, exhausted from another late night at the office. I frown, pausing with my keys in hand. Were Rowena and Nina coming over tonight and I spaced it? Who else would be listening to *Reputation*?

I unlock the door and step inside—and my jaw nearly hits the floor at the sight that greets me. Dylan is humming in time to the music, his broad shoulders swaying as he energetically mops the floor. He's wearing navy basketball shorts that hug his muscular thighs and a sleeveless gray hoodie with armholes so large they showcase his sculpted arms and offer a tantalizing peek of the tight muscles along his ribs. Each push of the mop makes his biceps and triceps ripple under his tanned skin. It's mortifying how stunning I find him.

On top of that, he's wearing a blue New York Knicks cap. Backward. Good heavens. Backward baseball caps are irresistibly sexy on a man. Paired with the way his blond hair curls at the nape of his neck... A brief pulse of heat thrums low in my stomach and my mind goes blank. The sight of him cleaning our apartment while singing Taylor Swift is apparently the domestic sex fantasy I never knew I desperately needed.

Wait, why is he even wearing a cap indoors? What on earth is going on with him?

I look away, tossing my keys into the bowl at the entrance, and notice a new vase, filled with violets, where the one he broke used to be. I'm about to ask him about it, but when I glance up again, I catch him twirling the mop and using it as a mock mic stand to belt out the high note. That's it. If this performance goes on any longer, I might lose my last marble. I clear my throat, cutting the show short. "Hey," I manage, but my voice comes out unnaturally high-pitched. Apparently, my vocal cords haven't quite recovered from the visual ambush of Dylan's biceps.

He turns at the sound, his face lighting up with an easy, wide smile, the kind that crinkles the corners of his bright eyes. "Brolin, you're home."

I lose a few feet of intestines as they melt at his enthusiastic greeting, warmth rushing to my core. The fatigue from my long day slaving over the North Shore project dissolves in the glow of his smile.

"Yeah, finally," I reply, unable to keep from grinning back at him. "It's been a beast of a day, but I'm glad to be home. And at least the week is over." I point at the vase. "New flowers?"

Dylan props the mop against the couch and walks over, his tall frame eating up the distance in a few long strides. "You said you didn't like flowers that die, so I got you a plant. It blooms year-round."

"T-thanks?"

"It's nothing." He leans against the wall, and I'm tempted to touch him just to confirm he's real and not a government experiment in male perfection. "Have you eaten yet?"

"No, I'm starving."

"Perfect. I was thinking I could make a quick run to that taco place around the corner you love." He definitely escaped from a top-secret research facility where they engineer men to ensure no one around them makes sensible choices. "Carne asada with extra guac and a Pineapple Jarritos, right?"

I'm surprised he memorized my order. "Tacos sound perfect."

"Great. Let me finish here and I'll head out."

For a second, I'm tempted to ask him to change before going out, you know, to prevent women from swooning and causing pedestrian pile-ups on the curbs. The NY emergency services are already overloaded enough.

But as my gaze travels over his athletic form again—the sleeveless hoodie highlighting his ripped physique, how that damn backward cap makes him look both boyish and hot as sin —I realize it wouldn't matter what he wears. Dylan could don a paper sack and women would still faint in the streets.

I keep my mouth shut and watch as he retrieves the mop and resumes cleaning and dancing spontaneously to "Shake It Off" as the song changes. Is he a secret Swiftie?

I flee to the bathroom because if I have to witness one more unintentionally sexy thing, my ovaries will explode.

The shower does little to calm the current of electricity zinging through my veins. I tilt my head back and close my eyes under the spray of hot water. But even with my lids shut, I see Dylan. How his eyes crinkled when he smiled. The flex of his muscles as he moved. The way he shook his booty to the music that I didn't find as ridiculous as I should have.

I shut off the water and wrap myself in a fluffy towel. Back in my room, I pull out the shortest pair of shorts I own, holding them up with a wry smile. They're more denim underwear than actual pants.

All week, I've been parading around the apartment in increasingly skimpy outfits—shorty-shorts, off-the-shoulder tops, messy buns. And... nada. No reaction from Dylan beyond his usual friendly smiles. It's like trying to seduce a golden retriever. A hot, oblivious golden retriever.

Tugging on the shorts, I figure if these don't get a rise out of him, nothing will. I twist my damp hair up into his favorite messy bun, then stop. With my neck already twinging in protest, I let my hair fall loose instead, the wet strands cool against my bare shoulders.

For my top, I bypass my remaining off-the-shoulder options and go straight for the nuclear option—the oversized Blue Devils shirt Dylan lent me when I got soaked by the sprinklers at his parents' house. Turns out I didn't even have to steal one of his basketball jerseys; he's already given it to me.

Slipping the worn cotton over my head, I catch a faint whiff of Dylan's scent still clinging to the fabric. Clean and crisp with a hint of something manly. The smell wraps around me like an embrace, and my eyes flutter closed. Gosh, the atomic plan has already backfired and is short-circuiting my brain instead of his. I let the shirt go and push it as far from my nose as possible.

I check myself in the mirror before going back out. The hem of the shirt skims my thighs, covering my shorts—kind of counterproductive. I knot the excess at my waist, letting a slice of skin peek out. It's a bold move. I'm literally putting *all* my skin in the game.

Time to see if Dylan is ready to play ball.

When I head back into the living space, Dylan is unloading the takeout boxes onto the kitchen counter. The scent of cilantro, lime, and spices wraps around me, but his presence makes the air thicker than all the spices. The baseball cap has come off, but now his hair is all messy and tousled, sticking up in a way that suggests he's run his hands through it too many times and that makes Dylan even more devastatingly sexy.

He lifts his head and takes me in, giving me the slowest of once-overs. There is a new boldness in the way he looks at me, being deliberate and unapologetic about it in a way that makes my skin slow-fry under that heated stare.

Dylan cocks his head. "Is that my shirt?"

I nod, playing it cool. "I told you it was comfy and that I might not give it back."

He holds my gaze a little longer than is comfortable, then says, "Nice shorts."

His voice is casual, but heat simmers each word, making my knees turn to jelly. I glance down at my exposed legs, suddenly aware of how much skin is on display. When I look back up, Dylan's eyes are still on me, a smirk playing at the corner of his mouth. *That's new.*

We bring the tacos to the couch, and Dylan takes control of the remote. I expect him to put on something boring like the news or sports, but after zapping through the channels for a while, he logs onto a subscription service and *Legally Blonde* begins to play.

A little dazed, I ask, "You like this movie?"

Dylan shrugs. "Nina's made me watch it so many times, it's grown on me."

I stuff my mouth with taco because otherwise, I might say something stupid like, *Will you please marry me?* or, *Can I bear all your children?* The taco is delicious—crispy, savory, everything I love—but the taste is a blur in the background compared to the presence of Dylan next to me.

As the opening credits roll, I sneak a glance at him from the corner of my eye. He's slouched back against the cushions, long legs stretched out in front of him, looking utterly relaxed. Acting like this is a normal Friday night for us, hanging out and watching rom-coms together.

But it's not normal, not even close. Because I'm sitting here in his clothes, the ghost of his scent surrounding me, hyper-aware of every single inch between us.

I shove another bite of taco into my mouth, forcing myself to focus on the screen. But with Dylan's solid warmth radiating beside me and the memory of how he looked at me earlier seared into my brain, concentrating on a movie is impossible.

But the story eventually wins me over and I get absorbed into the shenanigans of Elle Woods and her law-school drama. Unfortunately, the respite is short-lived because as we finish eating, Dylan clears the plates, and when he comes back, I'm on high alert.

He looks at me sideways. "You look tense, Hunt."

I shrivel under the scrutiny. When he concentrates all his focus on me like that, my walls become invisible and I wonder if he can see straight into the part of me that's been quietly churning all evening. I force a smile, saying, "Work has been intense. Just a little neck pain."

I stretch my head from side to side as if to demonstrate how easily the problem can be solved.

"Neck pain? We can't have that." His voice is low and smooth and sends a ripple of tension straight through me. "Do you want me to work out those knots for you?"

I stammer, "A-are you sure you know w-what you're doing? You could make it worse."

He grins at me, all confidence. "I'm a pro masseuse. Our sports massage therapist back in college taught me all the tricks." He wiggles his fingers at me.

The thought of Dylan touching me has my pulse skyrocketing, and I bite my lip, unsure if I'll survive a massage from him. "Okay, then."

I turn sideways, expecting us to sit side by side for the massage, but Dylan climbs onto the couch and slides behind me, placing me firmly between his powerful thighs.

His legs are warm and solid, pressing against me on both sides, and the sudden proximity sends a jolt of awareness through my entire body. My hair is still loose after the shower, for drying, but now Dylan brushes it aside, collecting it up. His fingers sliding through my hair send goosebumps racing across my skin as sensation explodes over my upper body.

"Do you have a hair tie?" His breath tickles the side of my neck.

Barely able to form coherent thoughts, I fumble to pull one off my wrist and hand it to him. He gathers my hair higher, his fingers grazing my scalp, and ties it atop my head. It might be the sexiest thing that's ever happened to me.

At least until he leans in, his lips nearly brushing my ear, and murmurs, "The massage might work better if the shirt is loose. Is it okay if I unknot it?"

"Mm-hmm," is all I can manage in response.

Dylan's hands sneak to the front of my borrowed shirt, his knuckles skimming my ribs as he unties the knot. The brush of his fingers against my stomach turns my veins into faulty wires, electrocuting me from the inside out. I focus all my energy on keeping myself upright and not fully collapsing back against his muscular chest.

Then his warm hands drop onto my shoulders, and I lose control of my mind and limbs, melting into his touch. The heat of his palms spreads through my skin, sinking deep into my muscles, and I have to bite my lip to keep from making an embarrassing sound. Our bodies are touching in so many places, and it's even more electrifying. At this rate, I could solve the energy crisis all by myself.

"What's more stressful, work or your love life, with all those dates you've been going on?" Dylan teases as his magic fingers knead the tense muscles at the base of my neck.

I barely have enough brain cells left to say, "I've given up online dating. I'm not seeing anyone at the moment."

My spine is too occupied melting under the contact of his hands to lock in place as I wait for his response. Otherwise, it would've gone ramrod straight.

And, oh, if he doesn't make me wait for an eternity. A long, loooooong pause follows, and then Dylan says, "Good to know," without adding anything, and still working magic with his hands on my shoulders.

I wonder what he means by that. *Good to know* because after having to save me from one of those disastrous dates, he hopes I have more sense? Or *good to know* because this massage is foreplay and next, he'll grab my hair by the knot he's made, tilt my head backward, and kiss me senseless?

I wish I had the guts to ask. But more than anything, as his fingers press deeper, I wish with all my being that he'd do something, make a move, shove me back, roll on top of me, take me right on this couch. But he doesn't. He keeps massaging me, loosening my muscles, and unraveling my entire soul one stroke at a time.

Dylan stops only when the closing credits roll on the TV, and I realize that I've missed most of the movie.

And then, just like that, Dylan slips up from behind me and tells me it's getting late and we should go to sleep. The sudden lack of his warmth makes me feel oddly exposed as if a protective shield has been taken away. He wishes me goodnight and walks down the hall, leaving me in a state of utter bewilderment.

I stare after him, my heart still racing, wondering how I can feel so utterly connected to him and uncertain at the same time. I listen as he uses the bathroom and, once I'm sure he's safely tucked away in his room, I lie down on the couch and start randomly punching and kicking the cushions because what was that?

A cocktail of adrenaline and frustration bubbles up in my hands, at my temples, and in the hollow of my throat, making my limbs restless. I fight to keep from screaming into the nearest pillow. How could he touch me the way he did and then walk away like it was nothing? The confusion swirling inside me builds to a point where I'm ready to burst.

All the touching, the massaging, and then *goodnight*? My skin still tingles, every nerve on fire from his hands, and now he's just... gone?

Dylan's door opens again. I quickly compose myself, stopping the kicking and punching, and pulling myself back into an upright position as he reappears in the living room, holding a paper bag.

"I forgot to give you something." He dangles the bag from his long fingers I'm now all too familiar with.

My pulse jumps the instant I see him, my earlier frustration momentarily forgotten, replaced by curiosity and—a dangerous hope. He walks to the couch and sets himself between my legs before squatting down, one hand casually draped over my lower thigh, the other holding the bag up for me. The heat of his hand resting on my thigh is a distraction; it makes it hard to focus on anything else but the warm weight of his fingers over my bare flesh.

"Thanks," I say, taking the bag from him.

We stare at each other intensely, the space between our mouths the smallest it's ever been.

He jerks his chin at the bag. "Are you not going to look inside?"

The intensity of his gaze makes the air in my lungs burn as my fingers tighten around the paper, crunching it. I don't want to break eye contact, but what choice do I have? I nod and look inside where I find a romance book from one of my favorite authors, but it's not any book; it's a special edition with sprayed edges.

My hands tremble as I pull it out, the shiny cover catching the light. "How did you know I liked this author?" I snap my head back up to meet his gaze.

Dylan shrugs, standing up. "Isn't this the one that got ruined at my parents' house? You said you were looking forward to reading it. I saw it in a bookshop window and thought of you."

The rasp in his voice contrasts with the way my chest tightens at the casualness of his explanation as if it wasn't the most thoughtful, heart-flipping thing anyone's done for me. I have no words; I'm floored. I'm torn between wanting to jump up and hug him or grab him by that ridiculously sexy hoodie and kiss him until he forgets his name.

Instead, I simply say, "Thank you, Dylan. This is so thoughtful of you."

He grins, that boyish charm of his in full force. "It's no problem, Hunt. But don't stay up all night reading, okay?" He punctuates his words with a wink that sends another ripple of electricity straight through me.

I manage a small smile, hoping he can't see how a simple book and wink can unearth me. "I'll try my best," I quip to match his playful tone despite the butterflies wreaking havoc in my stomach.

Dylan chuckles, giving me one last heart-stopping smile before he turns and heads back to his room. As soon as his door clicks shut, I collapse on the couch once more, the fancy paperback hugged to my chest.

I stare up at the ceiling, thinking it won't be a book that'll keep me up tonight.

36

HUNTER

The morning light creeps through the blinds, rousing me from a restless sleep. I stretch, my body tangled in the sheets, and it takes a moment for my sleep-addled brain to register that I'm still wearing Dylan's shirt. The worn fabric rustles against my skin like a secret.

I listen to the house, all quiet. I have to pee so, making as little noise as possible, I use the bathroom and then pad into the kitchen. The apartment is empty. Dylan must be asleep. I savor the stillness.

As I fill the coffee pot, my thoughts drift to last night, to the memory of Dylan's hands on my shoulders, the warmth of his touch lingering long after he'd gone to bed. What did it mean? Was there more to the massage than friendly comfort?

My anxiety spikes at the thought of him waking up, of having to face him in the cold light of day after last night. I pull my hair into a high ponytail, needing something to occupy my hands as my mind spins.

I should make breakfast, even though my baking skills are

nowhere near Dylan's level. Or I could ask him for a cooking lesson, just to have a reason to stay close.

His door opens, then the bathroom's. The sound of the shower running is next. I listen, trying to guess how long he'll be, each drop of water ticking in a distant countdown.

As I wait, I consider various poses I could strike for when he walks in. I try leaning casually against the counter, one leg crossed over the other, angled toward the hallway. No, too forced, not sexy at all.

Next, I hop onto the counter, legs slightly spread, hands resting at my sides. Nah, too staged, too obvious. What would I even say if he asked what I was doing perched on the fixtures like a pin-up calendar girl?

I slide off the counter. In a moment of inspiration, I stretch up to reach something on a top shelf, gauging how much the shirt rides up with the motion. Enough to reveal the bottom curve of my ass. I freeze. No, that's too much. *Good morning, this is my ass*, is not the message I want to send.

As a last-ditch effort, I lean forward over the kitchen bar as if inspecting something, my body stretched out, elbows resting on the counter. The shirt pulls tight against my figure. I rise on tiptoes, offering a teasing glimpse of bare back thighs. Sexy in theory but awkward in practice, and incredibly uncomfortable to hold for any length of time.

My muscles tremble from the strain, and I give up as the bathroom door creaks open. I straighten up and look around wildly, my heart lodging in my throat.

I pace in a frenzied circle to decide on a position, any position. But after all the rehearsing, I end up standing and pathetically gaping like a landed trout as Dylan emerges from the hall, still wet from his shower, a white towel slung so low on his hips, I'm not sure how he can walk without it slipping right off. Static blocks my hearing. I've seen him shirtless before, but this towel of scandal is a million times worse than swim trunks.

I can't stop staring at the V of muscles disappearing under the towel's hem, at the fine golden hair trailing downward...

My mind goes blank, any semblance of a coherent thought dissolving into nothing more than a silent scream at the sight of him—damp, nearly naked, and incoming. I forget how to breathe.

"Morning," Dylan greets, his voice raspy, not fully awake yet.

Instead of returning the greeting like a normal person, I blurt out, "Did you forget your clothes?"

Dylan shrugs, giving a pointed look at the shirt I'm wearing: his jersey. "You stole my favorite shirt. Did you sleep in it?"

Heat rushes to my cheeks, but I manage a nod, my throat so tight I can barely swallow.

I'm scrambling to find a half-decent response when Dylan adds, "Cool." One word, but the way he says it, all casual and yet heavy with subtext, makes my stomach perform an Olympic-level gymnastics routine.

Then, as if he hasn't already short-circuited my brain, Dylan opens the fridge, grabs the milk carton, and starts chugging straight from it. I'm pretty sure that's not allowed. My eyes widen, indignation bubbling up, but it fizzles out in record time as I watch his throat work, his Adam's apple bobbing with each gulp.

I should protest his lack of basic etiquette, but I'm too busy staring at the hypnotically sensual sight of Dylan drinking as if he were starring in a milk commercial not made for family TV. If the industry wanted to put a sexy spin on "Got Milk?", Dylan would be their man. I would've never guessed dairy consumption could be such a turn-on for me, yet here I am: hot, bothered, enthralled.

My mind takes it even further as it conjures an image of the milk spilling down Dylan's bare chest, and hello—apparently, I have a new kink. What is happening to me? I blink rapidly, wondering if I'm developing a fetish for the mundane—the mop last night, and now this.

When Dylan finishes drinking, he wipes his mouth with the back of his hand and puts the milk back in the fridge as if chugging half-and-half straight from the carton was a totally normal morning ritual. Not content, he taps my nose playfully.

"Got thirsty after that shower. I'm gonna go get dressed now."

"O-okay," I stammer, my voice reedy.

Dylan saunters off to his room, leaving me standing in the kitchen, my brain still overloaded from all that muscle. I grip the counter's edge to anchor myself back to reality. This is fine. Totally fine. Two platonic roommates sharing good mornings. Nothing to see here.

After a few, unending minutes, Dylan returns wearing gray sweatpants and that damn sleeveless hoodie again.

I regain my composure enough to make a joke.

"Ah, you had some clothes left after all," I quip, aiming for nonchalant but landing somewhere between breathless and over-eager.

Dylan smirks, tossing me a quick, lazy look as he moves to grab a pan. His eyes linger on me for a moment longer than necessary before he asks, "What's your mood for breakfast?"

"Pancakes? I-I mmm... was wondering if you could show me how to make pancakes without using a pre-made mix?" I surfed through so many highs and lows I sounded like a boy hitting puberty.

Dylan raises an eyebrow. "Can you handle the pressure, Brolin?" he teases, his voice low and playful.

I nod in response while thinking, *Can I handle the pressure? I can barely handle standing next to you without combusting. But sure, pancakes. Let's pretend that's my biggest challenge right now.*

Dylan switches the pan for a flat griddle and selects the ingredients from the fridge, setting them on the counter as he gives me the basics of the recipe.

I listen, but his voice is white noise, drowned out by the heat creeping up my neck. I grip the whisk, pretending to focus as Dylan steps behind me, his front pressing against my back as he guides me through the movements. His warmth seeps through my shirt—well, *his* shirt actually—and I'm hyper-aware of every inch of space, or lack thereof, between us.

His hands slide over mine, guiding the whisk in slow, hypnotic circles. The touch is maddeningly light, and my pulse thrums louder with each pass. I can't tell if he's aware of the tension building up. His touches appear deliberate, yet they're casual enough to keep me guessing.

I'm balancing on a knife's edge, almost anticipating the fall. He mumbles something about how whisking is all in the wrist. His voice is a spark, my spine a line of tinder waiting to ignite.

"Like this?" I ask.

"Mmhmm."

He's so close goosebumps race down my neck. I can't focus. By the time we're done, I might know less about making pancakes than when we started. The batter isn't the only thing that's getting mixed; my brain feels like it's been tossed into the blender. I wish I could whisk my way out of this mess as easily as I'm whisking the batter.

Part of me wonders if Dylan is naturally this seductive, or if he knows what he's doing to me.

As the batter smooths out, Dylan's hands slow to a stop, but he doesn't pull away. His chest keeps rising and falling against my back, the silence stretching between us like a rubber band ready to snap.

I struggle to find my voice. "Uh, what's next?" I wince at how breathless I sound.

Dylan's reply vibrates through me. "Now, we let the batter rest for a minute. Gives the gluten time to relax."

"Right, relax."

Dylan steps to the side, giving me back some much-needed space. I turn around to face him, to regain my composure, but one look from him nearly undoes me all over again. The heat in his eyes, the hunger, are new. But I'm not sure if it's my mind playing tricks on me, making me see what I want to see, or if it's real.

"Ready to pour?" he rasps.

I nod, not trusting myself to speak. We move to the stove, and Dylan hands me a measuring cup. I pour the batter onto the griddle pan in small, even quantities. As the pancakes start to bubble, it's a good visualization of what my skin's been doing all morning. Every nerve ending in my body is alive and screaming for his touch.

"Hunter." Dylan's voice makes me jolt. "You're going to burn them if you don't flip them soon."

"Right, sorry." I dutifully flip the pancakes. They're a little darker than ideal, but still okay.

We work in silence for a few minutes, the sizzle of batter on the griddle the only audible sound. I'm going to explode if something doesn't happen soon. Whatever game Dylan is playing, I wish he'd either stop or go further, because this in-between is torture.

When the pancakes are cooked, Dylan transfers them from the pan to a serving plate, forming a neat stack. He turns off the stove and sets the dirty pan into the sink. I expect we'll sit at the table now, but before I move, Dylan surprises me again by lifting me bodily onto the counter.

The sudden movement knocks the air from my lungs. My ability to breathe further deteriorates when his fingers grip my hips and he steps between my thighs. I gasp, my hands instinctively going to his shoulders to steady myself. Then I pull away, wondering what's happening.

With nonchalance, Dylan plucks a pancake from the tower and puts it on a plate, as if it were perfectly normal for us to stand this close, with him between my legs.

He grabs the syrup and begins to slowly pour it on top. Again, the gesture is inexplicably sensual, the sticky liquid drizzling over the pancake, strangely suggestive, obscene almost.

Dylan then grabs a fork, cuts off a bite of syrup-soaked pancake, and offers it to me.

I part my lips, letting Dylan slide the fork into my mouth. Once more feeling this is all very sexual. My lips close around the metal, the intimacy almost too much as the sweet richness of the syrup coats my tongue. But I barely register the taste. All I can focus on is the way Dylan's eyes darken as he watches me.

"Verdict?" Dylan asks, calm under fire. But maybe I'm the only one who's burning.

"G-good." My voice comes out breathy, and I wonder if he notices how completely undone I'm about to become.

Dylan takes a bite for himself and proclaims, "More than good, I'd say."

He sets the plate aside, and I think now he's going to pull away. But he leans in closer, his hand coming up to cup my jaw. His thumb swipes at the corner of my mouth, and my entire body goes still.

"You had a little syrup." He brings his thumb to his lips and sucks it clean.

A rush of heat pools low in my belly. The sight of his mouth around his thumb makes my head spin. But then the last sliver of rationality I've left takes over. I frown, confusion tempering the desire swarming through my veins. This is so unlike the easygoing, goofy Dylan I know. The one who cracks jokes and teases me relentlessly but has never crossed the line into blatant flirtation. This version acts like he's got secret training from the "How to Make a Gal Swoon" Academy.

"What are you doing?" My voice wavers. "Why are you spoon-feeding me breakfast like we're in a daytime soap? And why did you buy me a book last night?"

He doesn't answer right away. Instead, he places his hands on the counter on either side of me, caging me in with his body. I have to tip my head back to meet his gaze, my pulse pounding wildly in my throat.

"I think the real question is..." His face is so close I can count his lashes. "Why are you wearing my shirt and rolled-up crew socks?"

He raises an eyebrow, his expression amused and smug at the same time. It's the look in his eyes that makes realization wash over me: I've been caught.

37

HUNTER

My entire body seizes up with a heat so intense, I'm afraid I'll burst into flames.

"Did Tristan talk?"

Dylan grins and gives me a subtle nod.

I groan and, since I have nowhere to go, I hide my face in Dylan's hoodie. "What did he tell you?" My voice is muffled, but my mortification is clear.

"He informed me I'm on the receiving end of a seduction scheme." Dylan's tone is light, teasing.

I want to crawl into a hole and disappear. Burrowing my face deeper into his hoodie, I mutter, "I won't be able to look you in the eyes ever again."

Dylan works his fingers up my scalp and pulls my half-pony-tail loose. "That's a pity because I really enjoy eye contact while making love."

His words knock the little air left in my lungs out for good. My heart stops, the entire world flips upside down, and my ears ring as he gently but firmly tilts my chin up. His touch is soft, yet the control behind it is undeniable. When our eyes meet, the intensity in his gaze leaves me exposed. He's stripping me down to my core, and I can't stand the vulnerability of it.

"You want to have sex with me?" I ask on a breath, the question landing with a quiet force that fills the space around us.

Dylan brushes my hair backward. "Yes, I would very much like that." His tone is resolute, and a magnetic thrum starts at the base of my spine.

"But you said make love?"

Dylan's thumb traces my bottom lip, his touch light but deliberate. "I did." His voice is low, but the words echo through me like a shout. "Because that's what it would be with you, Hunt. Making love. Not sex."

My heart stutters at his confession, a warmth blooming in my chest and spreading through my every cell. I grip his arms tighter, my fingers digging into his skin as if I'm to hold on to this moment, to make it real.

"R-really?" My voice fails me, the words getting stuck in my throat.

Dylan nods, his gaze never leaving mine. "Really."

He cups my face with one hand, placing the other on my hip. His touch grounds me, anchoring me to this moment.

"It might sound absurd." His thumb strokes my cheekbone. "We've known each other forever. But something has changed, and I can't ignore it anymore."

I almost flatline. "What's changed?" Anticipating what he might say is the purest form of misery.

Dylan's eyes search mine as if he's struggling to find the right words. His thumb continues to stroke my cheek, the touch so gentle it makes my heart ache. "Everything has changed. In the past month, I've felt closer to you than I've ever felt with anyone. You're easier and funnier to hang out with than even Tristan. I can't wait to be home with you every night, to see your smile and hear your laugh. It's the best part of my day. I'm sad when I wake up and you've already sneaked out of the house. That I didn't get to tell you good morning."

His words lodge deep in my bones. I can't breathe, can't think, as he continues.

"I wanted you even when I was dating Olivia. That's the main reason the failed break-ups frustrated me so much. Because every time, I was looking forward to coming home and testing the waters between us but never could."

Each new confession sparks in my chest, lighting up something bright inside me as I process what he's saying. My mind reels, struggling to make sense of it all. Dylan wanted me? Even when he was with Olivia? The idea seems impossible, too good to be true.

"But you and Olivia... you looked so..." I trail off, unable to finish the thought. The memory of seeing them together, of the jealousy that twisted in my gut, is still too fresh.

Dylan's expression becomes solemn. "Olivia and I were never that serious, Hunt. It was mostly hanging out, a few kisses. But it never went beyond that. I never even once wanted to have sex with her."

Then he gives me a stare so dark my toes curl in my socks. His eyes rake over me, taking in every inch of my face.

"But with you... Those shorts you've been wearing around the house... worked wonders, Brolin. You have no idea how many times I've had to stop myself from reaching out and touching you."

The words rumble through his chest as his hands slide down to my hips, his fingers digging deeper into my skin through the thin fabric of his shirt.

"Every time you walked around in those tiny shorts, I wanted to grab you and kiss you until you couldn't breathe."

"W-why didn't you?"

"I didn't want you to think I was on the rebound from Olivia or something. That you weren't my number-one choice." Dylan's fingers tighten on my hips, his grip firm and possessive. "Because you are. And the only thing hotter than seeing you in my shirt would be dragging it off of you."

My skin prickles at the thought of his hands on me, slowly undressing me. I can almost feel the heat of his touch, the whisper of fabric sliding over my skin as he removes the shirt inch by tantalizing inch.

"I want to take my time with you," Dylan continues, his eyes darkening with desire. "Explore every curve, every freckle, every sensitive spot until I know your body better than my own. I want to make you shiver and gasp and moan my name."

Each word is a caress, igniting a fire under my skin as Dylan's hands slide higher, his thumbs brushing my ribcage over the light material of his shirt.

"I can't tell if it's love. If it's too soon to call it that." He drops his forehead over mine. "But it feels a lot like it. The way my heart races when you walk into a room, the way my skin tingles when you brush against me, the way I can't stop thinking about you even when you're right next to me... It's like nothing I've ever felt before."

Dylan's last confession hits me in a wave, crashing over me and sweeping me under. My fingers dig into his arms, clinging to him as if he were the only thing keeping me from drowning in the overwhelming rush of emotions. I'm not sure if I'm holding on to him out of lust, love, or a desperate need for support, but either way, my grip is shaky, my hands trembling against his skin.

It's my turn to confess. "Dylan, I've had a major crush on you since the day we met. You've been the guy I've compared every boyfriend to, and no one has ever lived up to you." The words spill out of me in a rush, letting go of a secret I've held inside for so long. But now that I've laid my heart bare on the kitchen counter, I float in the freedom of saying these words out loud. "I went on all those stupid dates because I wanted to forget about you and Olivia," I admit, my voice cracking. "Seeing you two together, it hurt so fucking much. I thought if I could find someone else, I could move on from this hopeless crush. But no one else could ever compare to you."

I will my hands to stop trembling as I continue. "Every time I went out with a new guy, all I could think about was how he wasn't you. How his laugh didn't make my heart skip the way yours does, how his smile didn't light up the room the way yours can. It was to convince myself I could be happy with someone else when deep down, I knew it would always be you."

Dylan's eyes widen. "Why didn't you say something sooner? In all the years we've known each other, you never once hinted that you had feelings for me."

I let out a throaty laugh, shaking my head. "How could I? When we first met, I was eighteen, a freshman who still had to figure out who I was. And there you were, this sophisticated investment banker already living in the city like a proper adult. I was such a kid compared to you."

I caress his shoulders, giving myself permission to explore his body. "If I had told you back then how I felt, you would've laughed in my face. Or worse, patted me on the head like some silly little girl with a crush."

"I would've never laughed in your face."

I smirk. "But you don't deny the possibility of a brotherly pat on the head?"

"I can't speak for the me of back then, only for the me of right now who doesn't have a single brotherly thought toward you." He's unapologetic, intentional. When I think there's nothing left of me to burn, another section of my body goes up in flames. It's my spine this time. "And you've been an adult and living in the same city as me for a few years now."

I let out a long sigh. "You're right. But by the time I moved to New York, I'd drifted naturally into an acquaintance zone with you."

Dylan raises a skeptical eyebrow. "Acquaintance zone? Is that even a thing?"

I chuckle at his confusion. "Okay, fine. The technical term is 'friend zone,' but that implies a level of closeness we didn't have. We were more... friendly acquaintances. We hung out in group settings, but never one on one. I was always Nina's best friend to you."

Dylan nods thoughtfully, his hands still resting on my hips, his thumbs tracing idle patterns that send little shivers through me. "I get that." He smiles, eyes crinkling at the corners in that way I love. "So now that you know me better and we're more than acquaintances... do you still want me?"

His tone is easy-going but with an undercurrent of uncertainty that makes my heart clench. I realize that as confident as Dylan may appear, even he needs reassurance sometimes. The thought that he could doubt my devotion to him is almost laughable. If anything, the more I've gotten to know Dylan, the deeper I've fallen.

I let the love, the longing, the pure, unadulterated want shine through my eyes as I meet his, expressing everything I've kept locked away without holding back.

"Yes." The word falls from my lips like a prayer, a promise, an inevitability. "I want you more now than I ever have before."

Dylan holds my gaze, his blue-green eyes burning into mine with an intensity that would've made my knees buckle if I wasn't sitting.

Our gazes hold, the truth we've admitted making it impossible to look away. Then slowly, deliberately, Dylan leans in closer. His nose brushes against mine, his breath warm on my lips as he whispers, "In that case, you wouldn't mind if I do this..."

And then Dylan Thompson kisses me.

38

DYLAN

I kiss Hunter. After weeks of wanting, dreaming, craving, and it's like coming home. Every moment, every interaction, every shared laugh and lingering glance has been leading up to this. Her lips are soft and pliant beneath mine, parting on a gasp as I deepen the kiss.

I slide one hand up her back and tangle it in her hair, pulling down, tilting her head to the perfect angle. She tastes like maple syrup and something I want to drown in.

Hunter's hands come up to clutch at my shoulders, her fingers clawing at my hoodie. She arches into me, pressing our bodies together, and I groan into her mouth at the exquisite contact. Even with layers of clothing between us, her curves mold against the hard planes of my body like we were made to fit.

I nip at her bottom lip, soothing the sting with my tongue, and Hunter makes a needy sound in the back of her throat that shoots straight to my core. That little whimper, the way she's clinging to me, ignites something primal inside me, a hunger I've never felt.

This is how kissing someone should feel: consuming, intoxicating, devouring and wanting to be devoured.

I grip her hips tighter, pulling her to the edge of the counter until she's flush against me. I trail open-mouthed kisses along her jaw, down the slender column of her neck.

"Dylan," Hunter gasps, and the sound of my name on her lips, breathy and pleading, it unravels me.

I find her pulse point, sucking lightly. Her fingers thread into my hair, nails scraping deliciously against my scalp. I want to undress her, to make her mine. And yet, I also want to savor every inch of her slowly, but the need to have her pulses in my veins and is too insistent to ignore. Weeks of pent-up desire, of imagining her in my arms, have me teetering on the knife's edge of my control.

"Do you know how much it drives me crazy that you're wearing my shirt," I whisper against her throat.

"I'm—I'm getting a-an idea," she pants back.

My fingers inch higher, teasing the sensitive skin of her inner thighs. I skim my hands up, and up, until my thumbs brush the edge of her shorts, dipping under the denim.

"Gosh, Hunter, these shorts," I groan, my voice rough with want. "They've been testing my restraint all week."

She lets out a shaky laugh that turns into a gasp when I nip at her collarbone. "That... that was kind of the point."

I lift my head to look at her, a smirk tugging at my lips. "Is that so?"

Hunter nods. "I wanted you to notice me. To want me the way I've wanted you for so long."

My heart gets rug-burned at her confession, at the uncertainty still shining in her eyes. That this woman, this gorgeous, smart, sassy goddess has wanted me for years seems unbelievable.

"Oh, Hunter." I cup her face in my hands. "I noticed you. If the past years have been for you like the last month for me, I'm sorry. Because I wanted you, badly. Even when I shouldn't have, even when I tried to deny it to myself." I stroke my thumbs over her cheekbones. "I've imagined this, having you in my arms, being able to touch you, taste you, a million times."

To punctuate my words, I claim her mouth in another searing kiss, pouring all my pent-up desire into the contact.

We kiss until we're both breathless, until the need for oxygen forces us apart. Hunter rests her forehead on the crook of my neck. "What now?" she asks, not looking me in the eye.

I caress down her long hair. "Are you asking what are my plans for the weekend? Because those include getting you in bed and not letting you leave until you have to go to work on Monday."

Her hands fist into the fabric of my hoodie. "S-solid plan, Thompson."

I lift her chin with a finger because I'm not sure she's clear on how serious this is for me. "But if you're asking what happens after I do all the things that I plan to do to you, is that we do them again, and again. Ideally, you'd move into my room or I into yours, and we make this a permanent arrangement."

Hunter's eyes widen, her lips parting in surprise. "You... you want to keep living together? Like, officially, as a couple?"

My head dips, eyes steady on hers. "I want to wake up with you every morning and fall asleep with you every night. I want to come home to you after a long day and cook dinner together, even if it's mac and cheese from a box. We can argue over who gets the first shower and end up sharing it anyway." I tuck a strand of hair behind her ear. "I want to build a life with you, Hunter. I'm all in if you are."

Hunter's eyes search mine. Emotions flickering across her

face—surprise, disbelief, and then, a tentative hope that makes my heart swell.

"You're serious," she says, more a statement than a question.

"As a heart attack," I confirm, my lips quirking. "I know it's fast, and if you need time to think about it, I understand—"

"No, I want it, but..." She frowns and looks away. "Aren't you worried about going too fast? What if we blow up and mess things up in our group?"

I get the sense that's not what she wants to ask me, that her fear is not about our group's dynamic but about me breaking her heart. "Nina and Tristan have already made that ship sail. And I can't promise this will be forever, but I can tell you that there isn't anything I wouldn't risk to see if it could be." I grab her jaw and gently tilt her face back toward me. "Now, why don't you tell me what's really on your mind?"

She struggles to maintain eye contact, but I don't let her look away. "Do you remember the conversation we had at your parents', t-the night we slept in the living room?"

I remember everything she tells me. Not just the words, but also the way she says them—how her voice softens or sharpens depending on what she's going through. "I do."

"Okay." She swallows, visibly nervous. Then she starts talking at top speed, without pausing as if she is afraid she'll lose her nerve if she doesn't get it all out at once. "This might sound premature, but since you're already talking about moving in together. Remember I told you I might not be able to have kids naturally? I might try IVF but the only road for me could be adoption. And before anything happens between us, I need to know that you can accept that. You have to understand that it's not an abstract possibility, but the most probable outcome for me. Because I can't let myself get... get swept up in this, if I already know you... you won't be okay with that. I've wanted this for too long. If you don't—"

I stop her, capturing her mouth in another tender kiss, before pulling apart, locking eyes with her, and making sure she hears me when I say, "I don't care, Brolin. Tristan has always told me my mom and dad felt more like parents to him than his own. Biology has nothing to do with it. Our kids come from your belly or from a situation where they need help and a loving family. I'm good either way."

"You are?"

"No. Love doesn't come from genes. We can adopt an entire basketball team. The important thing is that we'll be raising our kids together, me and you." I notice she's about to melt into tears, so I smile, whisper-singing, "I wanna be your endgame."

The song has the desired effect because it makes her laugh. "Are you serenading Taylor to me?"

"What if I was?"

"You'd have to stop because I can't take any more swooning."

My turn to grin. "If we're done with the hard questions, then, can we move on to the fun part?"

At the barest nod from Hunter, I scoop her up into my arms, her legs wrapping around my waist. She lets out a surprised squeak that evolves into a moan as I capture her mouth in a fiery kiss. I carry her down the hall, pausing, undecided if we should go to her bedroom or mine. My door's open, so I go in there, our lips never breaking contact. It's a miracle I navigate the short distance without stumbling, considering how thoroughly Hunter is kissing me back.

I kick the door shut behind us and press Hunter up against it. She gasps into my mouth at the sudden impact, her back arching off the wood. I trail my lips down her neck, finding that sensitive spot below her ear that I've already learned makes her shudder. "A word of warning, Brolin." I bite into her earlobe hard enough to make her whimper. "I'm not such a *nice* guy in bed."

39

HUNTER

"I'm not such a *nice* guy in bed."

Those are the last words Dylan says to me before he shows me just how wicked he can be. He is thorough, detail-oriented, and in control. He breaks me down and puts me back together only to start again.

I don't know if my past lovers were inconsiderate, inexperienced, or downright incompetent. Or if sex—*making love*—with Dylan is so much better because it's him. Because it's us.

But the next few hours pass in a haze of tangled limbs, sweat-slicked skin, and mind-numbing pleasure. Dylan takes me to heights I didn't even know existed, wringing orgasm after orgasm from my body until I'm a trembling, incoherent mess. He knows instinctively how to touch me, where to kiss, when to be gentle, and when to be rough.

By the time we collapse onto the rumpled sheets, spent and sated, it must already be afternoon. Dylan pulls me close, my back to his chest, his arms wrapped securely around me. I've never felt so safe, cherished, and content.

"That was..." I trail off, unable to find the words to adequately describe the life-altering experience we shared.

"Incredible? Earth-shattering? The best sex of your life?" Dylan supplies helpfully, his voice a low rumble against my back.

I turn, eyeing him appraisingly. "Definitely not the best sex of my life."

He frowns, the cocky smirk slipping from his swollen lips.

"I'm not even sure we can call it sex."

The grin slips back in place.

"It felt more like a merging of souls." I let my palm trail down his arm, still marveling at the notion that I can touch him where I want when I want. Kiss him whenever I feel like it. That he is mine. Dylan Thompson is mine.

Dylan smiles, eyes shining even if a little droopy; the guy deserves a nap. "A merging of souls, huh? I like the sound of that." He brushes his nose against mine in an Eskimo kiss.

I hum in agreement, running my hand through his hair. It's damp with sweat, but I don't care. Too many times before I had to stop myself from smoothing it. But now I want to explore every inch of him, learn every scar, every line, every texture.

"I have a question." I trace idle patterns on Dylan's chest with my fingertip. "Of the past twenty-four hours, how much of it was you?"

"What do you mean? It was all me."

"Oh." I prop myself on an elbow and tap his nose. "Am I to believe you routinely sing Taylor Swift while mopping the house?"

"Ooooh, that part."

"Yeah, what was that?"

He cute-frowns. "Little counter-seduction scheme?"

"So the book, the movie, the massage, coming out of the shower in a towel, it was all deliberate?"

"In my defense, you tortured me for a week." His fingers lazily trace the curve of my waist, probably to distract me—it's working.

"You tortured me for years."

"Unknowingly."

"Tristan tells you I'm into you and then what, you two scheme to ruin me?"

"Don't sound so indignant." He pinches my ass lightly. "As if what you did with my sister was much different. At least I wasn't trading with inside information."

"Nina wasn't a part of this?"

"No, only me and Tristan."

"How did you guys come up with what to do?"

"Easy." He shrugs. "The internet."

"You googled, 'how to counter-seduce my roommate'?"

"No, we used TikTok for research."

"TikTok? Please, I need to know the exact text of that search."

"Something along the lines of, 'what BookTok girlies are into.'"

I sag back on the pillows. "Guess I should consider myself lucky you didn't show up in fae-warrior wings."

"No." He kisses the swell of my breast. "But I'm taking notes for my Halloween costume. Do you prefer pure white or midnight black for the feathers? And should I go all leather—jacket, pants—or shirtless?"

I cut him a mock side glare. "We've established I'm into bare chests. Drinking the milk straight from the carton was a nice touch, by the way. Was that on BookTok, too?"

"No, that was a little improv from me. Glad to hear the performance was appreciated."

"It was *much* appreciated." I roll half on top of him again, pushing him into the mattress. "In fact, from now on, you're not allowed to drink milk any other way."

Dylan chuckles, the sound rumbling through his chest under my palms. "Duly noted. Drinking restrictions are now in effect."

His hands come to rest on my hips, his thumbs pressing into my skin. The casual intimacy of the gesture, the ease with which he touches me now, fires up my spine in a series of small bursts and tingles.

"So," I drawl, walking my fingers up his sternum. "Was there something else in store for me today?"

"I was going for casual pushups in the living room, and in case that didn't work, I would've gotten on my knees and begged."

I raise an eyebrow, fighting a grin. "On your knees, huh? Seems I got you there anyway."

Dylan chuckles, his eyes darkening a fraction. "I'd say it was more of a voluntary surrender. You make it hard to resist."

I bite my lip to suppress the flutter in my chest. "If you surrendered, does that mean I won?"

His hand slides up my back, pulling me even closer. "Call it what you want, but I'm pretty sure we both won that round."

I run my hand up his chest with a teasing smile. "Did you follow a TikTok tutorial on that, too, or are you a natural?"

Dylan laughs, his grin widening. "No tutorial needed for that one." Then he turns serious. "You know, I didn't really need TikTok to figure out how to get your attention. I only had to find the courage to show you how much I wanted you. How much I'm in love with you."

My heart does a slow somersault in my chest, and I blink. His playful demeanor fades into something more intense, more honest. The moment stretches and expands as if time itself is holding its breath, waiting for me to respond.

My mouth goes dry. "You said you weren't sure it was love?"

"Did I? Then I was wrong." He pushes a lock of hair behind

my ear and in the most natural tone, with the most open expression tells me again, "I love you."

"I—" My voice fails me. I have no witty comebacks, no banter to use as a mask, the raw truth staring me down.

He tilts his head, observing me. "You don't have to say it back. I already know. I already feel it."

But I want to say it. To make him understand what this— what *he*—means to me.

The words are swirling under the surface, waiting to be spoken. It's not fear holding me back, but the magnitude of what they mean. Saying them will change everything in the best way possible. I meet his eyes; they look at me, steady and patient, prepared to give me all the space I need to tell him when I'm ready.

The thing is, I *am* ready. "I love you, Dylan Thompson."

Dylan's gaze softens and hardens at the same time. "Say it again." He brushes his thumb along my jawline.

I let out a small laugh, the sound bubbling up from somewhere deep inside. "I love you, Dylan Thompson."

He groans, burying his face in my neck and biting down. If we were in a shifter romance, I'd be marked now. Then he lifts his head again, his face brighter than I've ever seen it. "You know, hearing you say that... I could get addicted to it."

I playfully narrow my eyes at him. "I'll have to ration them out then, keep you on your toes."

His grin turns wicked as his fingers tighten their grip on my hips. "Oh, I'll find plenty of ways to get you to say it again."

"Will you be using sex to bribe me?"

He leans in. "Not bribery, just... incentives. I can make it worth your while."

"Oh, I'm sure." I run my fingers through his hair again, savoring the slight shudder he gives me in response. It's surreal to be in his arms with nothing left unsaid between us. The years of wanting, they've all led us to this perfect moment. "I can't believe this is real."

Dylan pulls back enough to look at me, his eyes holding mine with such intensity the hairs on the back of my neck rise. "It is real, Hunt. We are. And we're just getting started."

I lay my head on his chest, enjoying the steady rise and fall as he holds me. "I love you." I test the weight of the words now that they're out in the open, now that they're ours.

"I love you, too."

His arms wrap over me, cocooning me in a fortress. I'm physically trapped, but for the first time in years, I am free. Free of doubt, free of all the walls I built around myself. I listen to Dylan's heartbeat, and the world clicks into place.

"I never want to wake up without you," I tell him, my voice thick with emotion.

Dylan presses a tender kiss on my forehead. "You won't have to. We've got forever, Hunt."

And as we lie wrapped in each other, I know that our ever after has already begun.

EPILOGUE
DYLAN

Five Years Later

The adoption agency office isn't flashy—just a standard workspace with a desk, cabinets, and a few chairs. The only real clue to its purpose is the framed children's drawings lining the walls. Hunter sits next to me in front of the counselor interviewing us, her knee bouncing with restless energy. The chair creaks under my shifting weight as I try to appear composed—a feat, considering I'm auditioning for the role of "Future Dad."

"Tell us a bit about why you're pursuing adoption," the counselor prompts, her pen poised above a notepad.

Hunter glances at me, her expression somewhere between hopeful and *if you mess this up, Dylan, I'll throttle you.*

"Well," I start, clasping my hands together to avoid fidgeting. "We've been trying for a few years. Turns out, my swimmers are less Michael Phelps, more synchronized flailing."

The counselor blinks, clearly unsure whether to laugh or maintain professional neutrality.

Hunter groans softly, elbowing me in the ribs. "Dylan."

"What?" I whisper.

"They value honesty," she chides. "He doesn't want to put me on the spot, but I'm the one with infertility issues. I can't have a baby."

"I see. Is infertility the only reason you've chosen to adopt?"

Hunter takes over, her voice steady, soothing. "We want to be parents. Biology doesn't matter to us. What matters is giving a child a loving home and a family. We're actually happy to be helping someone in need."

Her hand slides into mine, and I squeeze it, grateful for her composure. "Yeah," I add. "Plus, we've had practice. My goddaughter, Soleil, tests our patience every time she's over. She's a tiny hurricane. And she's adopted, too. Half-adopted: her father was a real jerk, but then her mom met this—ouch."

Hunter has kicked me under the table. "Honey, the counselor probably doesn't care about Rowena and Adrian's origin story."

"True, I don't." The counselor's lips twitch. "But it's good that you've been around adopted children."

Hunter smiles tightly. I give her hand another squeeze to let her know we got this. "Yeah. Anyway, we're ready," she says. "We're excited to share our lives and love."

She has this radiant glow, part hope, part nerves, and a lot of determination that reminds me why I married her. The counselor seems charmed too because her posture softens, and she moves on to the next question.

The counselor sets down her pen with a satisfied smile. "I think I have everything I need for now. The next step is for you to complete the formal written application." She reaches for a neat stack of forms on the corner of her desk and hands them to me. "Take your time. Once you've filled these out and returned them, we'll move forward."

I accept the stack, thumbing through the pages briefly before handing them to Hunter. "Better if she handles this," I say, keeping my tone casual. "I've got dyslexia, and forms like this are... not my strong suit."

Five years ago, the thought of admitting something like this would've left me paralyzed. I'd invented some sort of excuse not to fill in the modules myself. But Hunter changed that. Her love has taught me that my struggles don't make me less capable; they make me human. With her, I've learned that honesty isn't a weakness, and neither is asking for help. She didn't just accept my flaws; she made me see how they're a part of who I am.

Now, there's no shame in leaning on each other. It's second nature, like breathing. Being able to ask for help and own my challenges? That's real strength. Instead of letting my weaknesses hold me back, I've learned to navigate around them, and even laugh about them.

Hunter takes the papers and pats my arm. "Division of labor," she says lightly, throwing the counselor a smile. "He'll keep track of all the deadlines and reminders."

The counselor nods, satisfied. "Teamwork like this will serve you well as parents."

I glance over at Hunter as she patiently fills out the form, her pen moving steadily across the page. She doesn't complain, doesn't even hesitate, just does what needs to be done, like always. It's not about keeping score; it's about showing up for each other and taking on what the other can't. Real love is knowing you don't have to be perfect to be enough.

Yeah, we're going to make one hell of a team.

* * *

By the time we leave the agency, I'm riding a wave of cautious optimism. Hunter loops her arm through mine as we step into the brisk New York afternoon. "You really had to bring up your swimmers?"

"Hey, she liked my humor. And I think it went well. It'll be good if she remembers us as more than just names on paper."

She shakes her head, but her lips curve into a small smile. "I'm surprised you didn't tell her we're dog haters. Now, that would've been memorable."

I laugh, the familiar joke still sharp after all these years. "You're right, I should've brought socks: *Stepping Into Parenting*."

Hunter laughs. "*Toe-tally Into Babies*."

We pass a line of honking taxis as Hunter slows her pace. She frowns, something on her mind.

"Should we tell them?" she asks, her voice low. "About the application? Tonight, at dinner?"

I look at her, startled by the shift in tone. "You mean everyone?"

She nods, a flicker of hesitation glimmering in her dark eyes. "I don't want to jinx it. But... I also want to share the journey. And if I get too stressed about the wait, I'd like to talk to Nina and Winnie about it."

I consider this. Our friends are the nosiest, most opinionated group I know, my sister especially. Secrets don't last long around them. "You're right." I sigh. "Let's tell them so they won't think we're having a mid-life crisis or something."

Hunter laughs, her tension easing a bit. "I don't know. A bright-red sports car might suit you."

I smirk. "I'll stick with parenting chaos, thanks. I hear it's just as expensive."

She hugs me. "Alright. We'll tell them. Tonight."

I kiss her before flagging down a cab.

The ride to Tristan and Nina's place is short. We're the last to arrive, and the moment we step in, Soleil comes barreling toward us, her curls bouncing. "Uncle Dylan!"

I crouch down, bracing for impact. "Hey, sunshine! How's the reigning queen of chaos?"

"I'm not chaos!" she declares, hands on her hips in a perfect imitation of Rowena.

Adrian ambles over, holding his infant son. "She's more of a tyrant than chaos."

"Daddy!" Soleil protests, her little face scrunching up in mock offense.

Rowena appears, armed with a plate of appetizers and a raised eyebrow. "Don't rile her up, Adrian. She's finally calm."

Adrian shrugs. "Calm is overrated."

Rowena ignores him, beaming at Hunter. "You look different. Did something happen?"

Hunter turns to me. "Not even five minutes and we're busted."

Rowena smirks, smug. "Busted for what? Did you sneak off to get matching tattoos?"

"What is a tattoo, Mommy?"

Rowena pats her daughter's head. "Something you don't have to worry about for at least another thirteen years."

Soleil pouts. "I can google it."

Rowena sighs. "If you can spell tattoo, you deserve to know."

Hunter chuckles nervously, and her fingers dig into my arm in a silent, *You're the one who said we should tell them.*

I clear my throat, scanning the room for my sister. "Where are Nina and Tristan? Let's get all the tough love in one sitting."

"They're in the kitchen arguing about whether the napkins should be folded or rolled," Adrian says, adjusting his son in his arms. "It's riveting."

We move to the kitchen where, sure enough, Nina and Tristan are bickering over the napkin placement.

"I'm telling you, folding them into flowers is the way to go," Nina insists, keeping her hands on her round belly; at thirty-six weeks pregnant, she could pop out my niece at any time. "It's classic, elegant."

Tristan shakes his head. "Rolling them is trendier. Plus, it saves time."

Nina scoffs. "Are you in a hurry?"

Nina looks up as we enter, her eyes narrowing suspiciously. "What's with the faces? You two look like you robbed a bank and can't decide whether to feel guilty or excited about it."

Hunter shoots me a smile that reads, *I told you so*. Yeah, we could've never kept such a huge secret from our friends.

"Nothing that dramatic."

Tristan abandons the half-rolled napkin in his hands—I have to say, Nina might be right, her technique is superior—and everyone else stares at us expectantly.

"What did we miss?" Tristan asks, his sharp blue eyes darting between Hunter and me. "Please tell me Soleil did something embarrassing we can record for her wedding slideshow."

"Not yet," Adrian pipes up, lowering his son so Rowena can stamp a kiss on his tiny head. "But Dylan and Hunter have news."

Nina perks up, her gaze narrowing on me with the precision of a heat-seeking missile. "What news? Wait, are you guys...?"

"No," Hunter blurts out, her face going crimson. "Well, not exactly."

Everyone leans in, their collective anticipation palpable. I glance at Hunter, and she gives me the tiniest nod.

"We've applied to adopt," I announce.

For a split second, they're all silent. Then Nina lets out a delighted squeal. "Oh my gosh! That's amazing!" She sets the napkins down and wraps Hunter in an awkward side hug, her belly preventing a full range of motion. "I'm so proud of you guys!"

Even Tristan looks touched, though his default setting is sarcastic. "Wow. That's wonderful. I didn't know you two were ready for sleepless nights and a permanent glitter explosion in your house."

"Just as ready as you are," I quip back.

Rowena steps forward, her eyes tender as she wraps us in a three-way hug. "You'll be amazing parents. And if you need any advice on the adoption process..." She glances at Adrian, who's busy preventing Soleil from stealing the baby's bottle.

Hunter laughs, returning Rowena's hug. "Thanks, Winnie. And don't worry, we plan to be those annoying friends who constantly ask for parenting tips, then ignore all of them."

Her heist thwarted, Soleil tugs on my sleeve. "Uncle Dylan, can I show you my new dress?"

"Later, sweetie, I promise."

Nina points a finger at Tristan. "If you want a second one, we're adopting, too. I can't be pregnant again."

My sister has been complaining for the entire nine months that instead of a pregnancy glow, she got a pregnancy rot. Her gestation has had a few complications; she could've lost the baby. Nina jokes about it, but it hasn't been easy.

My sister throws up her arms. "I'm carrying the Prince of Darkness's spawn, what else did I expect?"

Tristan loops his arm protectively around Nina's back. "Been a few years since you called me that, Princess."

She turns to him, smiling like a love-struck idiot. "It's not foreplay, and stop fussing, I'm fine."

"You're carrying precious cargo," Tristan retorts, his tone half-serious.

Adrian snorts. "Is this your first reminder today, or are we past double digits?"

"I've lost count," Nina says dryly, but her eyes sparkle as she looks at Tristan—my actual brother-in-law now.

"Mommy, what is foreplay?"

Rowena makes a panicked face, her eyes darting to Adrian like she's passing him the *you deal with this* baton. "Something else you don't have to worry about for another thirteen years, sweetheart."

Adrian frowns. "Did you say thirty years? You did, right?"

Rowena slides up to him and kisses him on the mouth. "You just be glad she doesn't know how to spell anything yet."

A quiet, steady warmth fills my chest as I watch my friends—*my family*—laugh and bicker. These are my people—chaotic, flawed, fiercely loving. Adrian lifts the baby high into the air, making silly faces, while Rowena scoops Soleil into her arms, spinning her around as they both burst into giggles. Tristan dotes on Nina, earning affectionate eye-rolls.

And then there's Hunter, my wife. The woman who has been by my side through it all, who has seen me at my best and worst and loved me just the same. She catches my eye across the room, and the tenderness in her gaze makes my heart swell.

I cross over to her, wrapping an arm around her waist and pulling her closer. She leans into me, fitting perfectly against my side like she was made just for me. "We're going to be parents," she murmurs, resting her head on my shoulder.

"Yeah, we are." I press a kiss to her temple, marveling at how far we've come. From acquaintances—as Hunter likes to define the first eleven years we knew each other—to roommates to friends to being a couple, and now, soon-to-be parents. It's been a journey, filled with laughter, tears, and more love than I ever thought possible.

Her hand finds mine. "You okay?"

I nod, a slow smile spreading across my face. "More than okay. I'm just... happy. Really, really happy."

"Yeah, me too." Her dark eyes, soft and shining, find mine. "I love you, Dylan Thompson."

I lean in, whispering in her ear, "Say it again," and then I bite her earlobe.

* * *

MORE FROM CAMILLA ISLEY

Another book from Camilla Isley, *If the Ring Fits*, is available to order now here:

www.mybook.to/RingFitsBackAd

ACKNOWLEDGEMENTS

As I wrote the last line of this story, I teared up. Which is ridiculous, really, because Dylan biting Hunter's earlobe isn't exactly a tragedy. It's banter—a little sassy, a little sexy—but still, it got to me. Maybe it was saying goodbye to these three couples that I've spent the last year bantering with in my head... but there I was crying at the PC.

I want to thank you for reading this book—this series—alongside me. I hope you laughed, and yeah, maybe even got a little emotional—just like I did. You're the reason I keep doing this, and I'm constantly overwhelmed by your messages of love and support. If you've ever hesitated to tell me you enjoyed a story or tag me in a post—don't. Do it. Those messages keep my writer's heart going. And if you also leave a review, just know that somewhere, I'm happy-dancing in my pajamas in your honor.

To my editor, Megan Haslam, thank you for wrestling more depth out of this story. To my copy editor, Emily Reader, thank you for your keen attention to detail, and for all the "ha-ha," "I snorted here" comments that made me laugh too. To my proof-reader, Susan Sugden—for making sure nothing slipped through the cracks.

To my publisher, Boldwood Books. To the production team, for wrapping my stories in such pretty packages. To the marketing and sales teams, thanks for dealing with my anxieties, endless emails, and constant questions.

To my family—thank you for your unwavering support and your ability to tolerate my artistic moods.

And finally, to my new kitty, Sofia, for being the best furry procrastination enabler.

ABOUT THE AUTHOR

Camilla Isley is an engineer who left science behind to write bestselling contemporary rom-coms set all around the world. She lives in Italy.

Sign up to Camilla Isley's mailing list for news, competitions and updates on future books.

Visit Camilla's website: https://camillaisley.com/

Follow Camilla on social media here:

facebook.com/camillaisley
x.com/camillaisley
instagram.com/camillaisley
bookbub.com/authors/camilla-isley

ALSO BY CAMILLA ISLEY

The Love Theorem

Love Quest

The Love Proposal

Love To Hate You

Not In A Billion Years

Baby, One More Time

It's Complicated

The Love Algorithm

It Started With A Book

The Is Not a Holiday Romance

If the Ring Fits

The Roommate Experiment

Boldwood
EVER AFTER

xoxo

JOIN BOLDWOOD'S
**ROMANCE
COMMUNITY**
FOR SWEET AND
SPICY BOOK RECS
WITH ALL YOUR
FAVOURITE
TROPES!

SIGN UP TO OUR
NEWSLETTER

HTTPS://BIT.LY/BOLDWOODEVERAFTER

Boldwood

Boldwood Books is an award-winning fiction publishing company seeking out the best stories from around the world.

Find out more at www.boldwoodbooks.com

Join our reader community for brilliant books, competitions and offers!

Follow us
@BoldwoodBooks
@TheBoldBookClub

Sign up to our weekly
deals newsletter

https://bit.ly/BoldwoodBNewsletter

www.ingramcontent.com/pod-product-compliance
Ingram Content Group UK Ltd.
Pitfield, Milton Keynes, MK11 3LW, UK
UKHW041304010625
6178UKWH00022B/281